THREESOMES

A collection of twenty erotic stories

Edited by Miranda Forbes

Published by Xcite Books Ltd – 2011
ISBN 9781907016554

The stories contained within this book are works of fiction.
Names and characters are the product of the authors'
imaginations and any resemblance to actual persons, living or
dead, is entirely coincidental

Printed and bound in the UK by CPI Bookmarque, Croydon

Contents

Between Two Lovers
by Thomas S Roche

She shouldn't have worn something slutty.

It had made sense early that morning. *Get them both out to brunch*, she figured, *and wear something slutty. Get them tipsy at Verts Déchirées* (best mimosas in town, and where else can you get a breakfast salad?) – *and wear something slutty. They're men. They'll go for it, duh. Don't apologise; be honest how you feel, about the two of them, about the two coincident relationships; about* sex. *If you mention it to one of them before the other, it'll forever nag at the other one. Just tell them both at once, and wear something slutty.*

Without the wearing something slutty part, it ran the risk of becoming all process, no sex. And while Avery hated process, she did, however, like sex.

So she wore something slutty.

'Well,' Luke chortled, '*I'm* straight!' He sounded self-congratulatory.

Avery fixed him with a gaze that could have frozen Vesuvius.

'Well, I had planned on being there,' she said. 'So I don't see how that matters.'

'Hey, I'm not homophobic!' bleated Luke, having an urban-sensitive-new-age-guy-straight-male-homophobia panic.

Jacob grinned lasciviously.

'I'm not either,' said Jacob. He clapped Luke on the back. 'Promise you'll stay between us, Ave? Maybe we can use, like, sheets with holes in them – like the Mormons.'

1

'Jews,' said Avery.

'Excuse me?'

'Jews. Orthodox Jews are supposed to have sex through a sheet. They don't.'

'I thought it was the Amish,' said Luke.

'They don't either,' said Avery.

'So it's not Mormons?' said Luke.

'I was making a joke,' said Jacob sourly.

'Hey, guy, there's nothing wrong with gay sex,' spat Luke suddenly, with a self-righteously liberal air.

'Oh, I *love* gay sex,' said Jacob. 'I eat it up! Nothing I love like a big fat dick!'

Luke stared at Jacob, confused.

'Not really,' said Jacob sheepishly. Avery was more than a little satisfied to see him turn a deep pink.

'Look,' said Avery. 'Forget I said anything.'

Jacob recovered: 'Hey, let's not be too hasty here. I mean, we've got sexual chemistry, the two of us.' He added hastily, '*Avery and me!*' in a bark, violently waving his hand to indicate – without question – that he and Luke did *not* have sexual chemistry. Then to Avery, pointedly: 'I mean, it's intense, am I right? Maybe it'll spill over and ... you know ...' he made a cryptic gesture describing a triangle between the three of them, talking with his hand where his tongue seemed to fail him.

'You know, *what*?' asked Avery, annoyed.

'You know.'

'I *don't* know.'

'This thing could work,' he finally said, his voice a deep dark chocolate purr of suggestive energy. 'A threesome, like you said.'

'That would be weird,' said Luke.

'Forget I said anything,' said Avery, and gulped the second half of her mimosa.

Jacob peered at her, refilling her flute from the pitcher.

'It could work,' said Jacob, to Luke. 'I mean – look how she's dressed.'

'Ain't *that* a fact,' said Luke.

Jacob's leer radiated open lust, as his eyes took in Avery's face and upper body, the tight soft shawl-collar top moulded to the outline of her breasts, her chickens stiffening her undercarriage effectively, but not as effectively as Jacob's lustful gaze stiffened her nipples. In an instant, she knew they were visible, not just 'cause she could feel the tight hot hardness, but because Jacob and Luke exchanged a glance that told her so. She felt a wave of hot-cold-hot; her face was red, she knew. She was blushing. She shouldn't have worn something slutty. That was stupid. And as for proposing a threesome? That was fucking *stupider* than stupid.

She looked down. Her hot skin goosebumped. She squirmed uncomfortably under the two men's gazes. Her jeans were too tight and rubbed her places she really oughtn't to be rubbed right now. She wasn't quite down to her skinny jeans, and in any event, there was less to these jeans to begin with than there ever should have been at brunch.

She felt reckless, sick, nauseated.

When she looked up, Jacob and Luke were both staring at her: shameless, ravenous, consumed by lust – word up. From the way they were drooling, if there hadn't been a table full of mimosas and fucking breakfast salads between their crotches and their faces, Avery thought both dudes would be on their way to the hospital with boner-induced chin fractures.

'Is she hot, or what?' said Luke.

'Fuckin' *smoking*,' said Jacob.

Christ, boys, want a drool cup? she thought bitterly, trying to fight off the wave of immense gratification. As awkward as it was, she found it fucking hot to have two guys she was totally into – and, in fact, already sleeping with – looking at her with such open lust. For a moment she wasn't sure she really wanted to stop it.

'I don't think it's that weird,' said Jacob. 'She's fucking hot.'

'She's fucking hot,' repeated Luke, nodding fervently.

'I mean, who *wouldn't* want to fuck her?'

'Fucking *hot*,' Luke repeated.

'Forget I said anything,' murmured Avery.

3

'I mean, is sex with her the fucking bomb or what?'

'The fucking bomb,' said Luke.

'Forget I said anything,' whimpered Avery.

'The things she does?'

'The things she says,' purred Luke.

They high-fived. 'The things she *says*!' cried Jacob merrily.

'The mouth on that girl!'

'At the right moment,' said Jacob.

'She'll say the right thing–'

The dudes fist-bumped.

'But, you know, that's not what I like about her. Mostly it's the body,' said Jacob.

'It's a good body,' said Luke.

'Not like that. The way she moves. The way she reacts.'

'Oh, yeah, yeah, yeah, yeah, fuck yeah,' said Luke, consumed. 'The way she *reacts*.'

'I mean, erogenous?'

'Erogenous zone,' grinned Luke. 'One big one.'

'Called Avery.'

'Now you guys are just fucking with me,' growled Avery.

'You know that part in the small of her back,' said Jacob – whapping the back of his hand against Luke's shoulder in open camaraderie – 'where if you tickle it real lightly or kinda lick it there, she just goes fucking nuts?'

'I don't know that spot,' said Luke, bewildered.

'I'll show it to you,' said Jacob lasciviously. 'Avery, c'mere.'

'Fuck off,' she breathed.

Both Luke and Jacob grinned.

Luke said, 'You find that place at the ball of her foot?'

'What place?'

'Like you were saying with her back. Just tickle it, or run your tongue over it, and this girl goes–'

'Forget I said anything,' Avery hissed.

'–fucking nuts,' mewled Luke. 'The tongue especially.'

'Dude, are you a fucking foot freak?'

'Hey, lighten up,' said Luke. 'You were just saying you wanted to suck my dick.'

4

'Hah! I don't know what you think you heard, dude – but you heard something I didn't say. Wishful thinking?'

'Yeah, on your part.'

The two made mocking kissy faces at each other.

'Forget I said anything,' said Avery, once more. 'This was stupid.'

Both men ignored her; their twin gaze only got progressively more obscene as the silence weighed them down.

'Personally, I'm into her tits,' Luke finally said.

'Luke, *stop*.' She was shifting uncomfortably.

Jacob made that sound that "dudes" make: sort of a "chaw!" sound, meaning "Yeah, no fucking shit, of course, fuck yeah, dude," or something like that. 'What's not to like,' he elaborated. 'Perfect. Are they fucking perfect or what?'

'Forget I said anything,' said Avery.

Luke: 'Fucking perfect.'

'Sensitive,' said Jacob.

'Sure, not just visually perfect,' agreed Luke.

'But, like, *sensually* perfect.'

'Forget I said anything,' Avery murmured.

'The way she reacts?'

'Oh, yeah. You know she can come from her nipples–'

'Jacob! Luke! *Stop*!' she hissed. She could barely move, she was so nervous; the faint swirl of a mild mimosa-drunk did little to help. She couldn't believe she'd actually suggested this; she couldn't believe she thought that it would work. And most of all, for the thousandth time, she wished she hadn't worn something so slutty.

Avery was aware of a sudden throb in her clit; she felt clammy, *down there*; the seam of her jeans pressed in tight, reminding her that she was wearing even less by way of underwear under her too-tight, too-low-slung jeans than she wore beneath her too-tight, too-thin, shawl-neck sweater. And that only made things worse.

When Avery glanced up again, the two men were staring at her tits, openly lustful. When they took in the sight of her face, red and humiliated, they both obviously felt a great deal of pleasure at seeing her humbled.

5

'You guys are just fucking with me.'

'Speaking only for myself,' said Luke. 'I think we're mostly serious.'

'I'm pretty serious,' agreed Jacob.

'Fuck off. Offer rescinded.'

'You opened the door, Ave,' said Jacob.

'Yeah? Forget I did.'

Then Luke said it, in his richest let's-go-to-bed voice, 'You want us to *beg*?'

Jacob: 'I think she wants us to beg.'

'I *don't*,' she said. 'It was a dumb idea. I don't know what I was thinking.'

'You were the one who wanted to date us both,' said Luke.

'Yeah, after you broke up with me!'

'She's got a point there, dude,' said Jacob.

Luke: 'Yeah, well ... that was stupid.'

'And now you gotta pay the price for your indiscretion,' said Jacob, in his "Dr Evil" voice.

The two high-fived.

'That place on her back,' asked Luke. 'You'll show it to me?'

'Oh, *fully*, dude, I'll fucking *demonstrate*. Information wants to be free. You just kinda–' Jacob did a thing with his tongue. She remembered the last time his tongue did that on the small of her back.

'She wants us to beg,' said Jacob.

Luke smiled. Jacob smiled. They put their hands together.

'You want us on our knees?'

'That'd be nice,' spat Avery. 'No, don't–'

She turned 11 shades of purple as they both kicked their chairs back and got on their knees.

'Please have a threesome with us?' Jacob mouthed, no sound – but they'd both done a semester of sign language and he knew she could read his lips. Avery looked around desperately to see if there were any deaf people around.

'No! Sit the fuck down!'

'Please?' This time, Luke, in a moan.

'Sit! Sit! Sit! No, don't–'

'Only if you agree to–' Luke began.

'–even fucking say it.' Avery cut across. '*Sit*,' she snapped. She was actually getting pissed, or at least she hoped they thought so. Inside, she was glowing.

They both sat down politely. The brunch crowd was glancing over, smiling; it was San Francisco, so shit like this happened daily – on a Sunday, every *hour*.

They sipped mimosas in silence; the waitress brought the bill.

'Are we gonna do this?' she finally asked.

The two men looked at each other.

Jacob made his "chaw!" sound.

Luke shrugged and nodded.

Avery took a deep breath. 'My place?' she asked.

Luke shrugged. 'It's close,' he said.

'Sounds good,' said Jacob.

'Yeah,' said Luke. 'And let's make it quick. I'm fuckin' horny.'

Jacob guffawed.

'It's the shirt!' they both howled simultaneously, and fist-bumped.

Good Christ, thought Avery. *What have I done*?

She breathed three times, slammed her last mimosa and sprinted for the door.

Under the circumstances, she figured, her two boyfriends could split the bill.

It was only a few moments before they joined her on Fifth Street, but it felt like hours. She stood there, heat pulsing through her body; she wanted badly to back out, but now that she'd gotten them to agree to it, the deed felt like it was done – without an item of clothing ever being dropped.

Fifth Street was busy. Two dykes made out across the street. A guy passed in front of her and dropped his gaze; she crossed her arms in front of her. Was this actually happening?

Jacob and Luke came out of the restaurant, Jacob tucking cash into his wallet. They looked her up and down and smiled.

Jacob turned to Luke. 'Dude, I'm not holding your hand.'

7

Avery made a disgusted noise. She took one hand each, and the three of them formed a line across the sidewalk walking toward Avery's place.

Had she been a little less drunk, she might have had further second thoughts – which wouldn't have done anybody any good. When Luke broke up with her – he 'needed some space', same old bullshit line every guy used – she'd resolved to be more experimental. No more monogamy. No more jumping into relationships. Dating was awesome. Fuckbuddies were cool. Casual sex was even better. Jacob had fallen somewhere at the confluence of all those categories: sex on the first date, sex on the second date, repeat ad infinitum. It had stopped being casual sex when they'd started planning sex weekends together, and she'd figured they would need to have The Talk when Luke came blasting back into her life, apologising for being a dipshit – just what every woman wants to hear, right? She'd gone right back to bed with him, and the sex had proven far better than before; apparently he'd learnt a lot in three months being single. Avery found herself in an arrangement suspended between a love triangle, dedicated polyamory and negotiated sluttiness. Jacob didn't seem to mind. Luke was slightly more possessive, but Avery'd put her foot down: no relationships as such; no monogamy. She didn't want things to get complicated.

So how was it she was holding two guys' hands, walking them back to her apartment, about to fuck them both?

The definition of complicated.

But then, it wasn't like she hadn't planned it out a million times in her fantasies. In fact, when she'd heard Luke's voice on the phone, she'd had three thoughts. The first was *He's dialled a wrong number*. The second was *Luke and Jacob = Threesome*.

The third thought was so filthy and distracting she'd barely heard a word Luke had said for the first half-minute of his apology.

She was a very naughty girl.

'How do we do this?' asked Avery. Luke and Jacob stood on opposite ends of her, in the corners of her small living room.

Her skin felt electric. It seemed to repulse them both; they repulsed each other, forming some weird fucking science experiment triangle. She felt breathlessly suspended between the two of them. Her back was to Jacob; her front was to Luke. She felt desperately asthmatic, locked in desperate breathless anticipation. She felt like she was having a panic attack. She blushed deep, her face hot, as Luke looked from her eyes to her tits.

Neither man said anything.

'How do we do this?' she repeated.

'You're the expert,' said Jacob.

He had stolen up behind her, six-feet plus of surfer dude towering over Avery's five-ish feet. He took hold of her waist, big hands resting gently on her hips. She trembled. He moved nearer, 'til his muscled body grazed her shoulder blades and buttocks. His thumbs traced the outline of her thong, visible above the too-low waistband of her jeans.

Luke crept closer, smiling enigmatically. Jacob's hands went up under Avery's soft, tight cotton sweater.

'Expert?' she moaned softly. 'How big a slut do you think I am?'

'Not as big as you'll be in an hour,' said Jacob.

Jacob's hands went smoothly north. At first she thought he was just cupping her tits – then the shawl collar blinded her, as Jacob lifted it neatly over her head.

'Oh God,' she said nervously, her words muffled. She obediently put her arms up, letting him take off her sweater. Jacob tossed it on the couch. Luke moved closer.

'You're wearing my favourite bra,' he said.

She could *feel* Jacob smirk behind her.

'Nice one, isn't it? She always wears it when she knows she's gonna get laid.'

'Are you two enjoying yourselves?' she asked.

Behind her, Jacob got hold of her hands and gently held them behind her.

'Now I am,' he said, kissing her neck.

Avery stiffened; his lips on her neck combined with him sort of half-pinning her arms made her so fucking hot she couldn't stand it. She sank into the sensation of Jacob kissing her as Luke moved in closer and looked her in the eyes. He reached for the clasp of her favourite bra – the thing was notoriously difficult to undo. Luke got it on the first try; Jacob let go of her hand to help Luke take it off of her, then reached down to unbutton her jeans.

The zipper stumped him, so Luke nudged Jacob's fingers out of the way and pulled the zipper down. Avery could almost feel the sizzling energy from where their hands touched. Two straight guys partnering up to undress the girl they were both about to fuck; it was freaky for them. That was so fucking hot.

As Luke took over pants duty, Jacob moved his hands up to Avery's tits; her eyes rolled back as he started gently working the nipples.

Luke lowered himself to his knees. He pulled Avery's tight jeans down her thighs with some difficulty, peeling the tight fabric away – fuck, had she really worn those out in public? As he did, Jacob tipped her head back and kissed her, hard, his tongue easing into her mouth while his hands began to work her nipples.

She kicked off her wedge-heeled mules and let Luke lovingly ease her jeans over her feet; as she stepped out of them, she felt his tongue tracing its way up her thigh. Surprised, she squirmed a little, which put her more firmly in Jacob's grasp. His big arms around her, he pinched her nipples more firmly, following the rhythms of her body. She writhed between them, feeling suddenly awkward. Jacob never let up kissing her deeply, and he never stopped working her nipples, building the pressure quickly until she was trembling with the intensity. Luke got hold of her slim, slutty thong and pulled it smoothly down her thighs. It was soaked.

How they made it to the futon, she'd never understand. It just sort of happened. Her two boys picked her up bodily, Jacob with his arms beneath her shoulders and his hands on her waist; Jacob with his palms across her buttocks, arms supporting her thighs. She felt like she was flying. As they settled her into Jacob's lap, his hard-on pressed against her back. Luke took her panties off.

10

She let him take them, feeling a slight wave of panic as they slipped over her ankles and she was *naked*; she felt it acutely. Naked, pinned between two hot guys. She knew this simply couldn't be happening – but here she was, naked between the two guys she was fucking. The two guys she was *about* to fuck. If she'd stopped to think for a moment, or been less buzzed, she never would have let it happen – thank God for fucking mimosas, she'd tell herself later.

Luke spread her legs. He bent down low; his tongue worked up over her thighs, nearing her cunt.

Before he could reach it, Jacob's hand slid down and across Avery's flat, tattooed belly and between her smooth-shaved thighs. Her lips, too, were smooth; she'd shaved for the occasion. In fact, she'd taken to shaving almost always; it vastly improved her life's ratio of cunnilingus to fellatio, especially when Luke was around.

'You like her shaved?' purred Jacob in her ear as he caressed her smooth-soft lips and found her clit.

'I fucking *love* her shaved,' Luke answered, his breath against her cunt. 'Like, fucking love.'

'Me too,' said Jacob. 'It's a guy thing.'

Luke lowered his face between Avery's thighs and planted his mouth hard against her vulva. His tongue went sliding across Jacob's fingers; Avery could feel the pressure of Jacob's hand on her clit and the caress of Luke's tongue gliding over her pussy-lips. They changed places and Jacob's fingers eased inside her, stretching her tight, wet cunt gently while Luke began to lick her clit. Luke had always been a consummate pussyhound – making up for a somewhat sloppy technique with the fact that every lick was totally his gig – not for her pleasure. Most guys were willing, sometimes even eager. With Luke? He thought of little else. And when it came to technique, a loose-lipped, free-form style usually got the job done.

It also meant he wasn't that careful about where his face was in relation to Jacob's hand.

For a second, Avery thought Jacob was caressing his face.

Fuck, that was fucking pervy. *What if–* she started thinking; then, *Fuck it. That's not gonna happen. Unless–*

The phrase was in her mouth before she could stop it: 'Are you gonna kiss?'

'Probably not,' said Jacob.

Luke shook his head; it sent a shiver through her clit.

'I'd kinda like it if you did,' she blurted.

''Cause you're a perv,' said Jacob, matter-of-factly.

It was true. A shameless fag hag since adolescence, Avery got instantly wet whenever she thought of two guys doing it. The fact that she'd historically only ever slept with utterly straight dudes had been one of the tragedies of her life thus far.

But that wasn't why she'd figured it was time to make a play for a threesome with Jacob and Luke. When she'd hatched her half-baked plan, she hadn't thought for a second Jacob and Luke would obediently augment her turn-on by touching each other; in fact, she'd completely dismissed the possibility.

But Jacob did not remove his hand from Luke's face. It looked fucking *hot*. She might have been prejudiced, sure, since Luke's expert tongue was working her clit faster and faster as his hands reached up for her buttocks and the small of her back—

'Not there, dude. *Here*.' With his free hand, which a moment before had been pinching Avery's nipples, Jacob took Luke's hand and guided it up the curve of her buttocks, past her hips, to the place—

'Oh fucking Jesus!' she cried as Jacob's firm guiding hand put Luke's fingers right where Jacob loved to kiss her.

'See? It's special.'

Luke's face came up from between her legs; he grinned salaciously.

'Nice!'

Experimentally, he glided his fingertips in circles around That Fucking Spot, and Avery twisted.

'No, don't—' she gasped.

'No, don't?' asked Luke.

'Or no, don't stop?' asked Jacob.

Luke's fingers tickled her there; she twisted, writhed, cried out; Luke's face descended between her legs again; he started licking her rhythmically as he caressed; it sent uneven spasms of tickling pleasure through her, but Luke wasn't nearly as practised at it as Jacob. Once Jacob had spent an hour licking there – she had basically come, or something like it. Luke was doing a damn fine job; her eyes rolled way back into her head and she shivered, gently humping her body up against him. But he wasn't the expert.

She felt Jacob's hand at That Fucking Spot: big, strong, heavy. 'Do that thing with her feet,' he said. 'I'll take over with her back.'

'Oh, fuck, fuck – fuck fuck fuck,' she thundered. 'No. No please–' she didn't know what she was saying; she writhed spasmodically between them.

Jacob turned her slightly, getting on his knees on the couch behind her, and spreading her legs so that Luke could get more firmly between her thighs. Jacob grabbed her hair. He arched her back. Jacob put his other hand down at That Spot – caressing, while pulling her hair gently, while biting her neck, gnawing, sucking, while Luke put his tongue on her clit, while Luke put his lips around the upper swell of her cunt lips, and did that *thing* he did; she'd never understand it – it was like a suck and a slurp, with a pressure somewhere no other guy could ever fucking find – and as he worked her clit Luke took her feet, one in each hand; he pushed them up to tip her vulva back at just the right angle, and each thumb found That Other Spot in the balls of her feet–

Avery screamed at the top of her lungs.

'Bad scream or good scream?' asked Jacob.

She made a 'Gaaah!' sound, writhing back and forth.

'Good scream?'

'Gaah!'

'Bad scream.'

'Gaaaah,' she howled, and clawed at his thighs. She shut her eyes tight, the movements of her body going fucking *crazy*. If she hadn't been pinned between two humans vastly bigger than she, she would have spazzed her way across the fucking living room, and probably poured out the window to slop on to Fifth Street. As it was, she was helpless between them – as they played her like an instrument, two virtuosos playing in

13

different keys.

'Good scream,' sighed Jacob. Avery's back arched; her belly undulated; her thighs shook; her head rolled against the tight hard grip of Jacob's hand in her hair; they kept going. They just wouldn't stop. Neither guy would let up. They worked every fucking erogenous zone she'd ever known she had, and a few she'd forgotten about, minus the two she could reach with her hands – which she started to do, totally shameless, planting her hands on her tits and working her nipples hard, pinching, prodding, squeezing, digging her fingernails into her flesh as she mounted toward–

'Orgasm,' said Jacob, matter-of-factly. 'Our girl's about to have an orgasm,' said Jacob.

'*Our* girl?' said Luke, his voice thrumming through her pubic bone.

'*Our* girl,' said Jacob emphatically. He stopped gnawing on the back of her neck and tucked her upper body firmly into his arms, still holding his hair.

Then he kissed her. His tongue went in deep, thick and wet, stifling her moans as she mauled her own tits like a maddened little vixen. His mouth came off of hers with a big wet snap of spit, and she lapped at it, teeth working violently like she couldn't get enough of him – them – of herself. Of fucking everything. She was crazed.

'Come for us,' purred Jacob, one hand pulling at her hair, the other gently caressing her face. Her eyes popped open wide and that was what did it; she'd looked into his eyes as she'd climaxed before – as creepy and Tantra as that sounds – but never like *this*. She came so hard she felt her fillings crack.

And neither boy had ever really heard her *scream* before. In fact, no human ever had; no creature had, except her cat. Which was not as dirty as it sounded; that is to say, when she came as hard as she came that day, it was usually vibrator-driven after hours of porn – and no one was listening, because Avery was always too embarrassed to seriously let go.

But this time, people were listening; two people, and probably the neighbours; possibly much of this city block and some of the next. She screamed anyway, at the top of her lungs, thrashing wildly back and forth until she had to push Luke's face away and shut her thighs and beg them, 'Stop, stop, stop, stop, stop!'

'Really stop this time?' asked Jacob.

'Uh,' she said, and clutched him close. Luke took a seat on the couch, with her feet in his lap; she shot him a warning look and he grinned.

'So, whuddaya say, dude?' It was Jacob: the cheeky one.

She was so brain-dead from screaming and coming that she didn't follow the innuendo, until after it was over. Even as Luke shot Jacob a sketchball look, she just lay there gaping and drooling.

'She said it'd really turn her on,' said Jacob.

Luke sighed.

'Weird,' he said. 'Fucking weird.'

Jacob eased himself out from under her; he tucked pillows under her back and leant way over toward Luke.

'Let's try not to make it too gay,' said Jacob, as he came in for the kiss.

And then his mouth was hard on Luke's – not even tentative; not a girl-kiss; not even a girls-while-their-boyfriends-are-watching kiss. Just a kiss; a fucking open-mouthed, lots-of-tongue kind of kiss. And it lasted.

When their mouths came apart, there was spit. There was *spit*. Avery moaned.

Both boys looked at her, smiled, turned back; they kissed again, deep again, and Avery watched, gape-mouthed, moaning, wide-eyed.

It just came out of her mouth before she could stop it – in a low, soft, rapturous moan, rich with promise.

'Oh, my God. Thank you. *Thank* you!'

They finished kissing and high-fived.

One of them said, 'Let's go to bed,' and that was good enough for her.

The Untouchable Tabby
by Lana Fox

I was her student at college when we first met, and the way she fixed me with that sky-blue gaze I thought I saw whole worlds there. When she laughed, she did so lightly, as if she hadn't a care, and I alone could see the sadness in her face. 'Tabby is such fun,' the other girls would chime. 'The way she talks! What a cutie.' But sensing Tabby's wounds, I believed she ran far deeper. Like my father before he divorced my mum, Tabby possessed a kind of blackness, and this pulsed behind her flirtations in a low, sad beat. In her quirky pageboy caps and skinny, ribbed tops, which barely covered her pale breasts, she would scrawl spider diagrams on the board, calling, 'Come on, darlings! More!' and I always imagined her gasping those words in bed, and the thought would make me writhe in my seat. 'Read the next paragraph,' she'd tell me, with a cheeky wink, and I'd hear the others whispering, 'Why does she always choose *Val*?'

Many years later, when I was home visiting my father, I bumped into Tabby in the post office queue. She was mailing a bright parcel with coloured balloons all over it – a birthday present for her niece, she said. Her hair, still short and curly, had gone from brown to cherub-blonde, and she wore a pair of black-rimmed, mock-preppy glasses. The little, slender lines on her face betrayed her age – late 30s, I decided – but she was still covered in those sweet brown freckles, which covered her cheeks, nose and throat. She was sucking a sweet that smelt of cherries, and it bulged behind her cheek as I invited her to visit. 'Watch out, peach,' she said, laying her hand on my arm. Her

17

fingertips were cool. 'You might get what you ask for.'

A couple of months later I received the call. Tabby said she was going to a conference in London, and her train made a stop in Leicester where I lived. Might she visit and take me out to dinner? It just so happened, I had two free tickets for the theatre that night. When I told Tabby, she agreed to come along.

I met her at the station, looking radiant, in a pair of curly pigtails with an armful of red roses. On the train platform, with the throngs passing by, she thrust the scented flowers towards me and gave me a quick kiss. When we embraced like old friends, she felt so slender beneath her top, with her breasts pressing against my own. Now our teacher-student barriers were lifted, I assumed we'd screw like we longed to, and when, in the car on our way to mine, she leant in close and touched my thigh, whispering, 'This is nice, isn't it?' I took it as a come-on.

Back at my basement flat we had to change in a hurry. The play was starting in an hour, and we'd follow that with dinner. My bondage friend, Ray, phoned while Tabby was changing. Ray had been my sex-buddy for months and was part of the play we were going to see. 'What's cooking with the teach?' he asked.

'Kiss on the mouth. Red roses. Already groped my thigh.'

'If that doesn't spell *fuck me*,' said Ray, 'I'll eat my own eyebrows.'

'I'd say join us, but she might be kind of vanilla.'

'She's all yours, bad girl. Don't torture her too hard.'

I went upstairs to use the bathroom, but paused on the landing outside. Tabby had left the door open and, with her back to me, was pulling a top over her head, while a pair of black, lace briefs cupped her tight freckled buttocks, the scalloped edge sinking seductively into the cleft. And dear mother of fuck, those thighs! Lean and glossy as if she'd rubbed herself with oil! There I stood, gobsmacked, in my little black number, thirsting to lick and grind ... and as if this wasn't enough, when Tabby glanced back across her shoulder, smoothing the flared white dress about her hips, I saw no shock in her heavy-lidded eyes. Instead, she looked up with a sexy pout, and winked as she slammed the door, leaving a blast of tantalising scent.

In my room, I sent Ray a text. *Caught her changing. She's wearing lacy knickers.*

He replied, *Slut needs a spanking.*

But for all my bravado, I sensed something wasn't right. Don't be silly, I told myself. You deserve this. Enjoy it. So I applied my own perfume, which Ray called bitch's blend, dabbing my pulse points before spraying my auburn hair.

As I blew a kiss at the mirror, I jumped to see Tabby behind me. With her hair still in curly, blonde pigtails and her lips slicked with transparent gloss, she was wearing a Marilyn-style halter neck dress, white, like the starlet's, and plunging, revealing a lightly freckled cleavage. She looked so hot she made me catch my breath.

Leaning against my doorframe, she said, 'Come on, sweetie. We're late.'

In the auditorium, I hardly watched the play. Ray, who was the translator for folks who were deaf, was signing with his hands while mouthing the lines. His face, which had always been riotously expressive, seemed far more alive than the actors', and the way he gestured with his hands made me remember how he smacked my naked buttocks once a week, or teased me with his fingertips as they slid around the edge of my slit.

The play was *Twelfth Night*, my favourite of Shakespeare's, but as time went on I became more taken with the way the light danced across Tabby's face, glancing off the shiny lips and brightening the blue eyes. I was enchanted by her scent and the way she laughed, dropping back her head; yet when I laced my fingers through her own, she turned to me, alarmed, before pulling her hand away.

In the interval, as I handed her a G&T, she stared down into it, jingling the ice cubes. The entrance hall was so crowded with other drinkers that she couldn't help but stand close. I received a text from Ray. *How much touch?* But I didn't even reply. 'So, Tabby,' I said, with a gulp of my wine. 'You're not into women?'

She rolled her eyes behind her glasses. 'I don't do sex, full stop.'

'But the way you dress and your body language ...'

Her expression grew sour. 'You can rely on it too much, dear,' she snipped, before knocking back her drink. When she lowered her glass, she told me she didn't do intimacy, and pursing the gin from her lips, added, 'Sharing's overrated.' I saw then that she'd been hurt by a lover – perhaps this accounted for the sadness I'd sensed when she taught me.

'But you *want* sex,' I tried. 'And you want sex with *me*. It'd change us both. I'm not your student any more.'

She gave a hard laugh that softened to a smile, then stroked the hair from my face. 'You're right, dear,' she said, 'but I can't, OK?' And then a buzzer signalled the start of Act 2.

After the play was finished, Tabby went to the loo, so I gave Ray a call. 'Beautiful signing,' I said.

He laughed. 'Like you noticed! You were too busy stroking your teacher's pussy.'

I told him about Tabby, how she wouldn't let me touch her. 'All the way through the second half, I didn't even look at the play. I was too stunned that she'd brushed me off.' It was true, I'd hardly seen the actors in their Shakespearian corsets – I'd been too busy gazing at Tabby's freckled breasts, so delicately cupped by the halter neck fabric, and imagining kissing those full glossed lips that would slide so perfectly over mine.

'Shall I crash the party?' said Ray.

I asked him to join us for dinner.

'That poor woman needs seducing,' he said. 'Let's give her the time of her life.'

I chose the restaurant: a tapas bar nearby. When I explained my friend was joining us, Tabby gave the tiniest pout as if I'd somehow abused her. By the time Ray arrived, we'd ordered champagne along with a medley of tiny bowls and platters. Roasted red peppers drizzled in oil, almond-stuffed dates wrapped in crispy bacon, chilli-fried shrimp, griddled halloumi cheese and hasselback potatoes all brown and sweet. We ate from a glass-topped table with a candle at its centre, using our fingers to pick at the fare. Ray and I sat either side of Tabby on a curved bench that followed the line of the table. Her body language was prim at first, arms tight at her sides, but as the evening wore on she let us snuggle so close that our knees touched, and she even allowed Ray to feed her bacon-wrapped morsels. The first of these made her moan with pleasure, dropping back her head as she chewed.

I pressed my thigh against hers and said, 'My turn. Feed me something.'

She watched me for a while, her blue eyes growing, her distrust grappling with the lust that swelled her pupils; then eventually she gave half a smile and chose a strip of roasted red pepper, which she placed on my tongue. I overacted entirely, falling back into the seat, massaging my breasts through the lycra as I groaned with enjoyment; beneath the table I reached between my legs massaging my own thigh as I let a droplet of oil escape from the side of my own mouth.

I could feel the burn of Tabby's stare as Ray leant against her ear and whispered, 'Lick it off.'

But the droplet ran down my chin and throat, and she didn't move an inch. So Ray, in his brilliance, moved round my side of the bench, sitting right close to me, and licked from my tits up to my throat, catching the droplet on his tongue, before repeating the act with his hand on my thigh, his fingers gripping so hard that I felt a glorious shot of pain. 'Fuck,' he told me, 'you're a sexy little bitch.'

'Feed me more,' I gasped to Tabby, rolling my head her way.

I thought we'd snared her because her cheeks had flushed and she was sucking her finger as she stared at Ray's seductions. He was now lowering my strap, licking across my shoulder; but before we could argue, Tabby was sidling away, snapping, 'You've no right. I'm going to powder my nose.'

She spent the rest of the meal quietly eating, while Ray dangled his hand below my belly, fingering me through my silky briefs

– sometimes smoothly, sometimes roughly – until I was so wet I couldn't eat. Worried about Tabby, I tried not to show my pleasure, which made the whole scenario twice as hot. We ended up back at my place getting stoned in my bedroom, Tabby lying on her belly across my double bed, her prickliness slipping slowly away. I burned a sandalwood candle that gave the pot an exotic tinge, and lay on the rug with my head in Ray's lap as we shared a joint. I stared up at his lively brown eyes, which made him look as if he were constantly amused.

Ray and I steered the conversation away from *Twelfth Night* and towards sexuality, but Tabby would have nothing of it. She continually brought us back to the present day, speaking of her teaching work, her neighbours and the art classes she enjoyed. But as the smoke took her, she began to lounge, rolling on to her back and laughing as Ray cracked jokes. 'Silly boy,' she told him, taking off her glasses. I was struck by her pretty face, so blue-eyed and innocent. 'You're worse than my students,' she added.

'I'm offended,' I said, with a wry smile.

'You shouldn't be,' she said, with a smoulder. Softening, she added, 'You weren't just any old student.'

Woah! My jaw went slack.

'Well?' Ray asked Tabby. 'What *was* Val like? Spill.'

Tabby rolled on to her front, her dress peeling upwards, the fabric gathering around her perfect thighs. Her whole expression was relaxed, playful, sleepy. With curls coming loose from her little blonde pigtails, she purred, 'Val was the cleverest girl I ever taught.'

I glowed.

Ray laughed. 'So how come she can't use chopsticks?'

I slapped his arm.

'Seriously,' said Ray, reaching around my shoulders. 'Val's adorable as heck, and clever, but I can't imagine she was much of a boffin!'

'Don't have to be a boffin to be smart,' I said.

Tabby rolled on to her back so she was looking at us upside down, her pale cleavage exposed behind her jawline, as if one move might force those tight little breasts to just pop from the fabric, nipples and all. 'She was dreamy,' she said, taking a drag on her joint. Breathing out her smoke, she closed her eyes: 'In that whole damn class, all I saw was Val.'

I grinned, setting my joint in the saucer at my side. 'And all I saw was you,' I said, softly.

'So?' Ray asked Val. 'Why don't you screw the girl?'

Tabby smoked thoughtfully for a while before giving her answer. When she did, her voice turned cool: 'A cheating bitch called Layla.'

Ray and I exchanged a look, before he peeled away and crawled across to Tabby. Climbing up on to the bed, he grinned and tweaked one of her pigtails. She giggled, blue eyes glinting as he pulled in close. 'I know a good cure for heartbreak,' Ray said, fingers glossing the fabric between her breasts. 'You're a sweetie, you know? And hot as hell. And Val over there is besotted. And maybe I am too.'

Tabby's eyes met his. She watched him for a while, then reached up and ruffled his hair. Smiling, she said, 'Are you making a pass?'

Ray laughed. 'We're *both* making a pass.'

She stared at me, waiting. At last, she gave me a sultry wink. 'OK,' she said, smirking, 'but only because I'm high.'

Happy as a birthday girl, I skipped across to the bed. When I was next to her, she said, 'Kiss me.' So I did. Her mouth was as yielding as I'd guessed: her lips, which tasted of cherry-flavoured gloss, slid across mine, and her tongue was lithe and gentle, tasting of the joint. We kept on going, opening our mouths on one another. I felt her fingers on my breast, kneading gently. She moaned. Then I ran my fingers through those soft little curls and touched her nape and the curve of her ass. She rolled on to her side, settling into the kiss, and now I was able to reach right beneath her skirt, my fingers brushing up those supersmooth thighs – I'd always known she'd be cool to the touch, like the insides of shells. When I drew away, I saw Ray reaching round her, pulling the fabric away from her breast. The sweetest, hardest roseate nipple lay gorgeously exposed. He rolled her on to her back, both of them smiling. 'Naughty teacher,' he told her. 'No bra. How slutty.' Then he began to lick Tabby's perfect breast, and kept on going until it was glossed with saliva. I watched for a while, then joined in, running my tongue over her other tight little nipple, making her gasp and shiver. Ray, who was softly moaning as he licked, thrust his hand inside Tabby's skirt and began to pleasure her with that wonder-touch of his. She arched, lips parting, and let out a sudden cry, her lips and lashes quivering, and said, 'Oh God, it's been so long!' I felt her absently tugging at my hemline. 'Take it off,' she gasped, with a pleading look. 'Oh, Val ... please.'

I didn't need any encouragement. Beneath I was wearing silky briefs – pink, the colour Ray liked – with a matching bra that raised and rounded my tits.

As Ray began to bite Tabby's nipple, she groaned, staring down at him, hand splayed on the back of his head; when she focused again, she said, 'Val, honey, let me touch you.'

On my knees, I shuffled closer, letting her run a free hand over me. She smelt of pricey scent I recognised – something dry by Calvin Klein. 'My ex was never as pretty as you,' she murmured, entranced by my body, 'and never so clever either.'

Ray pulled back, so I lowered myself over her, and said, 'If music be the food of love, we're playing it, baby ...' Then I dipped a hand inside her skirt and found those lacy briefs and the perfectly waxed pussy beneath. I started softly, then pushed my fingers right into her, making her cry out and grab fistfuls of the sheets. Her scent, her little moans, her slick little slit, her wetness sliding smoothly from inside her ... all of this from the teacher I'd once watched so keenly. I was so wet and enchanted that I couldn't look away.

At last, I heard Ray unzipping, but didn't expect him to crawl behind me, pull my panties aside and fill me with his cock. As I shivered with pleasure, he started fucking me hard, telling me I was a bad little girl who shouldn't touch her teachers. My whole body jerked with Ray's every thrust, and I knew I had to taste Tabby again, if only to feel the yielding of her sex. As I lowered my mouth to her, I glanced up her body: her lips were parted, covered in saliva and she was watching me from between her knees, her eyelids heavy. 'Do it,' she whispered. 'Suck me.'

I was so aroused, I burned.

As I pressed my tongue to her slippery sex, tasting her, teasing the nib of her clit, Ray continued to slam himself into me. 'Dirty girl,' he told me, pushing my face into Tabby's pussy and, turned on by his brutality, I licked and licked and licked. Tabby moaned so loudly, her sex gushing, thirstily. 'Oh, baby,' she cried out, 'don't ever fucking stop ...'

What I realised while I was going down on Tabby was how charged it felt. This wasn't simply a fun-fuck. This was about recovery. Later, for instance, as Ray jerked off, watching me spank Tabby, while a thread of drool spilled from her lower lip, I realised we were purging that cruel lover she'd mentioned: the one who'd probably been hurting her while I was in her class and had sensed her pain. Now, she knelt on the sheets, gorgeous and naked, her freckled skin glossed with perspiration, and I knelt behind her, pulling down on her pigtails so she was forced to tip back her head. I loved controlling her and displaying her for Ray, who, with his jeans and boxers round his thighs, was jerking off opposite Tabby. His gaze was glued to her tits, and he soon began a crescendo of 'Fuck, yes!' reaching out with his free hand to maul her breast. Tabby laughed and cried, 'Is he coming on me? Is he?' And oh, it was so joyous an exclamation, that it made me burn. As Ray came all over those perfect breasts, the sound of his come spattering her skin, Tabby reached back into my wet pussy and I felt such pleasure at her wondrous, digging fingers that I came too – deep and hard – falling on her, with a cry.

Afterwards, whenever we talked about Tabby, Ray would say, 'She was hot, but you were the hottest,' as every good lover should, and I said the same to him, of course, except I called him *bad*. On future dates, we'd talk about how the three of us had lain there together, after we'd all come, tangled up and naked, the smile on Tabby's face utterly serene. Perhaps this moment sowed the seed that gave Ray and me the guts to fall in love – the gift of what she gave us, and what we'd been giving her.

As it happened, we met her again two years later, quite by accident in a London bar. A beautiful redhead was with her, arm draped around my old teacher's shoulders. While we drank together, Tabby couldn't stop touching me – my knee, my arm, my hair.

'You're different,' I told her.

She grinned. 'Thanks to you.'

'Later, you can express your gratitude,' I joked.

And, of course, she did.

Proxy
by Malin James

Peter had been told, on more than one occasion and in tones that varied from awe to disbelief, that his sex drive was truly a miracle to behold. It was a testament to the truth of this statement that he invariably agreed. At 32, he had slept with only slightly fewer women than a seasoned professional and a small but impressive handful of open-minded men. He'd had lovers of every discernible type, in countless positions and in various locations both exotic and discreet. What little he'd yet to experience he'd had no doubt he some day would – until the accident had cut him off (riding a motorcycle at excessive speeds on rainy nights can do that).

With four cracked vertebrae and a collection of other hurts, Peter was three months into a long and painful recovery – a recovery that had all but killed his once heroic libido. At first the loss hadn't caused undue alarm. Traction, surgeries and heavy drugs would slow anybody down, and Peter's sex drive, though titanic, was by no means immune. Now, however, that he was fairly mobile again (he could even sit up in bed with a certain rakish flair), his desire for sex was still fast asleep, as was his impressive cock.

He tried the usual stimuli – fantasies, porn, memories (lovingly catalogued) of particularly good fucks – but none of it seemed to work. Thinking that perhaps he needed something a bit more concrete, he tried fantasising about Sarah, his adorable live-in nurse whose long, tapered fingers were a masterpiece from God. He imagined those hands stroking him into a thoroughly rigid state. He imagined the ivory column of her throat swallowing him whole. He imagined her climbing on top of him with her neat little uniform tunic pushed up around her hips, revealing, what he imagined to be, her naturally auburn curls. Still, he didn't stir. The bottomless well of his sex drive had gone disturbingly dry. Finally desperate, Peter broached the subject with his doctor while the adorable Sarah waited outside.

'Well,' said Dr Bradley, an aging hippie with a tremendously kind face, 'you've endured quite a trauma. It's normal for secondary functions to take a back seat while the body is trying to recover.'

'Dr Bradley,' replied Peter, scrubbing his hands through his dark, curly hair, 'sex is not a secondary function for me. It's a primary function. Possibly THE primary function. If I lose my sex drive, I don't know what I'll do.'

Peter, who avoided emotional drama like the plague, heard his voice crack and gritted his teeth. Dr Bradley gave him a sympathetic nod.

'Perhaps you could try something tried and true – something that's never failed, so to speak?'

'I have. None of it worked.'

'Well then, the only thing left to try, short of medication, is something completely new.'

'Dr Bradley, with all due respect, I'm not sure my history allows for something completely new.'

Dr Bradley smiled. 'Well, just give it a shot. See what happens. If it doesn't work, we can always try medication.'

With an encouraging smile, Dr Bradley left, leaving Peter the rest of the afternoon to think. He thought while Sarah moved about the room, adjusting this and checking that with her long, elegant hands. He went through the list of things he hadn't yet done, but concluded that there wasn't much. He'd seduced a set of triplets the summer before, and the odds of finding a young, willing nun weren't terribly good at the moment. Other than that, there were only two things, or rather, two people, that Peter had yet to do – his best friends, Ben and Michaela.

Peter and Ben and Michaela had been friends for ages, and

in that time, nothing had ever happened between them – nothing except for that once. In their final semester of college, what had begun as a drunken wrestling match had turned into something else, and the three of them had ended up kissing on the floor. It hadn't gone further than that, but the thought of it teased him now as he remembered Michaela's hot, swollen mouth and the length of Ben's cock pressed against his leg. Before he could change his mind, Peter picked up the phone.

He told himself, when he made the calls, that nothing was going to happen, that it was all just an experiment to see if his interest piqued. He told himself more than once and in no uncertain terms, but his nerves still jerked like a puppet's strings when the doorbell rang that night.

'Peter,' Sarah said, in her adorably husky voice, 'Ben and Michaela are on their way up. If you don't need anything else, I'm going to go out for a bit.'

Peter's stomach pitched, but he gave her a nonchalant smile. 'It's your night off, Sarah. Go have fun.'

'Thanks. I won't be back too late.'

Sarah bit her lip and smiled with a slightly less-than-professional warmth. At least, Peter thought she did. Before he could process the possibility, Sarah was gone and Ben and Michaela walked in. Peter's nerves came back full force.

'Hey Peter,' Michaela said, dropping into a chair. 'Are you OK? You look kind of awful.'

From anyone else, it would have been bitchy, but from her it was totally sweet. Peter forced a smile and managed a half-shrug.

'I'm fine. Sarah's just cutting back the codeine, that's all.'

'And how is the lovely Sarah tonight,' Ben asked, setting a bag of Chinese take-out on the neatly organised desk.

Peter scanned Michaela's body from the lovely peaks of her breasts to the extravagant length of her legs while Ben moved to stand beside her with his hip against her chair. Suddenly, Peter felt the whisper of something he hadn't felt in months. Not so much a stirring, but the hint of a stirring. It was enough to make it worth the risk.

Michaela cleared her throat as Peter eyed the curve of her

collarbone. 'Peter? You there? Ben just asked about Sarah ...'

Peter shook his head and found Michaela's face.

'Sarah ... right. It's Sarah's night off. She said she was going out.'

'That's too bad. She's pretty,' she said with a wink. Ben rolled his eyes.

'Come on, like you haven't noticed. If Peter weren't recovering, you two would be waging war.'

Ben shook his head. 'Pretty though she is, she's not my type.'

'Since when do *you* have a type?'

'Since now.'

Ben pushed off her chair and prowled around the room while Michaela shook loose her hair. Her fingers combing those long, dark waves and Ben's obvious restlessness brought the whisper back to Peter's groin, a little stronger this time. He listened to them banter, watched their physical ease, appreciated, not for the first time, how unusually good-looking they were. Remembering what Dr Bradley had said, Peter opened his mouth. He had no idea what he was going to say, he just knew he had to say it before he changed his mind.

'Hey, guys? I have a request.'

Michaela smiled. 'Sure – you're the guy stuck in bed. Just don't ask to borrow my underwear again.'

An awkward silence followed as Peter tried to figure out what he wanted to say. Finally, Ben rolled his shoulders and leant against the desk.

'Seriously, Pete. What is it?' he said. 'Do you need a kidney? Because I'm sure Michaela would loan you one ...'

'No,' Peter said, 'it's nothing like that. This is just going to sound really ... odd.'

Michaela, who had a surprisingly tender heart for someone who looked like a Russian spy, leant over and took his hand.

'Just tell us, Peter. It can't be that bad ...'

Peter took a breath. 'OK. I need you to fuck each other. And I need you to let me watch.'

Michaela opened her mouth, but nothing came out. Ben tactfully stepped in.

'I'm sorry, you need us to what?'

Peter almost wished he could take the words back, but the looks on their faces clearly said there was nothing to do but press on. 'I need you to fuck each other, and I need you to let me watch.'

Michaela cleared her throat. 'And why would we do that?'

Peter recognised her tone, the incredibly reasonable tone that preceded her getting incredibly mad.

'Wait. Just hear me out.'

Michaela crossed her arms as Ben lounged in a chair, but not, Peter noticed, before his eyes ran up Michaela's long, long legs. Maybe there was some hope.

'Since the accident, I haven't ... my sex drive has dropped to zero. It's not just that I can't get it up, it's that I don't even want to.' Peter paused, both humiliated and relieved to finally tell his friends. 'I've tried everything and nothing's worked – porn, fantasies; I can't even jack off. But I remembered that night in college, and now, watching the two of you together ... it's the first time I've felt anything in months. I just need to see if I'm ... if I'm ever going to get it back.'

'I'm sorry, Peter,' Michaela said. 'I had no idea.'

Peter looked at Michaela, instinctively aware that Ben hadn't taken his eyes off her. Finally, Ben spoke up. 'I understand what you're saying, but I need to talk to Michaela alone.'

Peter nodded. 'Of course.'

Ben stood up and waited for Michaela at the door. Then they slipped out of the room. Peter knew they could refuse his request. He knew they probably should – what he'd asked them to do crossed about two dozen lines – lines that had kept the three of them close and uncomplicated for nearly 15 years. Still, he had to hope. The whisper of interest that had quickened his groin became something close to a hum. Peter strained his ears. He'd just managed to catch murmurs from the other room when the murmurs suddenly stopped. A long moment later, Ben and Michaela came back in.

Ben looked serious. Michaela looked flushed but calm. Then without saying anything, Ben pulled Michaela into his arms. He kissed her, lightly, playfully at first. Then his tongue slipped into her mouth and she sank her body into his. Peter tensed, floored by the fact that they were going to do what he'd asked.

Ben's hands skimmed the length of her body, settling just beneath her breasts, just close enough to brush the undersides with his thumbs. Michaela arched her back, a subtle, instinctive response that had Ben wrapping his hands in her hair. Peter watched them move as if it was what they were meant to do, as if all the years of their friendship should have been spent like that. When Michaela began to sway against Ben, Peter was very officially on his way to his first erection in months.

Ben lifted his head and unzipped her dress, dropping hot, wet kisses down her neck along the way. Michaela tugged at his shirt, but he stayed focused on her face, watching her dark, hungry eyes as her dress slipped to the floor to reveal her gauzy bra and gauzier panties and just about everything else. She'd only just gotten Ben's shirt off when his hand dipped below her lacy waistline and began to stroke her sex. She gripped his neck and moaned.

Peter watched, fascinated, as Ben brought Michaela right up to the edge, cradling her close as she moved against his hand. Suddenly, she cried out and Ben lowered his head, swallowing the sound with a kiss. A moment later, she opened her eyes. Peter watched Michaela look up at Ben as a profoundly sweet softness lit up her face. Then she gave him a drowsy smile and sank down to her knees.

Ben leant back, bracing his weight against the desk as she worked him out of his jeans. Then Michaela angled her neck, giving Peter an unobstructed view as she kissed the pearly drops of moisture from Ben's fully hardened cock. Both men held their breaths. Then, with a distinctly feline smile, she took him down her throat.

Peter knew that his cock was hard – really hard – and that he was stroking it like a friend. He didn't, however, know that Sarah had come home until she was standing near the bed.

'Here, let me.'

Peter looked up and flushed. He hadn't heard her come in

(apparently, neither had Ben and Michaela, or if they had they didn't care). Peter's hand slowed to a stop. He was about to start apologising, when Sarah shook her head.

'Don't,' she whispered. 'You don't need to explain.'

After warming a bit of lotion in her lovely hands, Sarah stroked him once, from base to tip as Peter groaned. Then she expertly went to work. Meanwhile, Ben, who'd been testing the limits of his control, dragged Michaela into his arms.

He laid the long, lush length of her down across the desk, as bottles, papers and a bag of take-out abruptly hit the floor. Peter, caught between Sarah's glorious hands and the sheer hotness of his friends, watched Michaela wrap her legs around Ben's waist and press her body into his. Sarah murmured something he couldn't quite hear, as she looked appreciatively on.

The muscles in Ben's back tensed and bunched as he lowered his mouth to Michaela's breast, sucking hard at the nipple through the barrier of her bra. She moaned and threw back her head, as if the sounds were getting pulled from somewhere deep within her lungs. She was panting by the time Ben raised her hips and slid off her panties.

'Jesus Christ,' Ben ground out. 'Tell me you've got condoms somewhere in this room.'

'Here,' Sarah said, tossing him one from the bedside drawer without losing the rhythm with her hand. Ben caught it, barely registering Sarah's presence as Michaela tore open the wrapper and took the length of him in her hand.

'Ben, hurry. Please,' she whispered, arching her hips after quickly sliding it on. Ben kissed her, and thrust in.

Peter listened with half an ear as Ben's breathing went ragged and Michaela mewled in relief. Then Ben began to move, thrusting deep. Sarah watched them for a moment, then matched her pace to his. Peter's own hips, immobile for so long, began to move.

'Careful, Peter,' Sarah whispered. 'Not too much. I'll take care of you.'

'Sarah, I need to feel you,' he said, barely hearing himself over the rush of his pulse.

'All right,' Sarah said with a smile. 'Just hold on a sec.' Then she leant over and kissed Peter gently on the mouth before stepping away. He watched her strip out of her winter coat and her boots and practical tights, before she climbed carefully on to the bed.

'You can touch me, Peter, but anything more will have to wait.'

Peter, who would have sacrificed an arm just to feel her creamy skin, nodded his assent. When her delicious weight had pinned him, he pushed her skirt up around her hips, revealing her thatch of auburn curls. She reached for the lotion, pressing her sex against his cock. She gasped and nearly dropped the bottle when he found her heat and stroked.

On the desk, Ben and Michaela drove into each other as Sarah gently cradled Peter's balls, never wavering once with the motion of her hand. Peter closed his eyes. He was harder than he could ever remember being, absolutely ready to come, but she was drawing it out, letting him enjoy, waiting for Ben and Michaela to come. But Peter, now intensely focused on Sarah, wanted to see her come first.

He placed one hand on her hip to steady her. Then he slid his fingers into the heat of her slick, ready cunt. She arched her back and sighed. Peter paused and let her get used to him before he began to move, stroking the internal length of her clit while his thumb circled the swollen nub. She whimpered and jerked her hips, but even as she toppled over the edge, she stroked his cock, matching her movements to his. Peter gritted his teeth as Sarah's body clenched around his hand. He wanted to wait for Ben and Michaela. Luckily, he didn't have to wait long.

Moments later, Michaela cried out, clutching hard at Ben's back. The second she started to climax, Ben let himself go and followed her over the edge. Then, as if she'd known what he'd wanted all along, Sarah pressed the base of Peter's cock, gently massaging his prostate through his thin, sensitive skin. Peter closed his eyes and came in one massive gush.

When Peter opened his eyes, Ben held Michaela in his arms.

'Hello, Sarah,' Michaela said, as if they were meeting each

other for tea. 'How've you been?'

'Not bad. How are you?'

Peter looked up at Sarah's pretty, flushed face and manfully cleared his throat. 'Sarah came home early.'

Ben lifted a brow, managing, somehow, to look both sleek and ridiculous, bent naked, over a desk.

'Yes. Lucky for you that she did.'

'Lucky for us both.' Sarah leant in and gave Peter a scorching kiss. 'I've been wanting to get my hands on him for ages.'

Michaela grinned.

'I think we should probably go.'

Peter watched Ben help Michaela down, then draw her close. Even rumpled and post-coital, they looked absolutely hot.

'Satisfied, Pete?' Michaela asked.

Peter looked at Ben and Michaela, then at Sarah, who had folded herself up on the bed. 'Yes. I'm satisfied.'

'Good. Always glad to help. Ben, will you drive me home?'

Ben looked down at her, a thousand things playing over his face. 'I don't know ...' he said, softly.

'Ben, will you drive me home so we can do unspeakable things all night?'

'Well, then yes. Of course.'

Ben and Michaela gathered their things and dressed in under five minutes, stopping only long enough to pick the food up off the floor.

'Here you two – dinner ... maybe for later,' Michaela said, as Sarah pressed her adorable mouth down the length of Peter's throat. Peter waved and watched them leave. Then he settled down to thanking Sarah for helping him to recover.

Saturday Night Takeaway
by Josephine Myles

It was a Saturday night in a dingy pub in Bristol when I first realised my boyfriend had the hots for another man.

It was our new local, and we didn't know many people in Bristol yet. That's why I'd been thrilled to see Rob returning from the bar with a bloke in tow. He doesn't usually make friends as easily as I do, see, so it was wonderful to see him chatting so merrily. I admit, I couldn't follow exactly what they were on about as I had no idea who this Isherwood fella was, but I nodded, smiled, and amused myself studying Phil. He'd said, in his sexy, rumbling voice, that he was an English teacher at the sixth-form college. You wouldn't think it to look at him, all kitted out in leather and studs, with a ring through his nose, but I reckon his students must have loved him. He had twinkling eyes and a wicked smile, and Rob seemed to be hanging on his every word.

It was when I returned from a trip to the bar, clutching my three pints, that I realised what was going on. Rob and Phil were both sitting on the same bench, talking. Not so suspicious, I hear you say, but it was that daft expression on Rob's face that gave him away. It's the same one he uses on me when he's had a few too many and he wants to get into my knickers. I don't put up much of a fight, mind you, but then I've never seen the point in playing hard to get. I've always been a straightforward sort of girl, and if I want something, I ask for it; you know?

Take Rob, for instance. I'd first met him when he was a regular customer in the café where I used to work. It took me a

37

couple of weeks to realise that the bashful Waterstones employee was a real cutie, all dark hair, trim goatee, big brown eyes and soulful gazes. OK, so he had his head buried in a book most of the time, but I caught him checking me out when he thought I couldn't see him. Bless; he never did figure out that I was watching him in the mirrors. I loved the way he pronounced my name when he ordered as well, sounding out each syllable in Bethany like it was something special, and not just some weird, old-fashioned name I inherited from my great grandmother.

I began to wonder if it was the tattoos and Goth clothing that were scaring him off, but I certainly wasn't willing to change my style for anyone, no matter how much I fancied them. In the end, I figured it would have to be me who struck up a conversation, so I asked him what he was reading. I reckon he was pretty shocked I'd even heard of George Orwell, let alone read *Animal Farm*, but like I told him, I was taking an English Lit module as part of my Access to Higher Education evening classes. I was going to get to uni if it fucking well killed me. He laughed when I said that, a warm, mellow sound that made me want to kiss him there and then. Instead, I asked him to meet me for a drink after work; and the rest, as they say, is history.

There we were, then; 18 months later, having moved to Bristol so I could take my degree in social work. Rob still hadn't found himself a job in publishing like he wanted to, but he was working in another bookshop – an independent this time – so he was pretty happy with his lot. We had this nice little flat over the shops in Montpelier and things were going great. They were even getting better in the sack. Rob had worked up the courage to tell me what he really wanted in bed, and I'm telling you, you'd never think it to look at him, but that boy's a kinky bugger. Had me tie him to the bedstead and peg him with a strap-on the week before, and he'd been in fucking ecstasies. I practically creamed myself just watching him thrashing and moaning beneath me. It was after that that he told me he thought he was bisexual. Fair play to him, I thought. Would never have guessed he might want to do something about it, though.

So, as you can imagine, I wasn't exactly pissed off when I saw Phil's gaze lingering on Rob's arse as he got up to go to the gents. No, I was more ... shall we say, intrigued? Oh, and excited. Definitely excited. Yeah, I figured this was a situation with potential. I mean, let's face it, what red-blooded woman *wouldn't* want to end up in bed with two gorgeous men?

I plonked the pints down on the table as gracefully as I was able, and flashed Phil a mischievous grin. He shifted uncomfortably and gave me a wary smile. I think he must have known I'd seen him flirting with my boyfriend, and was probably wondering why I was grinning like a madwoman. I sat next to him and slid closer, purring into his ear as I squeezed his thigh.

'So, Phil, do you fancy coming back to our place later? We could get to know each other better.'

I had to stop myself laughing when he choked on his beer. Well, there's nothing like the direct approach, is there? To his credit, he recovered pretty quickly, and gave me this searching gaze like he was trying to figure out exactly what my game was.

'Bethany, darling, you do know I'm a friend of Dorothy, don't you?'

I guessed she must be his girlfriend or something, but she wasn't here, was she? 'Well, I'm a generous girl and I'm willing to share Rob so long as I get to watch. I'm sure Dorothy can share you for one night.'

Phil stared at me for a moment then burst out in laughter. 'I like the way you think, sweetheart. Well, maybe we can work something out, if Rob's interested.'

'Oh yeah, I can tell he is. He's never been with a bloke, though, so we might have to persuade him.'

Phil licked his lips, and I watched the moisture glisten there.

'Sounds good to me.' His voice was rough, a little hoarse, and I wasn't sure if it was an after-effect of the choking until I looked at his lap and saw a distinct bulge in his leather jeans.

Rob looked puzzled to find us sitting so closely together. I wondered for a moment if it was jealousy, but which one of us would he be feeling jealous of? I wasn't sure I wanted to know, so I slid over on the bench and made room for him between me and Phil. Not much room, as it was a short bench, but that just made things extra cosy and interesting. Rob gave me a quizzical stare as he sat down, but I just smirked, and he got the same when he looked over at Phil. To be honest, I don't blame the poor sod for gulping his pint down like he was dying of thirst; it wasn't fair, having me and Phil ganging up on him like that.

'I thought Phil might like to come back to ours. You'd like that, wouldn't you, Phil?' I asked, fluttering my eyelashes at him.

Phil gave a smile so salacious it should have been x-rated, then murmured into Rob's ear, making it abundantly clear just how much he'd like that, thank you very much. I'm pretty sure I saw him sucking on Rob's earlobe afterwards as well.

'Beth?' Rob's eyes were like a rabbit's caught in the headlights. His voice cracked as he attempted to continue. 'I ... uh, are you, er, sure about this?'

I think my fingers stroking his inner thigh let him know just how very sure I was, and I noticed Phil doing the same on the other side. 'Oh Jesus!' Rob whispered, his eyes practically rolling back in his head. 'Christ! Er, give me a minute, OK. I don't think I can walk right now.' That wouldn't have surprised me, judging by the way his leg was trembling under my hand. Oh yeah, and the massive boner he'd just sprouted. I noticed Phil giving it a quick grope before we let Rob be for a minute.

We didn't get another round in – there was an unspoken agreement that what we all really wanted to do was leave as soon as possible. You could feel it in the air, in the spaces between our awkward words and our needy bodies. There was a cloud of lust around that table so thick I'm surprised the rest of the punters couldn't see it.

'Ready?' I asked my men, and they nodded, following me out into the cool night air. Phil and I chatted about films and TV shows on the short walk to our flat, carefully avoiding the subject I reckon we were all thinking about. Rob kept his trap shut and I worried that he was having second thoughts, but Phil slung his arm around Rob's shoulder so I snuck mine around Rob's waist, and somehow we managed to negotiate the narrow pavements without having to let go.

It was once we'd stepped through the front door that things became awkward again. I'm not sure what I'd expected. Maybe that we'd be ripping each other's clothes off in the hallway. As it was, once we'd separated to get through the door, Rob felt obliged to offer Phil the grand tour of the flat, all three rooms of it. I didn't think that's what Phil was after, so I suggested they make themselves comfortable on the sofa. There was a bottle of blackcurrant vodka in the freezer and I reckoned that'd go some way towards loosening us all up a little. Well, loosening the guys up, anyhow. I was already feeling pretty limber and lithe and oh-so-ready for a bit of action.

And so for the second time that evening I walked in on the guys while carrying drinks. Bugger me, they were sucking face! I nearly dropped the shot glasses, my whole body trembling with anticipation. God, there was something so fucking sexy about watching them kiss. Nothing gentle about it; just raw, animal passion. Rob's hands were everywhere, as if desperately making up for all the years of denial. Phil's hands were more relaxed, one holding Rob's head, the other kneading his arse. I could tell just how turned on Rob was getting by the tent in his jeans and the way he moaned into the kiss. Oh yeah, that and the way he started frotting against Phil's hand when it found its way down to his dick. Let's not forget that. That was hot.

I dropped on to the sofa next to them, happy to watch for the time being. Almost absent-mindedly, I pushed my hand up my skirt to my aching pussy. Rubbing myself through my damp knickers, I reached a fever pitch of excitement so quickly that I just couldn't help reaching out for Rob's erection, just as he was reaching out for Phil's. As I rubbed him through the denim, he groaned and bucked up against my hand, so I set to work on his fly. Freeing Rob's cock and taking it into my eager mouth, I caught a glimpse of him managing to get Phil's out of the confines of his tight jeans.

41

Sucking Rob's cock and watching him give his first fumbling handjob to another guy, I had a thrilling idea.

'Phil? How about giving Rob your dick to suck too?'

'Huh?' Rob said, as Phil scrambled to his knees. My poor love, he looked dazed and confused; his hair dishevelled and his face glowing. 'Oh, right. Yeah, uh, OK.' Rob gave a breathless laugh as he caught sight of Phil's prick. He went a little cross-eyed trying to focus on it, which made me want to start giggling too. I stifled it by swallowing down Rob's cock again, tilting my head so that I had a great view of Rob taking Phil's hard length into his mouth, just a little way at first, pulling back to kiss and lick. He looked like he was in heaven and I wondered if I should be feeling jealous, but just then he looked down at me, smiling around the head of Phil's cock. Yeah, there was love in that look, all right. We shared a moment, a special one, what with both of us having a mouthful of dick. The strangeness of the whole situation hit me squarely. I mean, if you'd told me that morning that this is what we'd both be doing before the end of the day I'd have said you were a nutter, but here we were, and it was bloody fantastic.

'Hey, third guy in the room here,' Phil protested. 'I hate to break up this little love-in, but shouldn't you both be sucking dick?'

Well, he had a point, but I couldn't resist giving his arse a slap before getting back to the job in hand – sorry, that should be the job in mouth, I guess. Mind you, Phil seemed to enjoy that slap if his whimper was anything to go by. Well, either the slap or Rob's rather messy but enthusiastic blowjob. Even with my attention half on what was going on above me rather than on Rob's dick, I felt him grow close alarmingly quickly. Not that I could blame him – there's nothing quite like having a mouthful of cock to get me going either. I took him deep, swallowed around the head then drew back as my mouth filled with his delicious salty tang.

I watched Rob as he came, his eyes closed and his mouth a perfect 'O' as his body bucked and heaved. He still had his hand on Phil's prick, but had abandoned sucking it for the duration. Probably wise – I wouldn't have wanted him to spoil

42

things by accidentally biting down in his ecstasies.

'Fucking hell, Beth! Jesus, I ... I never ...'

Whatever Rob had been about to tell me was cut off by Phil rubbing his dick over Rob's lips in a way that made it very clear what he wanted. Rob made a happy sound, the same one he makes when eating ripe strawberries, and opened wide for a mouthful. There was a moment when I worried he might be about to choke, but he managed not to. He wasn't deepthroating yet, but he'd be there with a little more practice. I decided I rather liked the idea of watching him practise.

I sat up to watch my boyfriend finish the job, which I judged wouldn't take long by the way Phil was groaning, his hands twisting in Rob's hair. Hand back in my knickers, it only took a few flicks of my swollen clit to have me creaming myself, just as Rob pulled back with a 'Mmmpf!' and received his first face full of come.

His shocked expression was priceless, and I couldn't help but giggle, pulling him over into a sloppy kiss while Phil collapsed back on the sofa, groaning. The taste of Phil's spunk in Rob's mouth tingled at my taste buds, and I felt like I was going to come all over again.

'You enjoy that, then?' I asked him as I broke our kiss.

'Uh huh!' he nodded, pulling his T-shirt off and wiping his face clean. The dopey smile on his face said more than his words could, and I grinned, handing him a shot of vodka to wash the unfamiliar taste out of his mouth.

There was this moment, then, that could have been awkward, the three of us sitting there in a post-orgasmic haze. Phil, this guy we barely knew who had just shot his load in my boyfriend's face – well, what do you say after that? I figured words were overrated, so I pulled my top off instead. Rob always says my tits are one of my best features, and that he likes a woman with a bit of cushioning on her. I reckoned Phil might have been of the same school of thought by the way his eyes widened.

'Nice pair,' he said, and I figured it was about time I found out just where on the scale of gay to bi he fell.

'Move over, lads,' I said, seating myself between them with

a wriggle. 'I think it's my turn for a bit of attention, seeing as how I've been so generous in sharing my man and all.'

'I like your missus,' Phil said to Rob. 'She's got balls.'

'Cheeky bugger! I bloody well haven't. Look, I'll prove it.' Well, I didn't need much excuse to show off my undies – a rather pricey black lace set Rob had bought me for my last birthday. After shedding my skirt, I was thrilled to find not one, but two pairs of hands exploring me and pushing down my bra. Two mouths dragging over my skin, my ears, cheeks, neck ...

I think I must have yelped when I felt a mouth close around each of my nipples. My brain short-circuited and all signals went directly from my nipples to my groin. I was sopping wet, aching for someone to touch me there. When I felt fingers pushing my knickers aside, I had no idea who they belonged to and that made it even more exquisite. They rubbed over my clit, sending sparks through my body, before plunging into my cunt and firing up an electrical storm that crackled through me and left me limp and twitching.

I don't know how long I was out of it, but when I sensed movement above me I opened my eyes. Phil and Rob were at it again, up on their knees, now naked, locked in a fierce kiss while their cocks did battle. Oh, for fuck's sake.

I cleared my throat. They both looked down at me. Rob's lips were kiss swollen and I just wanted to eat him alive. Now was not the time to be coy.

'So boys ... which one of you is going to fuck me then?'

'Umm ...' Rob looked at Phil, a question in his eyes. 'Beth, you do know Phil's gay, don't you?'

'He is?' I must say, it did come as a bit of a shock, considering he'd just been fondling me and sucking my nipple like it was going out of fashion.

'I thought you said you'd told her,' Rob said. He sounded angry.

'I did. In the pub. I told you I was a friend of Do–' Phil clapped his hand over his mouth, but he couldn't hide his laughter. 'Sorry, Beth. I thought you understood but I should have been clearer. I'm gay. I've never been with a woman before.'

I was confused. 'So what was all that about?'

Phil blushed, slumping down on the sofa next to me, his hard-on drooping. 'I was curious. And you're attractive, for a girl, and it felt fine with Rob here too. I just ... I don't think I could fuck you. Sorry.'

'Oh.' I wasn't quite sure how to take this revelation. One part of me was insanely flattered, and another part was a little put out, feeling like a third wheel. Should I offer to leave them to it?

But Rob, bless him; my Rob had an idea which saved the evening. His eyes lit up with dark fire, and he laced his fingers through mine, before doing the same with Phil.

'How about this: I screw you while Phil does me from behind? Sound good?' It certainly seemed to agree with Phil, whose face lit up while his cock took a renewed interest in proceedings.

'Oh yeah!' Phil said, as if there could be any doubt as to his feelings about the matter.

'Please, Beth? I really want you to be with me for my first time.'

Well, how could I resist a plea like that? A smile spread through my body, making every nerve ending tingle with anticipation.

We stumbled through to the bedroom, as that's where the lube was. I remembered to check that Phil had condoms first – I might be happy to share Rob, but I didn't really want to share anything else. He looked healthy and all, but you just can't tell, can you?

We landed on the bed in a mass of writhing limbs and hungry mouths. I lay back, spreading my legs. I needed to see this, to watch Rob's face as a man took his cherry. Rob slid into me smoothly with an ease born of much practice, then froze still, eyes shut and biting his lip, as Phil began to prepare him with his fingers.

'Rob, sweetheart, you need to relax.' I squeezed his arms, relishing the sensation of him trembling within me as Phil opened him up. 'Remember what it was like with the strap-on?'

Rob's eyes sprang open and he let out a shuddering breath. 'Yeah, you're right. I remember. Phil's bigger than that though.'

Phil chuckled. 'You two are super kinky for a straight couple, you know that?'

Rob jerked and moaned, falling forward onto me. I figured Phil must have hit his prostate, as that was Rob's usual reaction when I did the same. I wrapped my arms around Rob, feeling warm and fuzzy at the idea I could help him like this. That I could make it all less strange.

When Rob was penetrated I felt his whole body quiver, panting and dripping with sweat. I stroked down his back, making comforting shushing sounds and kissing his ear as his face was firmly buried in the crook of my neck. Phil caught my eye and winked. He had his hands on Rob's hips, his dick buried in Rob's arse and it looked so good my insides tingled.

'You ready for this, Rob?' Phil asked.

Rob raised his head, locked his big brown eyes on mine and gave a tremulous grin. 'Yeah, you ready, Beth?'

'God, yes!'

It took a while for Rob to sort out his rhythm, as I think he was overcome by the sensations. There was no letup for him; every time he slid out of me Phil thrust into him, which made Rob grunt and falter for a moment. I could feel the force of Phil slamming into him transmitted through the head of Rob's cock, and that combined with Rob's ecstatic expression tipped me over the edge, my orgasm rippling through me as I cried out my pleasure. By the time my climax had subsided the boys were sorting out their rhythm and I began bucking my hips to meet Rob's thrusts.

Rob was undone, incoherent; his body spasming wildly as he came inside me, pulsing hot and wet into my cunt. But Phil wasn't finished, and as he pounded Rob's backside I felt every thrust as Rob ground against my clit. I howled, letting another wave of glorious pleasure crash through me as Phil stiffened and shouted.

I gathered Rob and Phil in my arms, the three of us a shuddering, panting heap. Everything felt wonderful, and I let them both know with kisses. Rob accepted his sleepily, gratefully, before dozing off on my shoulder. Phil froze for a moment then opened his lips to mine, gently exploring my mouth with his tongue.

'I enjoyed that,' he said, sounding surprised.

I grinned at him, winking. 'Reckon you need a woman like me to turn you bi.'

'Dunno about that.' He looked over at Rob and stroked his cheek. Rob snorted and settled himself, dead to the world. 'Tell you what, though, I wouldn't mind you trying.'

One More Night
by Sommer Marsden

She was rushing past the cottage two doors up from hers when she heard, 'Hey there Little Red Ryder Hood ...' and froze.

The deep baritone with accompanying backup slammed her back ten years. The hair on Ryder's neck rose up in a ghostly wave of fine blonde down and she spun, feeling off kilter already. Her eyes sought but could not find the singer, until she heard a deep chuckle that slammed her in the belly like a cotton-wrapped fist.

'Hubie! Joe?' she called. Feeling a little desperate, a lot crazy. 'Guys?'

There was no way. She had not seen them in nearly a year. No way at all, and yet she knew it now. Could feel it in her bones, that heavy knowing that mimicked the feeling she got after recovering from a long illness like flu or a drawn-out bout with a fever. A deep-seated awareness came over her.

The song that was being hummed somewhere in the trees sealed the deal. It was the boys out there. Ryder stomped her foot. 'Hubert Sullivan Usher! Joseph Michael Palmer! Come out this instant!'

And then she waited. Was she crazy?

No. They stepped into the clearing, one tall and dark and gruff like a bear in a man suit. The other long and lean and ethereal. Ice blue eyes and pale blond hair. The boys.

They had been friends all through college. Inseparable – the three of them. Friends, only, no funny business. But for that one night.

'So no man yet? No marriage, no kiddies, no picket fences? It's been nearly a year, woman,' Hubie said. His deep voice was like a warm hand sliding up her neck and in the orange glow of the fire pit Ryder shivered.

'Nope. I have a thriving jewellery business. I have books, friends, good wine, nights out, invoices and paycheques.' She grinned. 'But none of that.'

Joe smiled, his eyes somehow surreal in the glowing flash of heated light. 'Hubie doesn't either, so don't listen to him. Nor do I.'

He said the last in that prissy, proper way that made him so endearing to her. She loved his almost stuck-up, uptight ways. But in Joe was a heart of gold and an old soul.

And a cock that could work miracles. Soft lips that know how to kiss. Really know how to kiss – and eat pussy. He rocked you to more than one orgasm while Hubie was ...

But she let that memory drift away on a curl of wood smoke. She couldn't go there. It had been one night a long, long time ago. Her 20th birthday. It had happened – just happened – after her drunken salute to herself and their youth. Her long monologue about their love for each other and how it would still fade, because nothing lasted for ever. It would fade and so would their youth. They were only going to be young once, only going to love each other this fiercely once. And how special were they that they had found each other. Three kindred spirits, friends, almost family but something more. She had let all the muzzy-headed words tumble out and then she had toasted herself and then them.

And then the boys had taken her. No one discussed it. It had just happened. A mix and turn and shift of three bodies. A mélange of forms and naked parts and soft words and cries. Orgasms and skin on skin and laughter and, at the end, a satiated peace and sleep.

The morning brought reality and no one had ever mentioned it again.

'... selling to?' Hubie said.

Ryder shook her head and tried to draw back the words that had come before the end of his sentence. She couldn't. 'I'm sorry. I spaced out on that. What?'

Hubie grinned, and cocked his head as if he had been tiptoeing through her mind. Reliving that night so long ago with her. 'I said, Ryder the daydreamer, your jewellery, who are you selling it to?'

'Oh! Tourists and some local new channels have been purchasing. Which is great, because then it ends up on TV and in the credits. And some local boutiques.'

'What were you thinking?' Joe said softly, grinning, poking the embers with a stick as he tapped his toe in the sand around the fire pit. His big foot was sheathed in his normal boat shoes, his khaki shorts knee length, his button-down shirt rolled and pushed to his elbows. Normal Joe – preppy chic.

'I was thinking about the jewellery show I'm doing tomorrow. How I should head off to my cabin and go to bed. I was thinking that this beer sucks ass,' she lied, taking the final swig.

'You were thinking about us,' Joe said, calling her bluff.

'Never,' she said, trying to tease with her tone.

'True story,' Hubie grunted, agreeing with Joe.

Ryder steadfastly refused to cave. It was that one time – a lifetime ago. No reason to even think about it.

At one point they were in you at the same time. You never thought that sweet full pressure could make you come, but it did. You straddled Hubie and drove yourself down on him over and over; he held your hands to his chest so you could feel his heart. All the while Joe rocked into your bottom, slipping into you on a cool river of lube. Working your ass, brushing your g-spot from a totally new angle. His hands on your hips, holding you so you didn't float away, or so it felt. Both of them. Holding you. You've never felt so safe.

'... fishing,' Joe said. His smile was ornery, knowing and smart-assed.

Ryder swallowed hard. Once they had been her very best friends. And for that one night they had been her lovers. Something she'd never been good at with Hubie and Joe was lying. She cleared her throat and steeled her nerves to admit it. 'What? I missed that.'

Joe laughed softly, drawing a heart in the sand with the stick he held. The tip was charred from him poking it into the fire every few moments. He drank the last of his beer and said. 'We are here on a boys' weekend. Haven't gotten together for months. Figured we'd come down for some fishing.'

'Oh,' she said and set her empty bottle on the ground.

'Yes, oh,' Hubie said and his voice was a little gruff. A bit clogged sounding. His eyes seemed to stroke her like a hand in the firelight – over her breasts, her belly, her legs in her denim shorts and flip-flops. Ryder wanted to eye up his jeans to see if he had a hard-on but she refused. She kept her eyes above his belt. Joe's too.

'I'd better go to bed. I have to get up early. Vendors need to arrive at seven sharp. Doors open at nine.'

She kissed them each chastely, hugged them too. She pretended not to notice Joe's hard cock brushing her thigh when he pulled her into the embrace. She hurried through the woods to her dark cabin and resolved to put it out of her mind.

For two hours she lay there, not thinking. Deliberately not thinking. When every decadent sinful image drifted into her mind, she resolutely pushed it aside. At midnight, she got up and poured a glass of wine. At 12.15 a.m., she considered it and at 12.16 a.m. she banished the thought. At 12.30 a.m. she knocked on their cabin door.

It was Hubie who answered. His dark hair in a tangle and his chin sprouted with dark stubble that clouded his tanned skin with shadow. 'Well, look what the cat dragged in,' he said softly and swung the door wide for her to enter.

Ryder still wore her white nightgown. She had tossed a grey cardigan over it and her feet were bare, and now dirty, from the beaten path from her cabin to theirs. 'Were you sleeping? Did I wake you?

'Hell, no, woman. We're watching some dumb-ass movie on cable and drinking beer.'

'What movie?' she asked dumbly.

'Shit if I know.' He touched her lower lip and Ryder felt her pussy go liquid and soft. A fierce surge of lust swelled in her chest and she breathed out like he'd squeezed her too hard.

'Who's there?'

She turned to see Joe and, when she did, her heart raced at his pale good looks. A smile lit his face and she realised that she still loved them. After all these years. Loved who they were, what they had meant to her once and what they still meant to her now. 'Little Red Ryder Hood,' Joe whispered and crossed his arms over his chest.

'I ...' Ryder lost her words then. It hadn't taken long to feel that old familiar belonging with them. Something she had rarely experienced thus far in her adult life. She loved her life and her business, but she was missing the rush of real life. The visceral reaction to love and lust and fucking. She didn't have time.

'You what?' Joe asked, cocking an eyebrow.

'You ...?' Hubie echoed.

'I want it back,' she sighed. She blew all the words out on a rush of air. She was so eager for them to hear her that she rushed it out of her mouth in a tumble of soft speech. 'I want it back. I want that night back. That feeling – you two. I want one more night.'

Then she waited. Her heart pounding like some tribal drum, her throat shaking with the force of it, her stomach dipping almost sickly from nerves. Joe turned on his heels and Hubie took her hand.

What did it mean?

'Come on, Ry,' Hubie said and tugged her gently.

'We thought you'd never come to your senses,' Joe said over his shoulder and her whole body seemed to relax.

It would be OK.

In the living room it was Joe who pulled her in for a hug. Engulfing her in his strong but lean arms while Hubie – his best friend in the world – closed in behind her. His broad chest pressed to her back, his cock pressing the small of her back. Joe kissed her, hands in her hair, his hard-on pressed to the cleft of her sex through the thin nightgown.

'I just want it back for one more night,' she said again.

'We can do that,' Hubie said, pressing his lips to her shoulder, her neck, the crown of her head. His kisses rained down along her back and his hands pushed up her nightie as she shivered like she was cold.

'No problem,' Joe said, pushing at the nightie too. Together they got off her cardigan, her nightgown, her panties. She worried briefly, stupidly, about her dirty feet but the thought drifted away as Joe's tongue touched hers and Hubie's fingers came from behind and started slow, lazy circles on her clit.

She gasped, tasting beer on Joe's tongue as his finger found her nipples and he pinched just a touch too hard. 'I remember you like a bit of pain,' he laughed softly and pinched her again.

The pain sizzled from her breasts to her cunt and it flexed, tight and eager around nothing at all. Hubie felt the swell of her hips as she tilted toward Joe and said, 'Let's see if it's still true.' He dipped his fingers, each as thick around as a cigar, deep into her pussy and he pressed against her g-spot with a precise kind of determination. 'Still true,' he said in her ear, and flexed again. He dropped to his knees, kissing a trail along the curve of her back, the wings of her shoulder blades, the swell of her hips. His fingers stayed buried deep in her wet pussy, his mouth never leaving her flesh. He trailed a wet line down until his tongue found the swell of her bottom and he started to lick and kiss her from one side to the other.

'Not to be outdone,' said Joe, with a chuckle. He kissed down the front. His tongue sliding in a slow, sinister dance between her breasts, over her belly button. He kissed one hip bone and then the other, all the while Hubie gave great attention to her ass.

Ryder clutched at Joe, Her hands buried in the pale floss of his short hair. Her one hand waved wildly behind her, finding purchase on Hubie's bare shoulder. He wore nothing but cut-offs and Joe nothing but gym shorts. They'd been drinking beer, watching movies, she thought wildly. Minding their own business until she had barged in and–

Joe sucked her clit in and nipped it. Hard enough that in her head a dark violet sizzle took up like a faulty neon sign. Ryder sucked air into lungs that felt too small to hold it and her pussy cinched tight around Hubie's thick fingers.

God how they made her feel. Singly. Together. She never

felt more free to be herself than with her boys. It had always been that way, still seemed to be.

The first orgasm slammed her and it was a blindside. One moment she felt so good, the next her cunt was rippling with harsh waves of euphoria. Tight, tight, tight around Hubie's probing fingers, her juices flowing out to meet Joe's ministering tongue. She held on to each one of them with a hand, swaying between them like a sapling in a storm.

Joe was the first to ditch his shorts. His cock standing out straight and true, ginger hair at the root and a birthmark on his right hipbone. Hubie laughed in that locker room way and Joe flipped him the bird. Joe's hands cupped her breasts, thumbing her pink nipples into small spikes of flesh. He drew her to the sofa as Hubie dropped his cut-offs. Hubie's cock was huge. He was a big man overall and not to be outdone in the cock department. A thrill worked through Ryder, she had forgotten. She stared at his thick hard-on and the nearly black hair at the base. His thighs, three times the size of hers, seemed like tree trunks.

'Don't' worry, Ryder, I'll go slow,' he said, meaning he would take his time. Let her adjust.

She nodded. She trusted Hubie with her life. Joe too. She could certainly give them one more day of trusting them with her body. Hubie dropped like a boulder to the sofa and she sat, her back to Joe's front, and watched him stroke his cock and watch her. Then Hubie leant in and kissed her while Joe tugged her hair enough to make her scalp sing.

The pain blended it all together. The soft kiss, the echoes of her orgasm. The feel of mouths and fingers and now cocks. She wanted them both now and later and in a million different ways. 'I feel greedy,' she blurted.

'Good,' Hubie said and patted his lap. She climbed on. Straddling his lap as he stroked her wet slit with the head of his cock. Ryder hummed low in her throat at the sensation of soft flesh on soft flesh. Of his hard cock pressed to her eager entrance. He held her hips almost reverently and she started to lower herself one inch at a time. Watching as her body swallowed his length and his mouth came down hot and insistent on her nipple. Hubie bit her and she jumped, but it was Joe who laughed.

'Come around here, smart ass,' she said, but there was no real heat in her name calling. She lowered onto Hubie, her eyes drifting shut at the pressure and the fullness of being stuffed with him. He lifted her and dropped her, lifted her and dropped her, as if she weighed nothing more than a sack of flour. And when he dropped her, the head of his cock nudged her g-spot and it winked to life. Some small secret thing waking for another go at pleasure.

Joe came to where she pointed. Standing behind the sofa that sat in the middle of the main room, dividing the dining space form the TV space. He stood facing her as she rode Hubie, his cock poking impudently over the back cushion.

Ryder took him in hand, meaning to make him suffer for laughing, but when she felt the silken slide of his hard-on in her hand, she caved, wanting nothing more than to make him feel good – to make him come. Ryder stroked Joe and Hubie fucked her, biting her again so that she hissed but her cunt went taut around his thrusting member. She lowered her lips to Joe and kissed the tip of him so that he groaned.

'A kiss?' he sighed.

'How about a French kiss?' she teased and pressed him into her mouth with her hand, before sucking down the length of him so that he had to clutch at the back of the sofa.

Hubie stopped for a moment, watching them and then he said, 'Jesus. Gonna make me come if I watch you.'

'Don't watch,' Joe laughed. But the laugh was breathy and high, as if he couldn't quite get it out.

Hubie held her hips tight, thrusting up and whispering words that she couldn't quite hear. When he pushed his broad finger into her bottom, she cried out, coming. Lips working around Joe who was shoving into her mouth, losing his manners a bit. He held twin hunks of her dark red hair in his hands like reins.

'Stop,' she said and they all froze. Both of them had been moving with a greater sense of purpose, almost frenzied. She knew it was close. It was close to ending and she said, very

56

calmly so they knew she was serious, 'I want you both in me. Again. Like last time.'

Neither of them argued. There were no jokes or jibes or teasing. It was a nearly solemn but rushed rearrangement of bodies. An almost holy (to them, anyhow) tableau. Hubie lay on the ugly brown rug and pulled her down. She lay flush to him for a moment while Joe waited, breathing shallowly, touching his cock to stay hard. Hubie kissed her, his big green eyes on hers. 'Hey, you say the word and it's–'

'Over. I know. But I won't. *I* came to *you guys*.'

'So you did, Little Red Ryder Hood, but still.'

Ryder kissed him. Loving him for protecting her, even if it meant from himself and then she sank down onto him again. Taking him in the second time was as good, if not better, than the first. The break had set her body on high alert. All the nerve endings in her pussy danced and clamoured for the feel of him. She whispered to Joe and he lubed himself well, his cock shiny with the stuff.

'I don't want to hurt you,' he said, pressing the head of himself to the tight eye of her anus.

'It always hurts at first,' she told him, and it was pretty much true. 'Plus, I like a bit of pain.' And that was pretty much true too.

She stilled and Hubie held her hands to his chest again. For some reason it reminded her of praying, the way he held her hands in his bigger ones. The temple of Ryder, she thought and smiled. And then Joe was in. That pinching bite of pain having passed as simply as a breath.

He started to move, her pushing back, relishing the feel of having both of them in her body at once. Loving both of them. The three of them joined physically the way they had always seemed joined emotionally and mentally. It was natural for her and that was good enough for Ryder.

And the boys.

Somehow it was not an awkward dance of three. They found a rhythm of give and take and up and down. She crested to orgasm only to crash down, her forehead to Hubie's hairy chest as he started to come, shaking under her as if he were fragile. Her fingers in his mouth and Joe's snaking around to press past her lips into the wet recesses of her mouth.

'I missed you, Ryder,' Hubie said as he came. His big awkward hips slamming up so that he could bury root deep into her. His heart beating so hard that his coarse rug of a chest jumped under her fingertips.

And then Joe was with him, holding her hips and slamming into her. He came with his lips on her shoulder and a simple, 'We love you, you know.'

And she did know. Which is why she wanted one more night. And that night wasn't over. Which made Ryder smile.

Three-for-All
by Emma Richardson

Just after midnight, I finally caught Rick alone. He was standing on our host's small balcony, looking down on Third Avenue. 'Isn't this city beautiful?' he said, turning to me with a smile.

'Mmm,' I answered. 'I never get enough of it. Or of you either.'

Rick bent forward and kissed my forehead. 'You look beautiful tonight,' he told me.

I laughed. Of course he would think so – I dressed for him. In spite of all the fashion industry's predictions that New York's official colour scheme was about to change, Rick never got tired of black. Or of seeing my legs, long and smooth and – for tonight – encased in sheer black stockings with a thin stripe of gold running from my high-heeled pumps to the bottom of my short velvet skirt. We both knew that the stockings ended right beneath the skirt, held up by a lace garter. I had given up pantyhose at Rick's suggestion, shortly after we started dating, and I loved the free and slightly dangerous feeling of walking around with nothing but a thin pair of silk panties between me and the fresh night air.

'Are you having a good time?' he asked me.

'Absolutely,' I said. 'Great people, and a great occasion. But Rick, you know, I wanted to give you a wonderful birthday present and I just couldn't think of what it should be.'

'Oh, Molly,' he said. 'Don't even think about that. This party is a great present. The best. I can't think of any way I'd rather spend my birthday than with you and all my best friends.

59

And some of the new people are interesting too. Who's that woman who came with Cathy? She's adorable.'

'She is, isn't she?' I agreed. 'Rose is her name. Isn't that appropriate? Those pink lips of hers are so full and soft they look like tiny pillows. I almost want to touch them.' I'd never said anything like that before, and I checked to see how Rick was taking it.

He laughed. 'Heyyy,' he said. 'I'm in charge of lust here.'

'Who said anything about lust? I just think she's adorable. Anyway, I'm not going to tell you who to be attracted to.'

'You're not jealous, are you?' he asked. 'Because I'm here with *you*. And with the way you look tonight, I'm taking you home with me if I have to carry you there over my shoulder.'

'No,' I said. 'I'm not jealous. You can look at anybody you like. In fact, I'm glad you like women.' Rick pulled me close and stroked my back. 'Mmm. You're a dream,' I said. 'Are you sure there isn't something I can get you for your birthday? Something to remember it by?'

'You're all I need,' he said, dropping his arm around my shoulders and steering me toward the door. 'Come on, let's go back inside and see what's going on.'

'Molly!' called Jake as soon as we re-entered the room. 'Hey, you guys, we're about to play five-card stud. Have a seat.'

'Cool,' said Rick. 'Deal us in. What are we playing for?'

'Oh, nothing,' said Jake. 'Just chips. You know, just for fun.' Jake handed chips around the circle and we played a few hands. 'Hey, Rose,' he said after a while, 'what are you doing for chips over there? You got a secret stash?'

Rose blushed a little. 'No,' she said. 'No, I guess I'm almost out. I just don't want to quit, I'm having such a good time.'

'Is this your first time at this?' asked Jake.

'Second,' said Rose shyly. 'But I don't think I really understood the game the other time I played. I'm starting to get the hang of it now.'

As I looked at the soft brown hair falling across Rose's furrowed eyebrows, an idea started to grow. 'Wait,' I said. 'Rose, if you want to keep playing, you can. But I think we need to raise the stakes a little. I propose that anybody who needs to can borrow more chips from the bank, but at the end of five more hands, whoever has the most chips *owns* whoever has the least. The loser agrees to do anything the winner says.'

'Like Truth or Dare,' said Rick.

'More like indentured servitude,' said Jake. 'What happens if you don't want to subject yourself to this?'

'No problem,' I said. 'You just lose the old-fashioned way, before the five hands are up. Then you're out. But if you can hold on, you just might win big.'

Jake laughed. 'Fine,' he said. 'I'm in.'

I knew Rose would never catch up in five hands. What I didn't know was whether she was truly a terrible card-player, whether she had drunk too much to have good judgment, or whether she was now secretly intrigued at the idea of losing under my rules. Pretty soon, only three of us were left. 'This is it,' I said. 'Jake, Rose and me. One of us will own another in just a few short minutes.'

'Wait a minute,' said Jake. 'Maybe we'd better clarify. "Own" for how long? What are the rules?'

'How about for the rest of the night?' I said. 'Until dawn.'

Jake raised an eyebrow. 'And what are the restrictions?'

'I guess that's up to us,' I said. 'Does anybody want to place restrictions on the winner?'

I looked around. Rose gave a little shrug and smiled down at her hands. Rick laughed and looked back at me. 'I'm out,' he said. 'Don't ask me. If Jake's not scared of you two, you can all go ahead as far as I'm concerned.'

'Fine,' said Jake. 'Sky's the limit, until daybreak.'

Rose dealt the cards and I slowly picked up mine. Three jacks. I felt my thighs tingle and I bit my lip, trying to hold on to my poker face. We placed our final bets, showed our cards and the game was over; Rose was mine.

'Jake,' I said. 'Thank you so much for having us here for the party. If you hear from Cathy, please let her know we took Rose home with us, and that she'll be just fine.'

I stood up and took Rose's hand, leading her into Jake's bedroom where our coats were tossed on the bed. 'Rose,' I said, facing her. 'You don't have to do this. I think you should – I think it'll be good for you – but you need to make your decision now, because if you do come with us you won't get any more choices for a while.'

She looked at me wide-eyed, and slowly nodded. 'I lost the game,' she said. 'I'm coming.' She slipped her arms into her soft blue coat and followed me back to the living room.

'Ready, Rick?' I asked.

'Whatever you say,' he answered with a laugh.

'No,' I said. 'From now on, whatever *you* say.' I took Rose's hand and put it in his. 'Happy birthday, sweetheart.'

In ten minutes, the three of us were at his large apartment where I poured one glass of wine and handed it to Rick. 'Sit down, sweetie,' I said. 'And tell us what you want. We're both here for you tonight.' He took the glass and sat on the smooth leather sofa, leaving Rose and me standing in the centre of the living room. I stepped behind Rose and put my arms around her gently. I was a little taller, but with her boots and my high heels, we somehow lined up just right so I was able to rest my chin on her shoulder. I smiled and winked at Rick. 'Molly,' he said, putting his feet up, 'Would you kiss Rose's neck?'

'Yes, please,' I said. I had never kissed a woman before – anywhere – but Rose looked soft and delicious and I slowly turned my head and touched my lips to her bare white neck. With my arms still around her waist, I felt her body tense slightly, but she didn't move away from me. I looked at Rick and he nodded.

'Go ahead,' he said softly. I brushed my lips against the back of her neck and then kissed her again, just below her right ear. She caught her breath and I licked my lips. I began covering the back of her slightly quivering neck with moist kisses. Looking up every few moments to make sure I was pleasing Rick, I moved slowly around to her front. Rose's low-cut white T-shirt left an expanse of pale skin available to my mouth, which was gradually becoming hungrier for her as I continued our gentle game. I found the outline of her tiny Adam's apple, and bent my head to kiss all the way around it. I pointed my tongue and placed it at the inner edge of her left shoulder blade, running it upward to the earlobe. I felt her quiver and wondered how she was feeling.

'You are beautiful,' said Rick. 'Will you kiss her face for me?' I nodded and moved my lips to Rose's cheek. It was plump and warm. I kissed again, moving slightly higher, and tasted salt.

'Are you all right?' I whispered. Rose nodded and I licked the tear away. She closed her eyes, allowing me to kiss both eyelids. Her soft face was gorgeous and my enthusiasm grew as I covered it with kisses.

'Her mouth, please,' said Rick. I hesitated. To kiss a woman on the mouth – I wondered whether I would finally know what men feel when they do that. I looked at Rose's bright eyes, which sparkled back at me. I placed my lips on hers for a second and then backed off in surprise. Her mouth was so small, so soft. The feeling was completely different from that of kissing Rick or any other man. And I wanted it again, badly. I put my hands on Rose's shoulders and turned her, to make sure Rick could see both of us. And then I wetted my lips and pressed my open mouth against hers. I nibbled and licked and tasted her sweetness and I felt her respond, pressing her tongue into me. I closed my eyes and kissed again and felt her hands on my waist.

Breathless, I stopped and rubbed my cheek against hers. I was excited by her gentle voluptuousness, and her compliance, but I did not want to hurt her. I turned to look at Rick, who seemed to understand what I was thinking.

'Rose,' he said. 'You are a beautiful girl, and I would love to look at you. How would you feel about that?' I watched her face. She shivered slightly and then the left side of her mouth curled up into a half-smile. 'Has a woman ever undressed you before, Rose?' he asked. She shook her head decisively and then smiled broadly, lowering her eyes in embarrassment. 'All right,' he said. 'I'm going to ask Molly to do this for me, but if you're unhappy, you just tell me and I'll stop her.' Rose nodded her understanding, apparently enjoying her passive role. No one had asked her to be silent, but it increased the sense of mystery for me. Our exquisite toy, willing but shy, was making me eager to see more of her too. I turned to Rick for instruction.

'Take her shirt off, Moll,' he said.

I gently turned Rose back to face him again so he would get the full view of her as I followed his orders. I pulled the cotton T-shirt over her head, and Rose lifted her arms to assist me. She wore a brassiere of white lace and Rick and I both gazed at the roundness of her young breasts. 'Sweetheart,' I said to him. 'What size, do you think?' Rick prided himself on his knowledge of women's bodies and my question gave us both a reason to ponder her longer.

'Good question,' said Rick. 'Rose, would you take two steps closer?' She approached the sofa. 'Good,' he said. 'Now turn around for me, slowly.' Again, she followed his instruction and his eyes followed her lovely breasts in their movement. '34C,' he said to me. I saw Rose smile and Rick said to her, 'Am I right?' She nodded. 'Beautiful,' he said. 'I'd love to see more of them, but first, go back to Molly.' She did. 'Now, honey,' he said to me. 'Would you mind touching that lace, just the sides?' I laughed. Would I mind? I wanted to touch her breasts as much as I wanted to touch my own, which, right now, was quite a lot. I had, of course, *seen* plenty of breasts, but my own were the only set I had ever fondled, and I was suddenly overcome with curiosity. I faced her and reached forward, cupping my hands around the bottoms of her underwire. She wriggled a little but did not move away. With flat palms, I stroked the sides, marvelling at their firmness. Rose closed her eyes, in what I hoped was pleasure. I curled my fingers around her. She moaned unmistakably.

Rick sighed and shook his head in wonder. 'Very, very nice,' he said. 'And now, Rose, would you unbutton Molly's blouse?' She nodded and I dropped my hands to my sides to give her room. She fumbled with the top button of my black silk shirt. I listened to my own breathing, trying not to move, not wanting anything to interrupt this dream. When she had completed three buttons, the top outline of my black brassiere was visible.

'Rose,' said Rick, firmly. She stopped and looked up at him.

(Oh, please, I thought. Don't let this be the end!) 'Would you please kiss Molly's chest?' he went on. (Thank God!) She leant forward and placed moist lips on my upper chest. 'More,' said Rick, and she moved aside the light fabric that was falling in her way. She kissed again. 'It's all right,' said Rick. 'You can finish unbuttoning.' She did. 'Now slide that thing out of the way,' he said. Without waiting for her to do it, I shrugged my shoulders and my blouse floated to the floor behind me. 'Good,' said Rick. 'Rose, please, kiss her again.' I smiled at him and then closed my eyes in ecstasy; nobody knew as well as Rick how sensitive my breasts were, and how they loved attention. She leant forward and kissed again, starting at my shoulders and working downward toward the upper edge of my bra. 'But gently,' he warned her. 'She's very, *very* sensitive.' He needn't have told her. Her touch was lighter than any man's had ever been.

'Now use your tongue,' instructed Rick, 'and lick your way all around the bra.' She began doing exactly that, tucking her tongue underneath the fabric and gently flicking at my most willing places.

'Very, very good,' said Rick approvingly. 'Honey,' he said to me, 'may she go on?' I nodded, not wanting to break the spell. 'Good,' he said. 'Rose, unhook her bra. The clasp is in the front.' I closed my eyes so I could do nothing but feel. She unhooked it and slid it backwards, caressing my shoulders as she removed it. The bra fell to the floor and Rose's cool, small hands held my bosom. 'You may kiss them,' Rick said to her. She bent forward and kissed, slowly and smoothly, beginning at the far sides, under my arms, and working inward toward the nipples. I felt Rick's eyes rub my tender breasts along with her hands, and the combination made me so wet my legs trembled.

'Rick,' I said breathlessly when I felt safe that she wouldn't stop. 'I wanted to give *you* a present.'

He laughed. 'Don't worry, sweetheart,' he said. 'You are.'

I sighed in pleasure as Rose's soft fingers traced wide circles around my nipples. 'But,' he added, 'there is something you could do for me ...' I smiled, knowing he would tell me when he was ready. 'You two look uneven now,' he said.

'Please take off Rose's bra for me too.'

I reached behind her and unfastened hers in one movement, slipping it off her shoulders on to the floor. My eyes met hers and we both giggled – maybe she had the same thought I did, about how easy those fasteners really are, even though they seem to cause men so much trouble. I noticed how our naked nipples faced each other and Rick said, 'Please step closer.' Without waiting for further instructions, I moved forward and bent my knees slightly so that I could rub my breasts against hers. The sensation was so extraordinary – like nothing I'd ever felt before – that I couldn't get enough of it. I pulled her body closer with my hands, pressed my breasts harder against hers, and surrounded her lips with my mouth. I pushed my tongue inside and felt hers grab hungrily for mine. As we kissed, I moved my hands to our sides and held all four breasts at once, feeling near tears from the intensity of my own pleasure. I was so engrossed in her soft warmth that I had almost forgotten we were not alone when, to my amazement, Rose spoke.

'Sir,' she said breathlessly, to Rick, 'may we ...?'

I heard a low, soft chuckle. 'I'd have to be a cruel man to stop you now,' said Rick. 'Rose, darling, you're perfect. Unzip Molly's skirt and get it out of the way.' She reached behind me, no longer seeming quite so innocent now that she had been aroused, and pulled the zipper down on my short velvet skirt, rubbing my ass as she did. I wiggled my hips to help her slide the skirt down to the floor and then, as I stepped out of it, she dropped to her knees on the thick carpet. About an inch and a half of thigh was exposed between the top of my stockings and the bottom of my panties and she pressed her mouth against it, licking and nibbling my nakedness. I ran my hands through her hair in ecstasy, and then I gently held her hand to stop her. My panties were soaked and part of me felt like begging for release, but I didn't want to finish yet – not without seeing the rest of her.

'Rick,' I gasped. 'May we ... can she take off ... can I ...' I couldn't make sense but of course I didn't need to.

'Rose, honey, lie down,' he said. 'I want you a little more comfortable.' She rolled obediently on to her back and closed her eyes, smiling at the ceiling. 'Now, Molly,' he said. 'Take off that poor girl's boots.' I slipped out of my own shoes and knelt beside her, pulling off her boots and setting them aside. 'And now, unzip those tight little jeans so our lovely girl can relax.' I crawled up to her midsection and put my hands on the button of her jeans, leaning over to kiss her smooth white belly as I worked the button out of its hole and moved the zipper down. Then, without waiting for further instructions, I straddled her and leant down to kiss her breasts again. I lapped at her hard nipples, before taking one in my mouth and sucking ... until I heard, 'Hey! Didn't I tell you to take off her jeans?'

'Sorry,' I mumbled. I moved off her and slipped my hands inside her pants. She lifted her hips to help me remove the jeans, leaving us equals once again – or almost.

'And now, sweetheart,' he said. 'Take off your stockings so we can see some more legs.' With my black stockings tossed to the side, it was only Rose in her white panties and me in my black ones and I didn't want to be stopped again.

'Yes, sir,' I said. 'And now, may I lie on top of her?'

'Absolutely,' he answered.

I moved my body onto hers, carefully balancing my weight on my arms so I wouldn't hurt her small form. I rubbed my legs against hers, amazed once again by the similarity. I had always loved the contrast of large, hard male limbs against my smaller, softer ones, but actually feeling another woman was almost like making love to my own body – except with twice as much pleasure; with another person moaning and gasping and searching for more. I moved my body down and rubbed my breast against her panties. Sure enough, they were soaked like my own, and the wetness on my nipple made me cry out in pleasure. I moved off her, suddenly desperate to have her naked, desperate to make her come – my alter-ego, my body-double. I positioned myself on my knees, between her legs, ran my hands all over her thighs, her bottom, her own desperate pussy, and then I pulled the soft white underpants all the way off her and pressed my face between her legs, rubbing my cheeks all over her wetness. She squirmed and moaned and –

just as I was about to locate her clit with my tongue – I heard a soft, low voice.

'Wait,' said Rick. 'You are gorgeous, Molly,' he said with feeling. 'I want you now.'

'I can't stop,' I moaned.

'You don't have to,' he said pulling off his own shirt and jeans as he stood over us. I watched him over my shoulder. In seconds, he was on the floor with us, yanking my dripping underpants off. 'Go ahead,' he said then. 'Lick that beautiful girl until she screams.' Rose laughed and spread her legs wider for me and I hungrily thrust my tongue into her, my bottom bobbing in the air as I bent my face down into her. Rick positioned himself on top of me and thrust himself upward into me. He had always been a great lover, but I felt him move inside me tonight with a force I had never known before. In what seemed like no time, I was moaning in pleasure, trying to hold back my orgasm. 'Moll,' he said breathlessly as he continued to fill me, 'It's OK. Come for me, sweetheart.'

'No,' I gasped, 'Not yet. I want Rose ...' And just then, we heard Rose begin to whimper, and then to scream. Thrilled by her ecstasy, I tightened myself around Rick and felt his heat gush into me as the waves of orgasmic pleasure crashed through my body.

As we sank together into the soft carpet, six arms and six legs intertwined, I gave Rose's tender cheek another kiss. 'When is *your* birthday?' I whispered.

Classifieds
by Darla White

The café was quiet, which was just how she liked it. Finding her favourite table was free, she carelessly threw her coat over the back of the chair and headed for the counter, desperate for her fix. The pretty blonde barista seemed rather underwhelmed by her order, but Jules had never bothered with the trendy caramel lattés, or any of the endless incarnations of frothy, sweet nonsense. All she ever wanted was a proper cup of coffee; strong, black and hot.

Picking up the local news rag off the bar she headed back to her table. Having a rare afternoon off Jules was looking forward to dwindling the day away, sat by the gas fireplace, drinking coffee and catching up with her city. It wasn't long before she was up to date on books and bands, and had completely stopped caring about the editor's opinion on the recent increase in property taxes. Her coffee was now at the perfect temperature, and she sipped it lovingly while flipping to the crossword. The café was still quiet. A few people had meandered in and out, most of whom she recognised; regulars like her. It was that kind of place. Looking up from her paper, Jules noticed a cute young couple standing outside smoking, and thought she could probably duck out and do the same, and still be done with her crossword before her coffee got cold. They never took her long anyway. If you do them often enough, you find that the clues are always repeating. One of these days she was going to pick up *The New York Times* and attempt the infamous undefeatable crossword, but she knew that she would probably just end up cheating by checking online for suitable answers. She stood up and reached for her smokes. Right! She didn't have any. A conscious choice. She was in the process of quitting and, cold turkey nonetheless, it was an almost impossible feat after ... *many* years of smoking. But it would be fine. If she just took 90 seconds, closed her eyes and took some nice deep breaths, the craving would pass.

Coffee drained, and crossword complete, Jules hummed and hawed over how to continue her lazy afternoon. It was then, while deciding whether or not to order another coffee, that she noticed herself absentmindedly thumbing through the classified section; a rarity at this stage in her life, save perhaps for searching for a used bicycle or neighbourhood garage sale. It had been years since Jules had last rented an apartment, and she couldn't remember ever actually looking for a job in the classifieds. But just as she was about to abandon the coffee-stained paper, she saw it: *Personals*. Jules smiled to herself, not really sure why, dropped the paper back on her table and headed to the counter. A second attempt to converse with the blonde barista was met with one-word answers, and the type of unimpressed glances that evolution has spent centuries perfecting in teenagers. So after finally receiving her refill, she abandoned the one-sided conversation and returned to her fireside nook.

With the personal ads open in front of her, Jules took a sip of her brew. It was much too hot, and the second cup was somehow never as satisfying as the first. At this point, Jules didn't care. The coffee was just a cover. Within seconds she had become completely absorbed in the raunchy desires of a hundred strangers: one-night stands, threesomes, bi-curious couples, gold-star lesbians. Powerful CEOs seeking a strapped dominatrix, and stay-at-home mums looking for after-school visits from the naughty girl-next-door. It was impressive, outlandish and deliciously intriguing. Before she had even circled a single ad, Jules had decided to answer one of the mystery requests, and try to make the most of this rare afternoon off. Today she would take a chance; leap head first into an experience that would either enthral and excite her, or ruin her completely. Either way, it would be new. Jules thought about buying a pack of cigarettes, but the idea of smoking – even just one – began to overcrowd her senses. *Just breathe*, she thought ... *90 seconds ... it'll pass*. Jules licked her lips. They tasted of cold coffee. When she opened her eyes, the first ad she saw read: "Willing female wanted. Experience appreciated", followed by the necessary contact information. At first it seemed so cold, and vague, but soon those five unassuming words had somehow managed to set a vivid scene.

She reached for her mobile phone, dialled the number and held her breath ... it was ringing. Her heart beat a little faster. The ringing sounded muffled somehow, like it was really far away, or maybe just an old phone – or maybe it was the sound of her own breathing echoing through the earpiece. Nearly seven seconds had passed before the anticipation became too much, but just as she was ready to hang up, a woman answered. Jules was slightly thrown. Truthfully, she had imagined a male voice at the other end, but before the mystery woman hung up, Jules managed to stutter out a reasonable 'Hello'.

The arrangements were made quickly, and easily. The mystery woman spoke with authority, and made her directions very clear. She stressed repeatedly the importance of anonymity, and that Jules's complete discretion would be necessary if they were both going to get what they wanted. They would meet that afternoon at the GoodNight Motel. It was out of town, just off the highway. Jules remembered driving past it now and then. It was cheap. It was dirty. It was perfect. Jules would arrive first, and rent a room under the name of Mrs Bartlett. She would then leave a note at the front desk for a Mr and Mrs Gray that would state the room number and nothing more. As Jules carefully copied down her instructions, so utterly aroused by this point that she was actually perspiring, she couldn't help but think that although it was possible that Mrs Gray had meticulously rehearsed these lines in hopes that a stranger would someday answer the couple's innocent little ad, it was much more likely that they had done this many times before, and had gotten very good at it. Jules was *really* counting on the latter.

They were to meet in two hours, plenty of time to head home for a seething hot shower. Jules considered the master bathroom her own personal sanctuary. She had put many hours of work into making it plush and perfect; luckily, the shower had always been overlooked by the energy police in the building. The head was old and powerful, and Jules liked the temperature set a fraction-of-a-degree below unbearable.

As the steam swirled and lingered around her, Jules began fantasising about her impending rendezvous. A twinge of fear gripped her stomach. Realistically, she had no idea what she was getting into. But she had made her decision and, brushing the unsettling feeling aside, she reached for her razor and focused on the task at hand. It had been at least two weeks since she had last shaved, and naturally, between the clouds of steam, her dull razor, and her absent-minded fantasising, she managed to nick her leg, just behind her knee, which is the worst. The skin is much thinner there, and cuts take for ever to heal. As Jules turned off the shower, basking in the lingering steam, she secretly acknowledged that it was this evening's shower that she was really looking forward to.

She took a cab, pondered stopping at the liquor store, but thought better of it, and arrived 30 minutes early. The GoodNight Motel parking lot was deserted save for a few choice cars. Colourful beaters that were easily 20 years old, with the dents and rust to prove it. Tipping the cabbie she headed for the front door. Renting a room and leaving the note with the front-desk attendant – an overly ripe, heavy-in-the-seat man, with greasy, slicked-back dark hair. He looked at her with a blank expression and coughed as he took the folded note – perhaps a practice he was well accustomed to; Jules didn't stick around to ask.

The room was sparse, with a double bed, a single bedside table, a set of drawers with a bolted-down television, a desk and a lone chair that had seen better days. The bathroom, with chipped mouldy tiles lay behind a dented door that neither locked nor closed properly. The air smelt stagnant, a combination of old smoke and stale sex, and it lingered in the walls – walls that were bare, except for small spots of peeling paint and brown patches that reached up to the ceiling. Jules turned and locked the door. Quickly pulling away from the handle, she thought about the documentary she had recently seen about the state of hotels, the underpaid and under-caring cleaning staff, the hidden dirt, the stains and lurking bugs and parasites at every corner. Pushing the thought aside, Jules turned in a full circle, as if a dog preparing to lie down; she wondered where to sit. Remaining standing she began to take her stilettos off, looked at the carpet and reconsidered. Moving anxiously around, she stopped in her tracks and tilted her head slightly to the right as she stared into the lopsided mirror precariously hanging over the desk. Checking herself out, she thought of herself as Mrs Bartlett: an oversexed, over-confident woman, a stiletto-wearing, ripped-stocking, leather-mini-skirt-and-black-lace-bustier character that Jules was growing to like more and more. It may have been the way her ass looked in the skirt, it may have been the nicotine withdrawal, but she liked the way she looked and she liked the way she felt, and for once it was great to be someone else. She could make Bartlett whoever she wanted and right now she wanted to be fucked – and hard.

There was a knock at the door and it quickly broke Jules out of her trance. Jules bent to the peephole before realising it was actually just a black dot that had been drawn on. 'What the fuck!' she muttered. Although she knew who stood behind the door, it would have been nice to get a split-second look first. She turned the handle and pulled the door open.

In front of her was a red-headed woman, masculine in face – square jaw, large nose, thick brows, with striking green eyes. Quickly her eyes moved to the man, of regular build, quite tall, tanned and with a mop of salt-and-pepper curly hair. Just as she scanned their faces, they did the same, and before three sets of eyes moved over legs, arms, asses and chests, Jules managed 'Hello'. The greeting reciprocated Mr and Mrs Gray walked past her and into the room. Awkward. Jules now noticed the large black bag that Mr Gray dropped by the foot of the bed. For some reason she started to fantasise the bag being filled with apple pies, whipped cream and chocolate milk; stifling a laugh she pictured the pies wrapped in a chequered red-and-white tablecloth. Why now, of all times, she was imagining a picturesque picnic was unclear. She was here for one reason – the same one as the couple standing in front of her. However, she conceded that whipped cream might be fun!

Not a word spoken, Mrs Gray approached Jules, her face statuesque except for a childlike twinkle in her eyes. She looked as if she had just left an office, her nine-to-five business attire – navy skirt, white blouse, navy blazer with beige stockings and pumps – suited her; she looked appropriate. Mrs Gray ran her hands through Jules's hair; Mr Gray was undressing behind them.

As he de-robed – jacket to shirt, pants to socks – he carefully folded his clothes and neatly placed them on the chair. God this woman's eyes were green; Jules stared intently at her eyes, attempting to see the rim of a contact lens, but to no avail. The black bag was still there, visible, calling to her, but just as she went to ask about it, Mrs Gray's tongue was in her mouth. It was hot; Jules liked it. She stepped closer to Mrs Gray, kissing her deeply and pushing her body hard against the navy-clad woman.

She always liked having her hair pulled and released a grunt as her head snapped back with a tug from behind; he was behind her, naked, his hand in her hair, his cock rubbing against her ass – she could feel his hardness through her leather miniskirt. He felt big, and she immediately wanted to be naked. As if reading her thoughts Mrs Gray ran her hands down Jules's neck, across her breasts, slipping her right hand up her skirt. Grabbing hold of Jules's stockings at the crotch she ripped them straight down and pulled hard. The cheap nylon snapped and burned as it tore from her skin. Jules was still wearing her stilettos, and was silently impressed with herself for this. She was warm and becoming wetter by the minute. Mrs Gray was bent by Jules's legs, strong hands running up her calves, her thighs, the bottom rim of her ass; one hand shot to her labia and the massage was soft. As she rocked back into Mr Gray's cock and forwards into Mrs Gray's mouth, her hands found the bobbed red hair in front of her. She pulled up,

74

wanting more and Mrs Gray obliged. Her tongue ran along Jules's lips, parting them and flicking her tongue back and forth, back and forth, in a motion perfectly timed with the hard cock now nestled between Jules's ass cheeks.

Her own hands went to her breasts and she squeezed just as she felt that hot tongue entering her; it was becoming fast, and she started to bend at the knee, pushing herself down onto the thick hot tongue. She was almost bouncing now; moaning softly, she was racing for immediate gratification, and instantly knew she wanted to slow down. *Savour this*. Reaching for the red hair she pulled, trying to pull the face to hers. She was met with resistance though. She tried again – nothing. This time she tried to turn around to face Mr Gray, and get a full view of that big cock she so enjoyed rubbing at her ass. He held her arms. She was quickly realising that she was here for one reason: for them to play with – for them to fuck. She would be taking it however they wanted to give it. Jules breathed in quickly. She wasn't used to not being in control; this was new to her, and she had two choices: stop now, run, forget this ever happened, or let the afternoon play out. It was an easy decision.

Still holding her arms he pushed her on to the bed. She landed face first and remained that way. She could feel him standing behind her, starting to push her legs open with his own thighs. Resisting slightly, he pushed harder. Jules licked her lips; she had hoped it might be a bit rough. Mrs Gray walked to the other side of the bed and, lifting her head, Jules came face to face with her. She was standing still, looking from Jules to him and back to Jules. She was smiling, and Jules joined her.

He pulled on her skirt from the waist, lifting her ass up into the air. His hands felt rough on her ass cheeks, his thumb started circling her asshole, gently pushing on it while two of his fingers found her pussy. His hand was working quickly and Jules could hear him breathing heavily. She was wet; she reached to his hand and pushed another finger in. It went deep and, just as she reached for another, his thumb was in her ass. It was intense and dry. As if hearing her thoughts, Mrs Gray walked to the black bag, unzipped it and pulled out a bottle of lube. She threw it on the bed and walked back to face Jules; she didn't skip a beat. He picked up the bottle and squirted her ass; the lube was cold, wet and it smelt like cherry. Fuck she hated cherry, but whatever, she could handle the smell more than the dryness and she wanted that thumb as far in her ass as possible.

God it was starting to feel really good, his rhythm in her pussy and up her ass was building. She knew instinctively that he was touching himself; she could hear his breath in sync with his movements both in her and with his free hand. She was on her knees now, hands spread in front, staring at Mrs Gray while thrusting her ass back and forth. She reached for her shirt and started to pull, when Mrs Gray reached over and pulled it off in one shot. That was two items of clothing ripped. She was starting to grunt and felt as if she was being prepped for something, and then – with no warning – his hand was out of her and he thrust his dick into her. He was big and thick and he reached for her waist and pulled her towards him. Mrs Gray was smiling and mouthing something Jules couldn't quite make out. She was pushing against him, and his hands reached for her breasts and squeezed, massaging and pinching her nipples, then running his hands down her back, and slapping her ass. She let out a yelp at the slap and he did it again, and again she yelped. Her ass stung and she licked her lips for it tasted good. Mrs Gray leant over and licked Jules's lips at the same time; again their tongues pulled and thrust against one another, as he fucked her pussy. He reached for her hair, pulling her back, and Mrs Gray stood up; she looked flushed and let her eyes fall on Jules's body, now naked except for stilettos. Pulling down on Jules's hips, pushing himself further into her, Mr Gray grabbed at her breasts and, grunting hard, their breath fell into rhythm.

She could feel him building, just as she was; it became faster, and harder, and his nails were now scouring down her stomach. She liked it – the simultaneous instant pain with the sweet thrust of his dick. He was fucking her hard, grabbing everywhere – her tits, her ass, her hair; he pulled her completely off the bed and, turning to the side, he pushed her down. Her hands found the floor and she was bent in half completely. As he pounded inside her, she desperately flailed to find a handhold. Finally grabbing on to her ankles she took him full force and the slap of his skin against hers echoed around the room.

With a barely audible roar he came, hard and fast, and she felt the rush. With that he threw her back to the bed. She turned over on her back, and looked up to find Mrs Gray still standing there staring down at her. The smile the same, her nine-to-five clothes the same, her masculine jaw somehow more square, and her brows furrowed. Their eyes broke apart and Jules looked to Mr Gray. He was rubbing his balls, his breath still loud and laboured, and his gaze was fixed intently on Mrs Gray. They were smiling at one another, and Mrs Gray walked to him, unbuttoning her blazer mid-stride. She undressed, leaving a pool of clothes at her feet; her pumps were kicked aside, and she stood naked in front of him. Bending to her knees, she licked the inside of his right and then left thigh. Moving his hand to the desk, she began sucking on his balls. Taking one, then both in her mouth she pulled back and just as quickly rushed forward and upwards with all of him in her mouth. His hand moved quickly up and down his dick; it was swelling and stretching all at the same time. Jules knelt on the bed and, as his hand grabbed the back of Mrs Gray's neck, Jules grabbed the back of her neck. She mimicked sucking his cock, and he was now watching her as he forced his dick into Mrs Gray's mouth. Jules watched; growing excited she started to touch herself, rubbing up down, slowly and then quickly, alternating in time to Mrs Gray sucking cock. She was building again.

Getting off the bed, she walked to them and knelt beside Mrs Gray. Kissing her neck, and reaching for her tits, Mrs Gray didn't pull away. She groaned, her mouth full of cock, before arching her back slightly so Jules could better reach her tits. She squeezed the woman's nipples and bit her neck. Turning to Mrs Gray's mouth she watched it slide back and forth along his shaft and reached her own mouth to his balls. They tag-teamed him that way, as his excitement grew; grunting louder and louder, he quickly pulled back and came over Mrs Gray's face. As he reached to steady himself with a hand on the desk, Mrs

77

Gray walked to the bathroom to wash her face and, when she returned, she stood directly in front of Jules. Instinctively Jules knelt up, and greedily pushed her mouth against Mrs Gray's pussy. Pulling and biting on her lips, licking from ass to front, Jules had to grab her ass from behind to give herself more leverage. She was engulfed in the woman's pussy, tasting every bit of her; juices rolled down her chin and she reached to wipe them off, rubbing them down her neck on to her breasts. Mrs Gray threw a leg over Jules's shoulder and pushed further and further into her mouth. Suddenly she pulled back, looked Jules in the eye and crossed to the bed.

Mr Gray picked up the black bag, laid it on the bed and opened it. He pulled out a strap-on and, still naked, walked to Jules. He was behind her, his cock growing hard again on contact with her ass. He bit her shoulder, pushed against her rhythmically and, from behind, used his hands to belt on the strap-on. It fit snug, and was not nearly as heavy as it looked.

Her nipples growing hard, Jules reached down and touched her dick; it was purple, ribbed and felt soft to the touch. She was excited; she had never fucked a woman before. Jules looked over to Mrs Gray who was laid on her back, knees bent and legs spread. She was propped on her elbows, her eyes begging Jules to walk the few steps to the bed and fuck her. Jules could taste her, and she wanted more. She wanted to bring her to the point of orgasm before fucking her. Walking over, she bent down slightly; with her knees propped on the edge of the bed, she dove in for more.

Mrs Gray's pussy was still hot and wet, and Jules circled her opening, flicking her tongue in and out. She groaned, and Jules smiled, crawling further on to the bed, hovering above her, adjusting the belt ever so slightly. Mrs Gray raised her hips and threw her head back. Jules felt to her own pussy and wet the dick with her own come. She pushed in, and heard her own moan. She started to fuck Mrs Gray, in and out, in and out. Balancing on her hands, her hips rocked back and forth and she bent to suck on her tits. She felt powerful, she felt strong and her excitement grew with each thrust. Mrs Gray was building; Jules could feel it – she could feel it in her mouth, in her arms and legs, and she started to fuck her faster and harder.

 Lost in her task, she had forgotten about Mr Gray, he was so quiet, but then he was behind her. His palm smacked hard across her ass, and she screamed. Surprise and excitement caught her breath and she realised only after it had come out of her mouth how loud the scream had actually been. He smacked her again and again and, standing behind her, his hands reached down and under her, grabbing for her tits. He pulled her up so she was kneeling and she pulled Mrs Gray with her. They shifted to the edge of the bed, Jules still fucking Mrs Gray with her huge, ribbed purple dick, waiting for Mrs Gray to climax, so they could come together.

 Mr Gray was hard yet again, she could feel him, and her stomach surged, God yes, if he started fucking her, she might not be able to hold on – it may be just too much. But that's exactly what he did; he pushed into her ass with his re-lubed dick, and the cherry odour hit her forcefully. But he was more forceful, ripping into her ass, grabbing her hair. Jules was precariously posed, taking it up the ass, while pushing into the pussy splayed out before her. She felt light-headed, unbalanced, and she opened her eyes. But somehow they found a rhythm; it was unbelievable – fucking while being fucked. Their groans combined into a singing sex choir, loud, pitchy and in unison.

 It was becoming too much. Her body heaved. Sweat against sweat, skin against skin, teeth on bodies, fingers in hair – it was building, she could feel it; they could all feel it. Jules was going to explode. She was going to come hard and she was going to come fast, and she did, all three of them at the same time exploded together. Their bodies crumpled into balls on the bed, chests rising and falling, dry mouths, wet legs, sticky thighs, burning asses and bruised pussies. Jules wanted to lie there for ever, basking in the intense emotions – satisfaction combined with a burning sensation she had never experienced; she wondered how she would get by without feeling it every time from now on.

 Her legs ached, her stomach muscles felt tight and the muscles in her arms quivered. Her eyes had been closed and now she opened them. The couple were off the bed, both half dressed, red faced and hair everywhere. Walking to the bed, Mr Gray ran his hand down Jules's chest, and grabbed hold of the purple dick. Jules rolled over and let him unclip the belt at her back. She couldn't bring herself to stand; she didn't trust her legs just yet.

Turning over she just lay there, watching them. Dressed, hair brushed, the black bag once more zipped tight and presenting an abyss of mystery, they looked at her. She met their eyes, and let them fall across each one of them, their prim and perfect suits, their office attire, their now combed hair. The rosy flush had left their cheeks; they looked like anyone else, everyone else. They looked as if they had just returned from a meeting, not a fuelled afternoon of hot three-way sex. They smiled, before he bent down and picked up the bag. And with that they left the room. No words exchanged; nothing had been said the entire time save a quick 'hello'. Then again what words would they have used? They all seemed trite. They each of them had known instinctively what the others had wanted. Words would have been useless. And now they were gone, Jules didn't even know their real names, nor where they lived, what they did ... She doubted she would ever see them again. Chills ran across her body as she rolled up and sat on the edge of the bed. She heard their car pull away and rose to her feet.

Her clothes were ripped, and she hadn't brought others. Quickly glancing around the room, it was as if they had never been there; nothing had been left behind other than the smell the three of them had added to the pre-existing stench of sex and cigarettes that now lingered more heavily in the air. She locked the door with the rusted key and walked to the reception.

Her legs were cold, her ripped stockings were tucked away in her purse, and she pulled down on her miniskirt. Dropping the key on to the desk, she lingered, staring at the man who hours before had gladly taken her note. Her blood had resumed to pumping normally through her veins, but she still had that great post-sex, faint-headed feeling. There was only one thing she now craved. A cigarette. It would be the perfect end to a perfect afternoon.

She leant across the desk, 'Do you have a smoke?'

He looked at her, her hair pulled back into a makeshift ponytail, her ripped bustier, her legs still faintly quivering. He opened his mouth to say something to her, but thinking better of it he closed his mouth, stood, and pulled a pack from his back pocket. He opened the squished packet, pulled one out and tossed it on the counter.

Her reflexes were dulled, her body in a state of relaxation and utter satisfaction, so she didn't even reach for the smoke as it rolled across the counter and bounced on to the floor by her stiletto. She watched him as he slowly put the pack back in his pocket and sat down. She bent down and picked up the smoke. Grasping it tight in her hand, she stood, attempted to straighten herself by pulling down on her skirt and smoothing her hair. She nodded to him and left.

Jules had no idea how much time had passed, but outside the air was getting cold – the afternoon was quickly turning to evening – and the cold air circled her mostly bare body, tingling her skin and raising the hair on her arms. She walked through the parking lot of the GoodNight Motel and stood on the sidewalk, eyeing the road for a cab.

Placing the smoke between her lips, she scrambled in her bag for a light. Finding a book of matches, she struck one and the cigarette crinkled to life; she took a long, hard drag. The inhale filled her lungs and burned. She stepped forward, steadying herself, closing her eyes as she exhaled. The buzz had caught her off guard – much like this afternoon's events – but once again she savoured the feeling. She took another drag, smiled and raised her thumb. She had a hot shower waiting for her at home, and tomorrow, well tomorrow was back to work, for it was such a rarity to have an afternoon off in her profession. But for right now she was completely in the present, and the smoke tasted better than any she had ever had.

An Up-and-Coming Area
by Elizabeth Coldwell

We hooked up with Jordan through an advert in a pub toilet, which makes the whole thing sound so much sleazier than it actually was. He was someone we already knew, he was legitimately offering his services, and we took him up on that offer. But I'm getting ahead of myself.

It started when they sold the Prince Henry. Jim and I weren't sorry to see the notice on the door announcing the pub would be closing at the end of the month. We had been living along the street from it for the best part of seven years and had only gone for a drink there once. That visit had been enough to persuade us not to bother going back. It was the archetypal backstreet boozer, run down and unwelcoming. The customers looked as though they stepped through the door at opening time and didn't leave until they were thrown out come last orders. A couple of old codgers nursed halves of bitter in the corner and a middle-aged man sat on a stool at the bar, three or four carrier bags of shopping at his feet, discussing his ex-wife in loud, unflattering terms. From the expressions on the faces of those around him, it obviously wasn't the first time they had heard this particular rant. The landlord gave the impression he was doing us a favour by serving us, and when I asked him for a Bloody Mary he told me curtly, 'It's not that kind of pub.'

Friday night was karaoke night at the Prince Henry. We would walk past on the way back from somewhere nicer to hear someone belting out an off-key version of *Angels* or *My Way*. We were never tempted to wander inside and join in.

When the "sold" sign went up, Jim became convinced the

83

pub would be turned into luxury apartments. A slow but steady process of gentrification was taking place in this pocket of London close to King's Cross, with the old businesses moving out as rents became too high for them to afford. They were replaced with sushi bars and little boutiques where a dress could cost as much as I earned in a week, or else the buildings were snapped up by property developers.

So it came as something as a surprise when the Prince Henry instead received a facelift. We walked past one Saturday lunchtime and saw through the open door that the brass rails surrounding the bar were being polished 'til they gleamed, and the old carpet with its arresting pattern of cigarette burns had been pulled up to reveal the floorboards below. 'They'll be turning it into a gastropub,' Jim predicted.

He was almost right. A story in the local free paper, which was pushed through our letterbox every Friday, revealed the pub had been bought by Finn and Liza Buxton, a husband-and-wife team who had started up a micro-brewery on the Caledonian Road. They saw this as an up-and-coming area, and intended to make the place their brewery tap, with half-a-dozen of their own ales always available. Eventually, they would be offering "meet the brewer" evenings and tutored tastings for those who wanted to learn more about beer appreciation. It was a big step up from sticky carpets and tuneless karaoke.

Within a couple of weeks of the grand reopening, Jim and I had stopped walking past in search of somewhere nicer. We found ourselves very much at home in the refurbished surroundings. The bare floorboards and mismatched tables and chairs, which looked as though they had been rescued from a skip, gave the place a lived-in feel. A bar billiard table had been set up, along with a jukebox whose eclectic mixture of CDs took Jim back to his student days. They served superior bar snacks: homemade pork pies and scotch eggs, and bowls of cockles and muscles accompanied by little salty crackers. The beer was, according to my husband, full of flavour and perfectly kept, and when I ordered a Bloody Mary, instead of being laughed out of the pub I was asked whether I wanted Worcestershire sauce, Tabasco or both.

But those weren't the only attractions the Prince Henry had to offer – at least, not for me. I soon struck up a rapport with one of the bar staff, Jordan. He was studying economic history at the nearby university, and he had a quick sense of humour I warmed to immediately. Though I didn't care to admit it to anyone, I also found him rather horny. He had shaggy black hair, pale blue eyes and the kind of complexion my mother would have described as roses blooming in his skin. His left eyebrow was pierced with a little silver barbell, and he dressed in black combat pants and two T-shirts – a black one bearing the name of some band I didn't recognise over a long-sleeved khaki one.

I didn't make a habit of eyeing up men so much younger than me, and certainly not ones who gave the impression they would be more at home in a skate park than a lecture hall. But whenever I spoke to Jordan I picked up a definite vibe. He might have made the same cheeky quips to everyone whose orders he took, but he seemed to take a definite delight in getting into some verbal sparring with me. He would hold eye contact with me just a little longer than was socially polite, and once or twice he trailed his fingers along my palm when he handed me my change. Little signs I couldn't easily ignore – signs indicating my attraction to him was very much reciprocated.

I found myself watching him as he moved between tables, collecting glasses, wondering how he would look stripped of his emo wardrobe, his cock hard and craving my touch. Sometimes, when I was in bed with Jim, his blond head buried between my thighs and his tongue dancing over my clit, I would fantasise it was Jordan down there instead. He wouldn't have the experience my husband had gained over the years, and so I would have the delicious task of teaching him all the things I liked best. I would tell him just where to apply his eager tongue, and when to switch from slow sweeps to furious little licks around the head of my clit, until the moment came when I no longer had the power to shape words and my blissful gasps and whimpers would let him know just what a good job he was doing.

But the fantasy wasn't just about teaching Jordan how to make me come. It also included Jim, sitting in a chair by the side of the bed, wanking his cock and telling me how good I looked as I writhed on my toyboy lover's tongue.

I would have kept all this to myself, if it hadn't been for the evening when Jim came back from the gents' to see me contemplating Jordan's firm arse as he bent over a table, reaching for an empty crisp packet.

'Enjoying the view?' he asked, chuckling when I started in my seat as though I'd been shot.

I didn't need to say anything. My burning cheeks were evidence enough of my guilt.

'It's not the first time you've been staring at him, either,' Jim continued. 'You might not think I notice these things, but I do.'

'You're not angry, are you?' I asked.

Jim shook his head and reached for his pint glass. 'Why should I be? I look at women all the time. If you must know, I was checking out the tits on the blonde over there while you were at the bar.' He gestured to where a group of three girls were chatting animatedly and laughing, a distinct Scandinavian edge to their accents. I realised immediately which one he'd been ogling. She was wearing her hair in schoolgirl-style plaits, something Jim always found a turn-on, and her plump breasts were almost spilling over the hem of her scoop-necked top. 'Mind you,' he added, 'in that outfit you can hardly miss them.'

He drained the dregs of his Buxton's Best, and went to get another round in. I assumed that was the end of the conversation. I was wrong. As he set a fresh glass of Cabernet Sauvignon in front of me, he said, 'I can't help feeling with you and Jordan it's a little bit more serious than just liking the way he looks.'

Wondering where this was leading, I replied, 'OK, so I fancy him and I'm pretty sure he fancies me too. But it's not like I'm going to do anything about it.'

In my head, I was preparing a little speech about how it was all just a fantasy. How, apart from the thrill of being with a

86

new body, there was really nothing a 20-year-old boy could give me I couldn't get from my weathered but still handsome 40-year-old husband. How I always used the image of Jordan to add to the enjoyment I was receiving from Jim, not replace it. I never got to say any of it, because Jim's next words rendered me speechless.

'That's a real shame. Because I would love you to do something about it.'

'I'm sorry?' I couldn't have heard him right. Was he suggesting I should have an affair?

Jim took hold of my hand. 'I'd love to see it. It's something I've thought about so many times. Bringing someone else into our bed ...'

'You mean have a threesome?' I asked, keeping my voice low even though the rock music pumping out of the pub's speakers was loud enough to drown our conversation. Jim nodded.

I didn't know how to respond. I glanced round. Everything was exactly the same as a moment ago. The three Scandinavian girls were shrieking with laughter as they picked their bags up to leave. A burly, shaven-headed bloke was racking up a break on the bar billiard table. Jordan, oblivious to the fact he was the subject of our discussion, was still gathering empty glasses. So why did it feel as though my world had changed?

Why had Jim and I never talked about this before? Our sex life had never exactly been dull: the toys in my bedside cabinet, the DVDs we watched to get us in the mood and the occasional spanked bottom I received as I squirmed on my husband's lap were proof of that. But those were things we did with – and to – each other, for our private enjoyment. Inviting a third party to join in was something else again. While it excited me to think we both fantasised about the fun we could have with a hot young stud, acting on that fantasy would be strange, scary new territory.

'So what do you say, Robyn?' Jim asked.

'Give me the chance to think about it,' I told him, 'and then I'll let you know.'

***

The more I thought about it, the more I began to believe we should give it a try. Jim did his best to encourage me in that direction. When we got home that night, we were barely through the door before he had pinned me up against the wall and was kissing me so hard I thought he would suck all the breath from me. As his body pressed against mine I could feel his cock, rigid and promising behind the zip of his fly.

'Come on,' he murmured urgently. 'Let's get you upstairs so I can really fuck that gorgeous cunt of yours.'

As he spoke, he reached between my legs, cupping my pussy through my tight-fitting jeans as though to emphasise the point. His dirty talk, combined with the way his fingers were pressing the seam of my jeans up between my sex lips, was getting me unbearably excited.

In the bedroom, we stripped in seconds. Jim urged me to get on all fours, then pulled the cheeks of my arse apart and began to lick between them, nuzzling into my pussy.

When he'd got me so wet my juices were coating the insides of my thighs, I heard him moving behind me and assumed he was getting into position to fuck me. Something nudged at the entrance to my cunt, but it wasn't Jim's cock. I recognised it immediately as the rainbow-patterned silicon dildo we'd bought from a sex shop in Shoreditch, thinner in girth than Jim so I could take it in my arse without difficulty.

'Pretend it's Jordan's cock,' Jim told me. 'Imagine him sliding into you, going deeper and deeper. Think how good it would feel, and how horny he'd be at the sight of you, all wet and open for him ...'

I didn't normally come at the moment I was penetrated, but Jim's words and the vision they were creating in my mind had my cunt spasming immediately around the silicon toy. That reaction, more than any words I used later, told him just how I felt about the idea of Jordan joining us for a threesome.

Even so, I suspect we would have kept it as a fantasy if my friend, Di, hadn't spotted the advert on the back of the toilet door. She had arranged to meet us in the Prince Henry one Saturday after she'd been shopping in the West End, simply because she was curious to see the pub I was always raving about. She was just as impressed with it as we had been, and we spent a happy couple of hours catching up on gossip.

Coming back from a trip to the ladies', she commented, 'Do you know anything about this handyman who's offering his services? Some guy called Jordan, behind the bar?'

As casually as I could, I replied, 'We know Jordan, but he's not here at the moment. He usually does the evening shifts. But I didn't realise he was any kind of handyman.'

'Well, the sign says he does work like painting and gardening, which would be useful. The garden's like a tip at the moment. Anyway, he's left a mobile number, so if you hear any recommendations from anyone else, let me know.'

I promised I would do my best, though I was aware of Jim's gaze on me. I was sure that at the first opportunity he would want me to nip into the ladies' and make a note of Jordan's number, though not so we could contact him in a professional capacity.

In that respect, I was wrong. When Di had left to catch a train back to Enfield, Jim said, 'We should have a word with Jordan. I could get him to clear out the guttering.'

Though it sounded like a euphemism for everything I wanted Jordan to do to me, Jim was being serious. The gutters of our property were clogged with leaves, left there by the high winds of a couple of winters, but since Jim suffered from bouts of vertigo, he wasn't allowed up ladders to remove them. I took Jordan's number, programming it carefully into my mobile. 'We'll get him to do this job for us,' Jim said. 'It means we can spend a bit of time with him away from the pub. Get to know him a little better. Decide if he really is the right one for a threesome.'

And that's all we were intending to do when he came over the following Sunday afternoon. When I'd rung him to offer him the work, he had accepted immediately, assuring me he had a good head for heights. Jim would be around to keep an eye on Jordan's safety, and I – well, I would make tea and get on with chores around the house.

Which didn't explain why I didn't bother to put on a bra

under my skimpy vest top and why, even though I had long ago decided the look was far too young for me, I twisted my chestnut hair into plaits. Jim clearly approved, from the low whistle he gave when I came downstairs, and when I opened the door to Jordan, his gaze swivelled down to where my nipples poked against my top before moving swiftly back up to my face. I'm sure he thought I hadn't noticed, but with Jordan, nothing escaped me.

The two men went out into the backyard to set up the ladder, while I started chopping vegetables in preparation for the evening meal. I didn't pay too much attention to what they were doing, though I heard various scraping and bumping sounds and the occasional shouted instruction. Then Jim called, 'Robyn, could you come here a moment?'

Wiping my hands on my skirt, I hurried outside. Jim was holding the ladder steady, while Jordan was descending at speed, carrying a short-handled rake.

'Could you take the rake from Jordan, love?' Jim asked. Not believing in such things being bad luck, I stood under the ladder and reached up. I still couldn't tell you how it happened, but instead of my hand wrapping round the rake handle, I instead found myself, just for a moment, touching the length of Jordan's cock through his baggy shorts. It was as though I'd completed a circuit: electricity seemed to flow through me, and I was sure Jordan felt it too. I couldn't just have imagined that the flesh seemed to pulse and harden beneath my fingers. Quickly rectifying my mistake, I took the rake, trying not to let either man see how my face was flushed with embarrassment and desire.

When Jordan joined us on the ground, he said, 'Is there something happening here I should know about?'

I shook my head. 'No, sorry, just me being clumsy.' I was trying not to remember how wonderful it had felt to have Jordan in my hand, hot and alive, for just a moment.

'Actually,' Jim chipped in, 'we did have a proposition for you. We – er – wondered how you might feel about joining us in a threesome.'

That was the moment when Jordan could have thanked us,

taken the money for the work he'd done and walked away. Instead, he bit his lip as though considering the suggestion, then said, 'I wouldn't be averse to the idea. But I need a better idea of what might be involved. Robyn, why don't you take your top off and show me?'

Standing there with a self-assurance which suddenly belied his youth, Jordan was giving every impression the threesome was his idea. I didn't argue with him. I simply pulled my top over my head, knowing the high wall which separated our house from the next gave us enough privacy.

'Oh, yes,' Jordan said, smiling at the sight of my bare, round tits. 'Now I know exactly what I'm getting into ...' With that, he took me by the hand and led me inside.

The three of us didn't even make it up the stairs. Jordan had stripped me of my skirt before we were barely into the kitchen. Jim quickly cleared enough room on the scrubbed pine table that Jordan could lie me down on it, and then the two of them went to work on me.

Whatever I'd hoped a threesome might involve, it couldn't quite match the reality of a hot mouth latching on to each nipple and sucking. If I turned my head one way, I could see Jordan pulling down his shorts, freeing the cock I'd had such a brief acquaintance with. It had risen rapidly in the last couple of minutes, and while it wasn't as long as in the fantasies Jim and I had created, it looked a good fit for my pussy. Jim had simply let his own cock flop out of his fly – though flop was hardly the correct word any more, given that it was standing as hard and proud as I could remember. The thought two men wanted me so much had my juices flowing, and I needed someone to lick them up.

Jim obliged, his tongue making a rapid ascent of my thighs before reaching the source of my wetness. He lapped eagerly, as Jordan continued to nip at my teats. I reached out and took a proper hold of Jordan's cock, rather than the inadvertent feel I'd copped before. His fevered response after I'd run my fingers along it a couple of times showed me how close he was to losing his load, and I slowed down, not wanting him to come just yet.

'The bathroom's at the top of the stairs,' I told him, 'and there are condoms in the cabinet over the sink. Bring back as many as you think we'll need.'

While he was gone, Jim continued to lick me. His tongue feathered over my clit, bringing me to the brink a couple of times but always pulling back before I could give in to the orgasm which threatened to overtake me. I glanced over to see Jordan standing in the doorway, strip of condoms in hand.

'Put one of those on and come over here,' I urged him. He did as I asked, sheathing himself in black latex. Jim relinquished his position, and I spread my thighs wide, letting Jordan climb on top.

This was the most gorgeously decadent thing we'd ever done, I thought, as Jordan's cock surged up inside me. Beside me, Jim was fisting himself, his eyes fixed to the spot where Jordan and I were joined. As he watched, Jordan slipped out almost all the way, letting Jim see the way my juices glistened on the condom. I groaned as he pushed back inside. As I'd predicted, he fit beautifully, hitting the right places without stretching me too wide.

'That's it, darling,' I murmured. 'Just keep doing that.' I didn't know whether I was referring to my avidly wanking husband or the young stud who was growing in confidence as he learnt just what I needed to make me come.

I knew he wasn't going to last long, not with his youth and the amount of stimulation he was receiving, and I needed that something extra to help my climax keep pace with his. Jim – wonderful, thoughtful Jim – slipped a finger into the folds of my sex, applying just enough pressure to my clit. That did it. At the same moment Jordan's back arched and he filled the condom with his spunk, the waves of sensation broke low in my belly and I came so hard I thought I was going to fall off the kitchen table.

'Maybe we should take this upstairs,' Jim suggested. His dick strained upwards, dangerously close to blowing its own load.

I shook my head. 'Not just yet.'

With Jordan's help, I climbed off the table and sunk to my

knees. I took my husband's shaft in my fingers and closed my lips around the fat, salt-tasting head. He caught hold of my plaits, setting the pace at which he wanted me to suck him, and I knew I'd been right to style my hair like that.

How clever the Buxtons had been, I thought, having the foresight to buy up the unpromising old boozer on our street corner. They had changed the pub for the better and, though they had no way of knowing it, they'd changed our sex life too. As Jordan guided my free hand to his cock, which was already beginning to revive, I had the feeling we really were in an up-and-coming area.

Peter and Pierre
by Alcamia Payne

Martha's life changed when Peter and Pierre moved into the apartment across the passage.

The lock on their door was broken and, as it swayed gently to and fro, Martha watched them through a crack as amid the packing cases and eclectic furniture the new-age hippies roamed around their apartment completely naked, and then proceeded to make love, their seduction alternately the soft serenade of rubbing bodies and the operatic crescendo of wild animals. Instantly, Martha was jealous, jealous of the passionate sex and angry at being the witness of something she couldn't share in.

The next day Peter and Pierre knocked on her door with a bottle of champagne and a box of chocolates. Apparently, Pierre was an artist from Marseilles and Peter was a doctor. Their affair had been love at first sight, a fact which made Martha experience a further pang of jealousy, but she couldn't dislike them, simply couldn't, it was impossible too. Peter and Pierre were the most likable gays she'd ever met and incredibly attractive. Peter resembled a Greek god with his wavy blond hair and fine frosting of baby blond hair and Pierre was the perfect Gallic seducer; swarthy and dark with smouldering eyes and a sexy French accent.

They stood with their arms around one another and apologetic grins on their faces.

'We came to say sorry.'

'What about?' Martha enquired.

'Our behaviour yesterday. The Yoko à la John Lennon

performance.' Pierre glanced at Peter. 'We knew you were watching us but ...' He nudged Peter in the ribs. 'The voyeurism was a bit of a buzz.'

Peter winked at her. 'Yes, it certainly was, luscious lips.'

Martha blushed.

'You still keep watching us, Martha.' Peter said a week later.

'You're both beautiful, that's why.' Martha remarked. 'And it's hard not to, since the lock's still broken.'

'It's all right, petal. But, we wanted you to know, we're not into voyeurism and kinky performances. We're simply two guys in love and about to get married.'

Pierre and Peter had evidently decided to adopt her because they were constantly leaving things on her doorstep; a trinket from the flea market, a book, warm croissants – perfect gifts all of them because they seemed chosen with a psychic precision. It was like a strange kind of ritual mating game. Either that or two men feeling sorry, Martha conjectured, for a poor girl jilted by her lesbian lover, and now in a flat she couldn't afford.

Soon they invited her to the movies where Pierre sat holding her hand and Peter fed her popcorn. One particularly memorable evening they made her dress up and they took her to a fancy jazz club where they both danced with her and she found herself being aroused and having her first disloyal thought about Melissa, as she compared the merits of their cocks as they pressed against her flimsy dress and wondered, just wondered, what it would be like to fuck her best friends in all the world, despite her being a lesbian and Pierre and Peter being gay.

The nature of the gifts began to change and became more romantic. Always flowers from Peter and chocolates from Pierre. She had no way of knowing this was a courtship though.

Martha received a visit from the landlord. She was behind again on her rent and this time he only gave her two weeks to pay. Martha felt a dark sense of consternation.

Peter will know what to do, she reflected. Peter was good at everything and especially problem solving; well, a doctor would be good at the finer details. She knocked on the door and Pierre opened it completely naked and indolently fondling his cock.

'Oh.' Martha said. 'Sorry to interrupt.' And her cheeks turned scarlet as her gaze dropped to Pierre's squat, thick penis. 'I was wondering if Peter was in?'

'Come in, *petit oiseau*, he's taking one of his long soaks.' Pierre said, grinning at her. 'I'll go and put some clothes on.' He gave his penis a tweak. 'So sorry about this, you can see why Peter calls me his Gallic missile. The trouble is he's my disease, Martha. Peter's the virus and I'm the host. He makes me perpetually hard. I asked him what the remedy was. He said there isn't one, not unless you count a diet of constant fucking.'

Martha studied Pierre's compact muscular body with its sprigs of dark hair. It was a very attractive body and it stirred her and filled her with the curious notion that Pierre and Peter were perhaps her illness too, and she'd somehow caught their unique love disease.

'Anyway, what problem do you want Peter the brain box to solve this time?' Pierre asked as he wriggled into a pair of tracksuit bottoms.

'I'm behind with the rent and Mr Nasty said he'll throw me out,' Martha said sadly.

Pierre made a moue as he frowned. 'But, you can't move out, cherie. It's impossible; we'd die if we lost you. You're our best friend.'

'I might have to.' Martha sighed as she leafed through a wedding magazine on the coffee table. 'God, you're getting married?'

'Yes.' Pierre grinned. 'Isn't it super groovy? Peter chose the rings the other day, didn't consult me, of course. He's decided he wants to make an honest woman of me.'

'Where have you been, lover? I thought you were going to join me in all the bubbles?' Peter said wandering out of the bedroom in a wispy caftan, and winding his arms lovingly around Pierre's neck. Through the thin material Martha glimpsed his long lean legs and his protuberant and exceedingly long cock, and she felt herself weaken. He hugged

Pierre while suggestively gazing at Martha.

'A tear trickled down Martha's face; she couldn't help it.

'My Christ!' Peter exclaimed. 'What did you do to Martha, Pierre? You didn't scare her with the Gallic missile, did you?'

'She's behind with her rent,' Pierre elucidated. 'Mr Nasty put the frighteners on her.'

Last night Martha had dreamt about Peter and Pierre. As their limbs entwined and tangled she'd somehow become caught up in the coupling; the cries and sighs and hands on flesh. She shivered as she remembered their cocks. First one and then the other pinning her to the bed.

'We love you, Martha,' Peter said. 'It's out of the question, you can't leave. It would be like amputating a limb or cutting a branch off a tree.'

Martha laughed. Well, that was one way of putting it, she pondered, as she studied them touching and caressing with their dancing fingers. Every time she watched Pierre and Peter it was like witnessing a unique event, such as the birth of a new species combining through symbiosis, or the functioning of a microcosm. And, they were so secure in their love, they didn't care what the world thought as they walked down the street hand in hand. They were the first truly secure people within love, she'd ever known.

'We're glad you came. You see, we wanted to talk to you about something anyway, Martha. We don't want you to feel left out when we get married.'

'That's sweet of you,' Martha remarked, as Peter stepped forward and insinuated his fingers between hers. He smelt fragrant. Martha loved the smell of Peter, soft and warm and comforting, whereas Pierre smelt masculine and feral.

'Last night we lay in bed and we talked about you. We want you to be happy.'

Pierre's eyes were bright with enthusiasm. 'Yes, we decided you ought to move in here. We know that you've been finding it hard to manage the rent since Melissa left and this is a huge apartment.'

Pierre had strong warm hands, capable man's fingers. He stepped forward and began stroking her other hand.

'It would never work. You don't want me around. I'd be the third cog in the wheel,' Martha objected.

'We do want you, Martha. We can't think of anything better.' Peter's fingers grazed her nipples and she felt herself light with inner fire as a fabulous shot of erotic arousal pulsed down her spine.

'It's the perfect solution.'

The next day Martha heard nothing from the apartment and when she knocked on the door it was locked. It was unlike Pierre and Peter to go away.

And then she heard a curious sound remarkably like a whimper and, pressing her head to the door, she shouted. 'Pierre, Pierre is that you? I shan't go away until you open the door.'

When Pierre opened it, he'd been crying and his face was streaked with tears.

'Peter left me.'

'No ...' Martha shook her head. 'Peter would never leave you. I realise you have mad arguments, but you always make up in the most delicious way.' She hugged him tightly and, before she knew it, she was kissing him.

Pierre made no objection. He pulled her closer and she felt the prodding of his taut penis between her legs, just like the dream but better. So much better.

Pierre's fingers started to play a symphony over her body.

'I thought you were gay. I thought I was gay,' she said, almost to herself.

'Love's infinitely imaginative. Never black and white, but all shades of grey.'

'You're such a philosopher, Pierre.'

'And you're a real bombshell.' He tickled her ear with the tip of his tongue.

'So, what was the silly spat about this time?'

Pierre hesitated. 'It was about you actually. We love you, Martha.'

He bit her neck gently. It was much better than Melissa, Martha sighed, as she felt her womb expand in pleasant ripples and wondered if, after all, a throbbing penis might feel rather good. Peter's hand slipped open the top button of her blouse, experimentally pinching first one nipple and then the other.

'He'll be back,' she said. 'Unlike Melissa, Peter always comes back.'

Martha still found it surprisingly hard to talk about Melissa and the memories stabbed like hot knives. Only yesterday, when she'd gone out to get a loaf of bread, she thought, she'd seen Melissa's bright cap of blonde hair disappearing round a corner. It wasn't Melissa, of course, but it was still intensely painful.

Pierre expertly unfastened the rest of her buttons, before bending down to flick each of her nipples in turn with his tongue.

'God, I've wanted to do that for ages.'

'Pierre, I really don't know ...' Martha's voice tailed off.

Pierre was easing her French knickers down her legs and reaching under her skirt to expertly comb her luscious thick thatch, igniting tantalising ripples all across the surface of her skin.

'Martha, I love you. Shall I spell it out, L-O-V-E? Real love.'

'Pierre, that's all very well, but ...' she objected, as he placed his finger on her lips, drawing her down beside him on the couch as he smothered her mouth with his.

'I give you full permission to fuck me,' he whispered taking her hand and placing it on his cock. 'I bet you never had sex with a bisexual man who loves you?'

'Pierre, for goodness sakes, you can't possibly love me – and what about Peter? This is the worst kind of treachery.'

'Peter won't mind.'

She stroked his beautiful cock. It was plump, upwardly curving, the perfect fit to massage her velvet walls. Martha was instantly seized with such passion she straddled Pierre's hips and gently lowered herself towards the Gallic missile as Pierre rubbed her clit. The penis nudged her open, the arousing friction making her wetter than she could remember, and then in it went; in and out, in and out, in a delicious pump action.

And, all the while, Pierre was smiling at her until, just as he was about to come, he pulled her forward and kissed her lips and face.

Martha couldn't believe she'd done it afterwards and the worst part of it was, she'd meant to ask Pierre why they'd been arguing about her, but in the heat of the moment, she'd totally forgotten. She was still wearing her shoes and skirt and she was ashamed of herself, so ashamed in fact, she clambered off the couch and, running across the landing, slammed her apartment door. God, what had she done?

Martha felt so guilty she stopped answering her door and the chocolates and flowers piled up on her doorstep. She'd rapidly become like a spy, peering furtively around corners and creeping around the flat. The trouble was she dreaded the thought of bumping into Peter and Pierre because she felt she'd betrayed them.

One lovely crisp autumn morning Martha was just crossing the road, when she caught a glimpse of Peter coming out of Selfridges. It was impossible to miss the tall rangy posture and the stunning blond hair. She tried to hide but it was too late; he'd already seen her.

'Martha, there you are, I was sure it was you!'

'More gifts for Pierre?'

'He's been a bit moody lately, needs cheering up. He told you about the horrendous argument, didn't he?' Peter linked his arm through hers. 'I think it was a bit of the old wedding jitters to be honest – anyway, we had such a fabulous making-up session.' He stroked her cheek as he looked her up and down. 'Shit, doll, we were getting so terribly worried about you. We haven't seen much of you for days. Look, let's have a coffee in the bookshop.'

'I don't want a bloody coffee,' Martha snapped.

'Whatever's the matter?'

'Oh hell,' Martha cried, bursting into tears.

'Martha, Martha, don't cry.' Peter kissed her. The kiss was long and lingering and she felt herself dissolving.

'I hate myself because I'm jealous,' Martha said.

'OK, well we can easily solve that one. You know how me and Pierre enjoy lovers' tiffs. The making up's so jolly. Come on, you ought to tell me about this jealousy thing. How could you be jealous over two old bisexual fags?'

'Peter, I wish you'd be serious.'

'What's the matter? Is it Pierre? If it is? He told me all about it, and I'm cool about the whole thing. I wasn't about to chain him to the bed and cut his balls off, well not unless he wanted me to. We've talked about it a lot. Loving you that is ... and we never keep any secrets from one another. We share our most intimate and dirty fantasies, everything. And, it wasn't as if it was a case of a fast fuck, was it? You're our extra-special friend, Martha, and we only want to make you happy. Now ...' He stroked her cheek. 'Paint on a smile and we'll go home.'

'Pierre.' Peter called. 'I brought our favourite girl home.'

Martha was filled with a heady mixture of conflicting thoughts as Pierre walked into the room. She flushed bright crimson when she saw him.

'Good thing too. Where have you been hiding, *petit oiseau*? We were about to call the police.'

'I told her it was cool, the sex thing. The best possible thing,' Peter explained, beginning to shrug out of his clothes.

'Ah that.' Pierre sighed, cupping her face in his hands and kissing her hard on the mouth.

There was nothing to say, Martha thought as she enjoyed the kiss. Nothing at all.

'Let's eat her. What do you think?' Pierre was staring intently into her eyes. 'My God, you smell divine, honey – all strawberries and cream.'

'Ah, please don't,' Martha said weakly.

Peter grinned. 'Don't what? Eat you? Oh, I think we should.'

'We both love you so much,' Pierre said. 'Personally, I love your buns; I'm always studying them when you're in your tight jeans.'

'And, I love these,' Peter exclaimed, squeezing her breasts;

first one and then the other.

'I ...' Martha said, her voice trailing off.

'This is long overdue. You know how much you want it, Martha.' Pierre was unbuttoning her blouse and slipping it from her shoulders.

Pierre turned her and, slipping his arms around her from behind, he smoothed his hand over the bulge beneath her skirt. Even the gentle stroking was enough to awaken her, to begin her juices flowing.

'Take out Martha's haircombs, Pierre. I love her hair, don't you?' Peter whispered.

Pierre unfastened the combs and, loosening her hair, he teased it across her shoulders in soft waves. Martha sighed. She was full of a curious euphoric sense of rightness, as with a sharp pang she knew she'd loved Pierre and Peter from the first moment she'd seen them. Passionately, deeply.

'I'm now going to undress you for Peter's delectation,' Pierre said. 'Because you won't do it, I think we'll have to do it for you.'

Pierre began kissing her ear, sucking her earlobe into his mouth, tracing his tongue over the erogenous places that Melissa had never seemed able to find. Martha was filled with delightful feelings as the arousal exploded all over her skin at the same time in multi-orgasmic fizzes, and she started dissolving in a flowing wave of ecstasy.

'Don't stop,' she breathed.

'We're going to make you stop thinking about Melissa and we're going to fill your head with us.'

'Ooh ...' She sighed as Pierre clasped her breasts, palpating them, before smoothing his rough hands down across her belly, rubbing her sex through her panties and sliding his finger up and down her cameltoe.

Peter unzipped her skirt and, dropping to his knees, wriggled it down over her hips. Pierre was still fondling both her breasts and her cunt, pinching her nipples between his thumb and forefinger, making everywhere sensitive for Peter.

Peter clasped her buttocks, drawing her to him, and bit her nipples with his teeth as he alternately tongued them and rolled

103

them around and around. At the same time, Pierre was stroking between her thighs, feathery caresses across her skin and up between her legs, making her warm and wet and flowing.

It was hard to hold back from such sexual attraction. Much better to surrender and think about the consequences later on. And it was so difficult to focus on which sensation to immerse herself in first; the fluttering orgasmic tingle in her nipples, or her fevered cunt, aching now for the touch of Peter's skilful doctor's fingers.

'Adorable Martha,' Peter crooned.

'Yes, lovely Martha,' Pierre echoed, as she arched her back like a cat, cried out, and Pierre's hands worked over her in wonderful firm strokes, full of the Gallic charm of seduction. There was nothing, Martha speculated, nothing in the world so delightful as being made love to by two equally fascinating men at the same time.

Peter had wriggled her panties right down to her ankles and was kissing her belly, moving insidiously as he created a fiery trail down over her trembling flesh and between her legs. Shit! He was now kissing the tender insides of her thighs and, God help her, she was thrusting her hips out to meet his tongue, her passion inflamed by Pierre who was still squeezing her nipples violently as his squat penis thrust between her butt cheeks and tantalised her anus; retreated, came in again and she surrendered to the sweet invasion of finger and cock, lips and tongue.

Her legs gave way and she crumpled, however, Pierre held her, his hands supporting her as Peter's fingers forced her legs further apart and, separating her fleshy sex lips with his hands, he pressed his nose and mouth and his questing tongue into her. He had a fantastically mobile tongue. It slithered all the way up and down, practically into her vagina and back out again.

Peter's fingers stroked her lubricious folds as the tongue came back and bit her clitoris gently and expertly enough to spark her orgasm and then, absolute heaven, he followed the triumphant orgasm up, by sucking her. A gentle sucking fucking by Peter, she smiled. Soft, feminine and patient.

Pierre carried her into the bedroom and laid her on the bed, holding her tightly from behind in his lover's embrace. She rose and fell in sublime ecstasy pushing her hips forward, greedy for the penetration of Peter's appetising, feminine cock.

It was like eating a box of chocolates, knowing it was sinful to consume the lot but knowing you couldn't help yourself.

Peter slithered up the bed, eyes half-lidded with lust, his cunt-flavoured mouth, teasing her.

'You're gorgeous, Martha.' Their hands clasped above her, so she was sandwiched between them, the tantalising friction growing.

Martha raised her leg to cover Peter's thigh and drew him in, felt the dick probe, enter, recede. And then Pierre pushed, gently at first, very gently opening her other hole with his fingers as he pushed in his cock, coaxing it.

The tips of her fingers and toes, even the roots of her hair seemed to be responding to the stimuli as Peter began to thrust and they entwined their man's fingers and held each other as they fucked her, pressing her tighter and tighter between them.

When she orgasmed it was as if her flesh was fused with both of them, pushing and dissolving into both Pierre and Peter in a molten volcanic explosion embellished with cries and moans and purrs, before the comforting downward descent into after love; of butterfly kisses and caresses like a gentle summer breeze. The most perfectly consuming sex.

Martha was best man at the wedding – or should she say best lesbian woman. She wore a stunning crêpe de chine dress, held the rings and felt fêted and adored, as Peter and Pierre introduced her to their select circle of friends.

'Oh, this is Martha. We don't know how we'd live without her ... She's our best friend in the whole world and we adore her.'

Martha walked upstairs to the hotel room and, easing off her shoes, she sat on the bed. She'd miss Peter and Pierre when they went on honeymoon. She wondered if things would change now they were married. Her eyes misted nostalgically. She'd caught Peter's bouquet, a perfect spray of roses, rosemary and love-in-a-mist. She held it to her nose, experienced the resurfacing of just one melancholy thought, one tiny prick of jealousy.

'Here she is.' Peter laughed as he pushed open the door. He looked splendid in a white suit and crisp satin shirt and her heart stirred, gave a leap. And then Pierre grinned over his shoulder. Pierre in a tailored morning suit, Gallic, darkly handsome, sexy as ever. She held out her arms, and they ran to her, hugged her.

'You did such a perfect job and the cake was simply divine. Clever girl.'

She started to cry, she couldn't help it. The marriage separated them, broke the circle and she wondered how that circle could ever again be complete.

'We've got something for you, babe.' Peter grinned. 'Give her the envelope, Pierre.'

Pierre slipped an envelope out of his pocket. 'I forgot, should have given it to you earlier, honey, but I was so nervous.'

Martha drew out the air ticket and frowned.

'You're coming with us to Bali and on the beach we're going to marry you. We intend to make an honest woman of you, Martha,' Peter said, beaming. 'What do you think of that? Of course, you'll say yes because we'd die if you jilted us.'

Martha felt a rising sense of incredulity as Peter placed his arm around her waist and Pierre held her hand.

'You didn't shut the hotel door,' she whispered, as Peter brushed her lips with his.

'Fuck the door,' Pierre said. 'We've only got half an hour until the taxi picks us up for the airport. I hope we packed you the right clothes. However, I doubt any of us will be wearing much in Bali.'

'You dirty bigamists,' Martha said with a sigh, as Peter began to unbutton her dress and Pierre, gazing up at her, wriggled her panties down her legs.

The Fuck-Me Cabbie
by Kay Jaybee

'That's him over there.'

'The one stood on his own? Brown hair, tight jeans, cute arse?'

'That's him.'

'Does he have a name?' I put my drink down onto the sticky plastic-topped table before us, not taking my eyes from the back view of the man leaning against the bar.

'Well, the men call him Mr Greedy.'

'And the women?'

My friend smiled at my expression, she knew me very well. 'They call him the Fuck-Me Cabbie.'

'Really?'

'Oh yes.' The satisfied lilt to Jenny's voice made me drag my eyes away from the self- styled Adonis at the bar, to the air of happy memory plastered across her face. 'He claims to have had sex with nearly every female passenger he's carried in his taxi between the ages of 18 and 50.'

'Is that so?' I picked my cola up and took a long thoughtful draft as I rocked back on my chair.

'So he says.'

'And you believe him?'

Jenny said nothing, but her smirk spoke volumes as she peered at me over the top of her glasses.

'And was it worth it? Is he that good in reality or is it all arrogant attitude?'

'I can't argue with the arrogant bit, but the man's bloody hot. Annoying, but true.'

Running a finger around the rim of my empty glass, my eyes returned to the cabbie, mentally willing him to twist round so I could get a proper look at his face. As if picking up on my mute signal, he turned, a pint glass in his hand, and stared directly at me. Unashamedly, I stared back.

It was his eyes that struck me most. They screamed non-stop endless desire; a desire which would somehow never be satisfied. The square cut to his chin and his bulky, yet toned frame, simply bellowed sex, as if a neon sign was permanently flashing above his head saying "Get it here – NOW."

The other signal he gave out, perhaps even stronger than the aura of lust, was conceit. He'd been told once too often that he was good in the sack. This cabbie needed taking down a peg or two.

'Go and talk to him.'

Jenny's eyes flickered at me mischievously, 'What are you thinking?'

'He needs cutting down to size.'

'How?'

'You'll see.' I kept eye contact with him. He didn't need to say anything to let me know what he was thinking. 'I want you to tell him there is a threesome on offer. Do not tell him who'll be involved, but feel free to let him make his own assumptions. It's not our fault if he jumps to the wrong conclusion, is it?'

Jenny looked momentarily disappointed, 'Won't it be us?'

I couldn't help but smile at her. Jenny's neat chest had been poking at the flimsy covering of her T-shirt and bra ever since we'd started discussing the taxi driver.

'Of course it will be us. But it might not be him ... Are you game?'

'I'm game. Tell me.'

Pointedly ignoring the cabbie, I shifted our chairs closer together so that no one could overhear what I was about to divulge to my companion.

Regarding me with renewed interest, Jenny was obviously eager to get our plotting underway immediately, but was still a little unsure about my plan, which I had to admit, was a bit complicated. 'Do you think he'll go for it? He's not known for

108

sleeping with a woman more than once. No return fares as it were.'

'I'm sure you could lay it on strong. After all, he's had you, but not me. You're a beautiful woman, honey; use that to our advantage. Sod feminism for once! Paint him a picture he can't refuse. Tell him about our casual relationship, and I'll see you and him at the back of the car park in an hour. And don't forget to switch your phone to vibrate.'

Jenny stood up, readying herself to approach our quarry, her short floaty skirt swaying suggestively around her long legs. I re-focused my blue eyes on to the cabbie's gaze, communicating what I hoped was an expression of mutual understanding. Then, with a deliberately seductive glance at Jenny, I trailed a polished fingernail down my pale neck, with the intention of planting the idea of all three of us being together firmly in his mind.

My plan set in motion, my mobile switched to silent vibrate in my jeans pocket, I watched as the black cab drove into view. I felt my phone ripple twice against my thigh. Jenny was signalling to let me know he'd gone for it, and they were awaiting their third party.

Using my phone to send a signal of my own, I took a deep breath, aware that my crotch was already twitching with anticipation at what I had scheduled for the self-styled Fuck-Me Cabbie. A reassuring movement at the corner of my eye told me that all the players for this production were in place.

Striding purposefully, my black boots clattered reassuringly on the tarmac. The taxi's back windows were already steaming up as I rapped on the passenger door. It opened at lightning speed, and a strong yet surprisingly soft male hand grabbed my wrist and yanked me into the cab.

Jenny was sat on the far side of the bench seat, her breasts free, her skirt rucked around her waist, showing me how damp her satin knickers had become. 'Hi, Sally, this is Nathan.' She greeted me, nodding to the cabbie perched on the small pull-down seat opposite her.

Ignoring him was more difficult than I'd imagined. His

chest was already bare. Perfectly toned, but not horribly overworked. Without giving my approval of his physique away, I raised my chin, and looked down my nose at him, freeing my wrist from his grip. I swivelled towards Jenny, who, as our plan dictated, immediately drew me in for a kiss.

Nathan gave a whisper of appreciation as he watched us make out. I could see the glint of power shining in his eyes. He truly believed that we were doing this to please him alone; it obviously hadn't occurred to him we might just want some fun. This man had taken being a control freak and twisted it. He didn't have to do anything; women would perform for him anyway. They were competing against themselves, against all the women that had gone before them. I groaned inwardly. It appeared that I had arrived on the scene in the nick of time.

Tracing my hands over Jenny's glorious chest, I enjoyed the familiar spring of her nipples as they hardened beneath my palms. All but dismissing the presence of our observer, whose hands were now placed firmly over the crotch of his jeans, I picked up Jenny's legs and swivelled her round, so her short pale limbs were lying across my lap. Knocking her shoes to the floor, I rolled down her hold-ups. In normal circumstances this was a job I savoured, kissing each portion of newly exposed flesh. Now I moved quickly, aware that the clock was ticking.

Taking both nylons I began to coil them together and instructed Jenny to pass her wrists to me. Nathan shuffled forward in his seat, eager to watch me restrain Jenny. He still hadn't spoken, but his interest in witnessing one woman tie up another was more than apparent.

My binding constructed, I lifted it towards Jenny's outstretched arms and nodded at her. We acted quickly. Jenny leapt across the tiny space between her and Nathan; sitting astride his lap, she grasped both his wrists. I shot a hand out, and shoved him back by the neck, 'You are going to do *exactly* what you're told, Mr Cab Driver.'

His eyes flashed rage, and he struggled to flip Jenny to the floor, but she'd been prepared for this, and pushed her weight down firmly on his legs

Leaning close to his face, I said, 'You were only sat

watching us anyway, what difference will it make to you? And besides, if you don't let me do this, we're leaving.'

The silence in the cab lasted long enough to become uncomfortable, before he said, 'OK.' His voice was far deeper than I'd imagined, clearly betraying signs of his arousal.

Nathan's eyes hinted, just for a second, at a shade of uncertainty as Jenny relaxed her grip and I fastened the hold-ups around his suntanned skin.

'Good boy.' I leant towards his stubbled face and kissed him slowly, taking a heady lungful of the undeniably sexy scent that emanated from his body, 'You see, good boys are rewarded.'

Jenny inched forwards and tugged at Nathan until he was sitting between us on the cab's bench seat. She ran her hands over his chest, while I crept a finger around the top of his jeans, easing it a little way inside his waistband.

From what Jenny had told me, Nathan was used to calling the shots; manoeuvring and manipulating his female passengers into whichever position he wished. I wondered how out of his depth he felt. That speculation alone was enough to send a few extra shots of electricity around my pussy.

My mobile juddered again. The time had arrived. I inclined my head enough for only Jenny to notice. She twisted immediately to face the cabbie and, raising one of her luscious tits, proffered it to his mouth. He sucked her flesh greedily, and by the way Jenny's expression altered and her eyes closed, I could tell that even without the use of his hands the taxi driver was skilled at the craft – but then if rumour was to be believed, he'd had plenty of practice.

Behind Nathan's back, I picked up his discarded T-shirt and twisted it into a makeshift gag. I touched Jenny's knee, and she opened her eyes, understanding what she had to do next. Pushing her tit further into Nathan's mouth so that his vision was obscured, she distracted him further by pressing a palm over his bulging crotch. Quietly I opened the door next to me, slid off the seat, and gave the gag to the person waiting outside the taxi, beautifully naked in the summer evening.

I could hear Jenny telling Nathan how good his mouth felt,

111

and that I'd opened the door to let some air into the car. She didn't mention that I was now standing outside, and someone else was sat in my place

The newcomer wasted no time. Placing warm hands on the cabbie's smooth back, they slipped them around his body, caressing the light spattering of hairs at the top of Nathan's otherwise clear chest.

Going around the vehicle, I opened the opposite door.

Everything that happened next happened very fast. Jenny pulled her breast from Nathan's mouth. Obviously sensing something wasn't right, he began to utter confused protests. At exactly the same time, my secret assistant lifted the gag and slipped it over Nathan's head, clamping it between his parted lips, and securing it with utmost efficiency.

Shaking his head and raising his bound arms, Nathan's expression was black as he attempted to see who was behind him.

'Look at me.' I snapped out my words, cutting through the moment of chaos. Meeting Nathan's angry eyes, my tone challenged him to ignore me.

He looked, his teeth biting hard into the crunched material.

'Are you telling us, that the Fuck-Me Cabbie – Mr Sex on the Road himself – can't cope with a little bondage? How odd. I wonder what your customers would say if they knew ...? Aren't you even a little bit curious to know what I've planned for you?' I gestured to Jenny, 'After all, my friend here promised you a threesome, although I think she may have forgotten to mention that you'll be watching and not necessarily taking part.'

The sound that escaped from beneath the gag was almost animal, and for a split second I wondered if I'd bitten off more than I could chew, but the hunger in Nathan's eyes shone as strongly as ever, adding heat to my own thermostat.

'You *will* move to the fold-down passenger seat in the corner. You *will* stay still and watch, and then, *if* you behave, you'll be freed. *If* you have learnt your lesson, then I'll ensure you're rewarded.'

I could virtually hear him thinking, *Learn what lesson?*

What do I need to learn? Nathan's bafflement at the idea that he needed to be taught anything was written all over his handsome face.

Without wasting any more time, I introduced the latest addition to the taxi. 'Nathan, may I introduce my other part-time partner, Lee. Fit, isn't he?'

The expression of dislike that flicked across the cabbie's face was so strong that it was borderline loathing. 'Now, boys, I hope you're gonna play nice.'

As fair as Nathan was dark, Lee's naked body shouted "I go to the gym every day" from every muscle. His sheathed cock was long, thick and pointing directly at Jenny. Nathan, still in his constricting denims, couldn't help but drop his gaze to his competitor's cock, before tearing it away, but peeking again, every few seconds, his gaze like a compass continually fighting the urge to swing North.

'Let's begin.'

No sooner had I spoken than Lee half picked up, half manhandled Nathan into one of the pull-down seats.

I hopped back into the taxi and closed the door. The space was cramped, but somehow Lee had moved himself to the middle of the bench seat between Jenny and I, and was eagerly yanking off my shirt and releasing my breasts to the stifling air.

Twisting so that he was facing me, Lee began to slide his hands over my chest and face, his mouth attacking every millimetre of my bare skin, while Jenny moved behind him, rubbing her tits against his back, her hands snaking around him, grasping his cock in her fist.

All the time I watched Nathan. Although obviously fuming at the unexpected turn of events, he'd edged as far forward as the seat would allow, and his eyes never left the erotic tableau before him. His dick was visibly digging into his denims, and his gorgeous chest was breathing deeply as his gaze flitted from Jenny's tits to mine, to Lee's crotch, our hands, our faces and on and on, taking in every movement, undoubtedly wishing that it was him at the centre of all the attention.

Reaching around Lee, my hands found Jenny's lap, which she instantly thrust forward so I could press my fingertips against her knickers. Frustrated by the fabric's presence, I pulled back, 'Take them off, Jen.'

Wriggling herself free of her remaining clothes, her arse teasingly close to Nathan, Jenny was about to sit back down, when Lee grabbed her, and pushed her to her knees on the dusty floor. She didn't need to be told what he wanted and, as Jenny engulfed Lee's shaft, two simultaneous groans echoed around the backseat, one of appreciation and the other, a muted, rather strangled whine of longing from the voyeur in the corner.

Stripping, I squeezed behind Jenny, my back against the divider that separated the driver from his passengers; I crouched behind her, my fingers busy over her left teat, while my other hand wove its way to her wet snatch. Shifting slightly, I stretched a finger to her opening, and eased it inside, making her sigh around Lee's dick. I worked fast, feeling her excitement rise as I pinched her nipple and kissed her back.

Sensing Jenny was about to come, Lee thrust his groin deeper into her face. Almost instantly, Jenny overloaded on sensation. As she shivered and jacked against us, sandwiched by lust, she dropped Lee's dick, her chest heaving as she caught her breath. She didn't have time to recover however, for Lee spun Jenny into the seat next to him and, switching his attention my way, hoisted me into the air, impaling me onto his cock.

As he filled me, I locked my eyes into those of the cabbie. 'This could have been you,' I gasped through Lee's thrusts, 'but from what I hear, you've had more than your fair quota of women lately.'

I moaned as Jenny's mouth came to my right tit, while her fingers found my left. Meanwhile, Lee's chest began to blotch red with the signs of his fast-approaching climax.

'Lee's gonna come, Nathan. I wonder how much you'd like to swap with him right now.'

Nathan blinked, but his jaw remained set around the gag.

'I can't believe you don't want to be in his position.' I paused, swallowing down my own need to come, 'Perhaps we've all got it wrong? Perhaps you'd like to suck some cock rather than pussy?'

Nathan began to swear into his T-shirt, 'Now, now, honey, it was only a suggestion. You shouldn't be afraid to explore your sexuality, you know.'

Lee tapped my leg urgently. It was now or never.

I leapt off Lee's lap, making him yelp with loss; a yelp I would have echoed if I hadn't been concentrating so hard on what was going to happen next. Pulling Nathan to his feet, I dragged down his jeans and boxers, watching with satisfaction as his cramped dick sprung forward, his neck and back stooped.

'This is your one chance for some action, Mr Cab Driver. Are you listening?'

He must have sensed from the edge to my voice that I was serious, as this time he nodded without hesitation.

'Right. You see this cock; the price for an orgasm of your own is to make it come.'

Nathan shook his head frantically.

I shrugged and began to gather up the clothes heaped around our ankles, 'OK, honey. Up to you, of course, I'd never force you.' I turned to the others, 'Come on, guys, we'll finish each other off at my place.'

'Shame,' Jenny spoke ruefully, her hands crossing Nathan's chest, tracing his muscles with the very tips of her fingernails, 'I was really looking forward to feeling that shaft between my legs again.'

Watching the cabbie intently, I saw him struggling between the desire to fuck Jenny and the idea that he'd have to rub a man off to get what he wanted. Continuing to make "time to go" signals, I turned to Lee. 'Don't worry, babe, I'll sort that cock out as soon as we get to my flat.' Continuing to talk to Lee, but looking at Nathan, I said, 'Such a shame, all it would have taken was a well-placed hand or mouth, and all four of us would have been satisfied.'

With three pairs of hungry eyes on him, the Fuck-Me Cabbie appeared genuinely uncertain for the first time. Had he finally realised that we weren't bluffing – that we really would leave him unsatisfied, and go off to continue the fun on our own? I held my breath as Nathan licked his lips. My whole body ached for a continuation of the stimulation it had received. Lee, his dick still tight and stiff didn't look far from begging for relief himself, and I didn't dare glance at Jenny. She was always up for a fuck anyway.

'Would it be so bad?' I asked, a smile forming at the corner of my mouth. 'Surely it would be worth it?' I eyed his desperate cock meaningfully. 'You could decide where that dick of yours ends up. I wonder what you'd choose? My cunt? Jenny's? Maybe a mouth, but I'm guessing not up Lee's arse, although that option is available ...' I let me voice die slowly away, dripping speculation.

The heat in the cab was becoming unbearable, and we couldn't stay there much longer without someone coming to see why an obviously occupied taxi had been still for so long.

It was the act of Jenny putting her shirt back on that finally broke Nathan's resolve. He began to mutter frantically, the words distorted by the gag, which Lee hastily undid. 'Untie my wrists.' He spoke firmly, if a little huskily after his jaw had been clamped in place for so long, but there was no disguising the pleading lilt to his voice.

I nodded to Lee, who complied immediately.

There was a second's total silence, and then Nathan said, 'Take those fucking clothes off, girls', as he grabbed Lee's cock in his right palm. Pointedly not looking at what he was doing, Nathan reached out with his other arm and grabbed Jenny, pulling her to his lap, before beginning to kiss her with fierce passion.

Sitting back in my small space, I couldn't take my eyes from Nathan's hand as he jerked off my male lover. Either he'd done this before after all, or his solo efforts at home had made him an expert in penile manipulation.

Lee, breathing deeply, his pleasure at being attended to by a male hand plastered all over his face, pulled me closer, and fastened his mouth to my chest, using my flesh to stifle his grunt of desire.

I could feel Lee's climax rising again as his kisses turned to nips and bites against my nipples. Nathan also noticed, and shifting in the cramped space, moved Jenny to his side, and shoved me to the floor. 'I want to make him spunk all over those hot tits.'

Seconds later, warm come spattered across my breasts, and Jenny was on her knees licking it up. As her agile tongue soothed up the sweet-salty liquid, I felt my body spasm with longing, and an orgasm to flutter in the pit of my stomach.

The moment Jenny's last lap had cleaned me up, Nathan yanked me upwards, banging my head against the ceiling, before turning me to face away from him, and lowering me onto his dick. Hastily pumping up and down, I was stilled as Jenny's mouth came to mine, while Lee lowered himself into the remaining gap between our legs and started to lick my girlfriend's clit.

Nathan came fractionally before I did, in a haze of swirling, dizzying colours that sent me collapsing back onto my spent lovers and the sweat-dampened plastic seats.

Only moments afterwards, we caught our collective breath. Lee picked up the clothes he'd discarded on the floor outside, while the rest of us dressed, our knees and elbows clashing in the small space.

Lee was the first to leave, closely followed by Jenny. I scrutinised Nathan carefully. He'd said nothing since he'd been allowed to join in. 'Lesson learnt?'

'What lesson?' Arrogance smirked in the depth of his beautiful eyes.

I should have felt incensed. I'd probably just allowed Nathan to fulfil yet another of his undoubtedly endless fantasies. Instead I just laughed and left him to his cab. I might not have scored the victory for the women of the area I'd hoped to, but I had the priceless memory of watching his body flood with insecurity, however briefly, and that was more than worth the effort. With my body glowing in the aftermath of a thorough seeing too, I found I simply couldn't be annoyed that the Fuck-Me Cabbie was as good a shag as Jenny had told me he was ... But that didn't mean I wouldn't try and take him down a peg or two another day. In fact, I already have another plan ...

Anything for Her
by Rachel Kramer Bussel

Emma's girlfriend, Jenny, prattled on and on and on, her sweet, high voice getting higher the more animated she became. The girl could talk, which was one of her charms, along with the adorably tiny lips the words came out of, lips that perpetually glistened with some kind of glittery gloss the femme seemed to naturally produce. Emma wasn't butch, but she didn't go much for make-up; it was all a bit of a mystery to her, one that was never solved no matter how many times her lips pressed against her girlfriend's shiny, sticky, sweet, perfect ones.

For herself, Emma preferred the simple look, a short, flattering cut of her deep brown hair that didn't require much maintenance, clothes that she could easily mix and match in grey, black, white and olive green, with the occasional splash of purple, nails short and clean, maybe with some clear gloss, never anything more colourful. All the primping and fussing were best left to girls who enjoyed it far more. She preferred buying clothes for Jenny, fun items in red and pink and purple, glittery and feminine, ones she enjoyed holding out for a naked Jenny to step into, then later gliding her hands under and easing off of her sensual body.

The same way Jenny could get lost in telling a story, Emma could get lost in Jenny, in those luscious brown ringlets of hair that coiled and coiled down her shoulders and back, in the way her face lit up, her eyes sparkling, in the fantasies that were always lurking in Emma's mind of just what she wanted to do with her. She knew Jenny was infatuated with her as well, but Jenny was also more easily distracted, her head turned by a hot

119

ass or a sexy smile, while Emma, for the most part, only had eyes for Jenny.

Emma paused then when she heard the same name pop out of those sweet, luscious lips, again and again: Damon. It was "Damon this" and "Damon that", so many times that the two-syllable name seemed to take on an echo, became a poetic tool, the anchor to whatever Jenny was trying to convey. He was Jenny's new co-worker at the gourmet shop where she worked, and apparently he was covered in tattoos, an earful of earrings, tall, with shaggy black hair hanging in his eyes, and sexy, with a punk rock bent.

Emma wasn't conventional by any means, but that wasn't her; she didn't show her unusualness on the outside in quite that way – though she'd never get mistaken for a prom queen or cheerleader – and she could tell by the way Jenny was talking about him that her girlfriend liked *him*, not just the idea of him. She didn't just admire his unusual looks or in-your-face attitude with customers, she liked him on an altogether more intimate level. From their boozy barroom whispers about which girls they wanted to bed, and occasional public flirtations, Emma recognised the lustful look in Jenny's eyes. 'And he said, "If you don't like what we have to offer, why don't you shop somewhere else?" No one ever talks like that to–' Mid-sentence, Emma reached out a finger to shush Jenny.

'What?' Jenny managed to mumble around the digit.

'Sweetie, tell me what you're really trying to say.'

'What do you mean?' Emma could sense tears threatening to spill from Jenny's eyes; the girl was much too sensitive for her own good.

'I'm not mad, but I can tell – you like him. I want to know why. Tell me what you'd want him to do with you. To you. With us. Don't censor yourself. I know you think I'm not into guys, and I'm not, really, not like you are – or were, before me – but if a guy turns you on that much, I'd be willing to consider him, as long as he knows you belong to me. I used to fuck them, remember?' She laughed at the memory; it had been such a long time, and she preferred to be the one with the cock in her relationships these days.

'Are you sure?' she asked, her voice breathless.

'Yes,' Emma said.

'Well, if you really want to know, I had a dream about the three of us the other day. And, well, you were sucking his cock and I was playing with your pussy. And then we switched and I was sucking his cock and you were fucking me, first with your fingers, then with your cock, you know the one; I was stuffed full on each end, and he was holding my hair tight while you held my hips down and pumped me hard. It was so hot, and you were so into it, all of it, and then we shared his cock, licking up and then down, kissing around it, and then I kissed him while he fucked you.' Emma didn't hear all of what Jenny said after that, because she was picturing this mysterious stranger somehow entwined between the two of them. It had been so long and yet a part of her remembered the kind of longing Jenny was describing, the sheer male energy a guy could offer, a live, pulsing, hot cock that could fill her all over.

Though it had been quite a while, so long Emma couldn't exactly recall, that didn't mean her head didn't turn on occasion when a particularly hot man, maybe one with his top off, muscles bared, so proud and secure in his masculinity, walked down the street. But this was different. She wasn't lusting after a man she saw on the street, or in an ad, or even someone she'd met. What was making Emma's pierced nipples hard at that very moment was Jenny, with a little something extra. It was the idea of Jenny getting what she wanted, of being able to give it to her, of sharing her perfectly slutty, sexy girl with a man who would surely be as thrilled to have her as Emma was, yet Emma would be the one to take her home.

'Show me his picture,' Emma demanded, and Jenny raced to the computer and pulled up his profile.

'That's my favourite picture,' Jenny gushed. In response, Emma reached between Jenny's legs, feeling exactly how wet the prospect of what they were considering, of their two become three, had done to her. Emma fucked her with those same fingers, adding three, then four, as Jenny rocked against her and they both stared at the man on the screen. Emma made her decision as she felt Jenny's pussy clench around her

121

fingers, then release a stream of juices. Emma twisted her fingers and turned to gaze deeply into Jenny's eyes.

'Yes, we can do it. I want to watch his cock as it goes right here, as he fucks you so hard you scream. I want to fuck you while you suck him. I want to torture you with him as my co-conspirator. I hope you know what you're asking for, Jenny.'

Like a bride, she said, 'I do,' and like a bride, Jenny had no idea what she was truly assenting to.

Emma had seen plenty of photos of Damon, but though they're rumoured to be worth a thousand words, a photo can't hold a candle to being up close and personal, to standing next to the man who's going to fuck your girlfriend and, when you see him, you decide perhaps you as well. Damon was one of those men who practically smouldered in person, who, without looking like he was trying at all, managed to take both women's breath away. Emma knew instantly, as she surveyed their plush hotel room, the one Damon had volunteered to pay for, why Jenny wanted him, because she felt it too – felt things for him she'd never felt with a man before.

'Hi,' he said, almost shyly, as he held out his hand. She took it, feeling the sparks at their touch. Jenny stood there, red coat covering her, crossing one ankle over the other. 'I'm Damon. I guess you know that.' He laughed, and Emma did too, followed by Jenny. 'Good to meet you. Uh, thanks ...' he tailed off, and she smiled.

'No need to thank me,' Emma said. 'I think we all want to be here as much as the next. Isn't that right, Jenny?' Emma asked, knowing that her girlfriend, for all her fantasising, was a little nervous too. When she didn't answer, Emma pulled her over and presented her to Damon, as if they were the ones meeting for the first time.

'Yes, yes. I can't wait,' Jenny said, her glossy red lips glistening.

'Then don't,' Emma said, pulling the belt of her coat and letting it fall open to reveal the red and black lace bra and matching panties Jenny wore. Emma pulled the coat the rest of the way off and let it drop to the floor; they had more important matters to attend to. 'Get on your knees,' Emma growled, and felt the charge in the room at her order. They all wanted Jenny on her knees, mouth at the ready; a quick glance at Damon's cock revealed his eagerness, while Emma could sense Jenny's arousal as she rushed to do Emma's bidding.

Emma moved behind her, admiring the way Jenny's pert ass rested against the shiny black daggers of her heels, her long, glossy brown hair falling down her back. Emma tugged her head back by grabbing a handful, smiling as Jenny's lips parted. 'I think you should show Damon what a good cocksucker you are, don't you?' It was a question that didn't require, or even warrant, a spoken response. Damon was already undoing his belt buckle, any shyness extinguished as his zipper lowered to reveal a long, cut cock, with precome as shiny as Jenny's lip gloss at the tip.

Emma pressed Jenny's head forward, her pussy starting to tighten as she looked down at the first live cock she'd encountered in so long that she felt almost like a virgin again. In truth, this was her first proper threesome; they'd shared some make-out sessions, and she'd watched an ex-girlfriend go down on another woman in a bar bathroom, but she'd never truly shared sex with two other people, a mutually gratifying exchange of bodies and wants. Her eyes met Damon's hazel ones as she led Jenny's mouth along the head of his cock then urged her to take it down her throat. Emma's throat ached as she dropped her eyes to watch its length disappear into Jenny's mouth inch by inch.

She reached for Damon's hand, squeezing it, then bringing it to Jenny's cheek, recalling how much her girl liked the silent encouragement of a slight pinch there when she swallowed one of the many dildos Emma owned. She kept her fingers pressed over Damon's, as the sound of Jenny sucking filled the room. Emma guided her girlfriend's head up and down until she couldn't stand the pressure in her panties any longer, and reached to unbutton her tight jeans, baring simple black bikini bottoms. She lifted her thin black T-shirt over her head, followed by her bra, until her breasts hung in front of her, the nipples perked up, the piercings offering an invitation Damon couldn't refuse.

While Jenny went about her business, Damon lunged for Emma, drawing her close then bending his head to suck one nipple while toying with the other. 'Yes,' he murmured as his warm tongue greeted her nub, licking tentatively at first, then sucking more firmly when she immediately responded. Maybe it was because she could see him doing it, was actively watching, or maybe it was something in his actions, but she knew his sucking was manly in a way Jenny's, no matter how fierce, simply wasn't. Emma shut her eyes and put one hand on Damon's arm, one in Jenny's hair, enjoying the way the erotic energy flowed from one to the next.

'God, you are both so sexy,' he exclaimed after fully mastering Emma's right nipple, before diving down to suck on the left. Emma's body rippled at his touch, and his words. She was used to watching Jenny lap up the attention of men and women whenever they were out, proud to have such a hot babe on her arm. Occasionally another tough girl dyke eyeballed her, or a busty femme, but men for the most part looked at her as an equal, not a potential seduction. They figured, she supposed, that she wasn't interested, so why should they be, but it wasn't like that at all. She wasn't about to chase them down, but bring her one like Damon, lanky and tall and into both her and her girlfriend? That she could more than handle.

She reached for his chest, her fingers crawling under his shirt to stroke the firm muscle beneath. While he was thin, her hand met a solid wall of sheer strength, and she sought out his tiny bud, teasing it with her fingers until he rose up from her breast, his face contorted with pleasure. 'Do you want to come in Jenny's mouth, Damon?' Emma asked, tightening her grasp on Jenny's hair, letting the girl know the decision would be theirs to make for her.

'Yes. But no. I mean, yes, but not yet. I want to fuck you. And her,' he said directly to Emma. She paused, just for a moment, long enough to realise she did, indeed, want his cock inside her. She hadn't planned on wanting that, hadn't thought much beyond the image of watching Jenny take him in, of teasing her while she did so, but this was something new, and his eyes were directly telegraphing his desire. She leant forward and kissed him full on the lips, softly at first, getting used to him. Jenny rose and soon the three were exchanging kisses, bodies grinding together, hands groping. Emma wound up naked first, the two of them lifting off her shirt, then Jenny unbuttoning her jeans. Usually when she knew they were going to fuck, she wore a strap-on, but tonight was different.

Damon easily lifted her onto the king-size bed, and Emma sank into its sumptuous sheets. She was going first, apparently, and for a moment, as she looked into Damon's eyes, she almost forgot about Jenny. She blushed, even though the other two didn't need to know her naughty little secret, that she was getting wet at the idea of his cock. Or maybe they did need to know, because Jenny pressed Emma's knees wide open, leaving no doubt as to how excited she was. This wasn't how they usually fucked. It was usually Jenny who was exposed, opened wide, on display.

Emma wasn't used to one pair of eyes staring at her, let alone two, but when Jenny met her gaze, then boldly dipped her head between Emma's legs, while Damon leant down to again suck on her nipple, she sighed and sank back against the bed. Jenny ate her pussy all the time, but usually it was at Emma's command, a subservient act. There was nothing deferential about how Jenny was plunging right in, owning Emma's clit, sucking hard and then driving and twisting her fingers inside her. Jenny wanted something from Emma, and so did Damon, and clearly, they were going to get it.

Emma let herself surrender to the surreal world the three of them had entered, one where roles were toppled and the past meant nothing. There was only here, now, lips and tongues and bodies, and she came as Jenny licked her, as Damon squeezed her back hard. But it wasn't over. 'Both of you, lie on your back,' he said, and Jenny shucked off all her clothes save for the sexy heels, and lay next to Emma. She giggled, but then stilled when Damon got on top of Emma. Jenny turned over, curling against her girlfriend, watching something she'd never thought she'd see. She was eager for this front-row pleasure trip, and she wasn't disappointed. The cock Jenny had delighted in sucking was now sinking deep into Emma's cunt, and Emma clutched an extra pillow on one side, Jenny on the other, as she wrapped her legs around Damon. He didn't wait long before hoisting her legs onto his shoulders, but instead of the fast fuck to ease the ache inside her, he went slowly, excruciatingly slowly. When she tried to buck her hips, Damon tsked at Emma. 'Be patient. You don't want Jenny to be denied, do you?'

For another guilty millisecond, Emma did, or rather, she wanted to get hers first, but she smiled at them each in turn before simply enjoying the push of Damon's cock into her extremely wet folds. When he pulled out, she was disappointed, but only for a few seconds, because then she got to do more than play voyeur; she watched him turn Jenny over so he could fuck her doggy-style, holding on to that perfect ass, while Emma moved closer to Jenny for a juicy, deep kiss. She found she couldn't stay in her place, couldn't stay still, but had to keep touching them both. She sat up and reached for Damon, who kissed her as he slid just as slowly into Jenny.

They shifted so Emma was beneath Jenny, getting fucked by proxy. Damon had meant to go slowly, meant to alternate and draw out their pleasure, but Jenny felt too good in that position and he started stroking into her harder, his hips bucking, while Jenny lay trapped between her two lovers. Emma found herself bucking again, this time with her hand between her legs, her clit on fire as she felt the passion sweep through their bodies. She had a brainstorm as her orgasm took over, sending heat sparking from her pussy on out. She slipped out from beneath the pair and pushed her tits together. 'Come on us,' she told Damon. 'Let us share it,' she said, having never felt the splash of come on her bare body, never having wanted to until now.

'Yes,' Jenny moaned, as Emma watched her climax, watched Damon's shiny cock, slick with her girl's juices, emerge. The girls were once again on their backs, but everything was different now. Damon held his cock, sliding his fist over its wet length, making each woman ache with a fresh round of desires for where he would put it, for what they'd like to do to him. He straddled Emma, offering her a taste, and she sucked him once, moaning, before he got between the two women, shut his eyes and got ready to come. When he did, he wasn't watching where it landed, but only going by the cries of the women, the ecstatic yells as his cream landed on its targets. He opened them to find the women smearing his come all over their bodies, feeding it to each other, and watched as they shared a sweet, tender kiss.

He pulled back for a second, shy again, afraid of intruding, but when he tried to get up from the bed, Emma and Jenny tugged him back down. 'Where do you think you're going?' Emma asked, and he smiled before sliding between them so they could all spoon and recover before going further.

Emma had thought she'd do anything for Jenny, but found that was only half true. She would do anything for her girl, but this had not been for Jenny alone. It had been for all of them, and Emma had found a new side of herself. Maybe next time she'd be the one to go on the prowl and bring home a tasty treat for them to share. Smiling as she felt Damon's arms circle her waist, she knew she was ready for anything.

The Psychic Harem
by Giselle Renarde

The whole situation seemed utterly sordid, but after everything Dianne had been through she felt she deserved a reward.

'These girls,' she asked the Madame, 'they *want* to be here, don't they? They're not being held against their will?'

The woman tossed back a fringe of salt-and-pepper hair and let out a sympathetic cackle. 'Heavens, no, little darling! They want to be here every bit as much as you do. Now, my dear, you said you've got $200 burning a hole in your purse? That'll get you half an hour with the harem. We take cash or credit, and I can give you an immediate appointment.'

This process was happening too fast for Dianne. She needed to know more about the girls, about what to expect. 'I've heard they're clones. Is that true? They're *clones*?'

'Heavens, no!' Madame chuckled. Her gaze flitted about the room like a caged bird. For a moment, she seemed hesitant to say more. 'Strictly speaking, no. It's more a matter of natural selection, my dear. These girls have been chosen down the ages for their powers of empathy as well as sexual generosity. Those who are most giving, with the most heightened sense of intuition, are bred with spermatozoa whose genetic materials have been overwritten by DNA from our girls' ova.'

Dianne puzzled over the process. She'd never conceived of such things. 'Female sperm?'

With a smirk, Madame patted her hand and said, 'There was no other choice. Have you ever encountered a *man* with an intuitive sense of what women want?'

Dianne couldn't help but laugh, though her experience with

men was limited. 'Do you see many female patrons?'

'Oh, heavens yes!' Madame squeezed her hand. 'More women than men some days.'

Could Madame possibly have realised what a relief that information represented? Perhaps she was psychic too. The thought made Dianne strangely nervous, and she stumbled over her words. 'That's good to know. I only hear about men coming to these harems.'

Madame nodded. 'Yes, because there's an extensive history of men consulting ladies of the evening. Historically, men have been taught to know what they want and take it. Women, throughout the ages, have learnt to give and give until we are nothing but hollow shells. Nobody has ever granted us permission to lie back and receive pleasure. We don't even know how to ask! When I invite the women who walk through these doors to tell me what they want, how do they respond? 'Oh, I don't know. Whatever. Doesn't matter.' And, in partnerships, that's precisely how they are treated – like their deep-seated desires don't matter.' Setting aging fingers across Dianne's forearm, Madame gazed deeply into her soul. She felt utterly naked. 'That's the difference you'll find here, my darling. The girls know precisely what you want. Even if you can't name your desires, they see every inclination embedded deep in your mind, and they act upon your impulses. They give you everything you never knew you wanted. How does that sound?'

'Wonderful.' Even her *mouth* salivated. 'Can we start right away?'

'Of course, my pet.' Madame squeezed her arm with surprisingly strong fingers. 'Payment upfront.'

Dianne undressed in a changing room with art on the walls and fresh flowers on the lowboy table. Madame had assured her the space was secure, and she could feel free to leave her belongings there, safe and out of harm's way. Naked, she pinched her nipples until they drew into pleasant little buds. She wanted to look her best for the girls.

Wrapping a wide pashmina around her womanly hips,

130

Dianne took a deep breath and stepped into the harem room. Reams of velvet ran the length of the floor. Bolts of the lush fabric bled from the ceiling and down the walls. The elegant furnishings were precisely what she'd anticipated, but she was surprised by the women's diversity. Somehow she knew there'd be an Indian girl with flowing black hair playing the sitar – maybe she'd heard the music from the lobby, or maybe her unconscious was simply clinging to antiquated images of harems in Orientalist paintings. Her skin tingled. A half-naked girl with olive skin and shimmering curls came to her left side, and a curvy black woman took her from the right. Both wrapped their arms around her waist, and she immediately wanted more touch, more fingers, more love.

'You're Dianne,' said the olive woman. 'It's lovely to meet you. My name is Francesca, and this is Georgette.'

Georgette offered a brief bow. 'I'm so glad you've come here today. I hope you'll come again and again.' With an impish smirk, Georgette escorted her on a brief perambulation about the harem quarters. 'We are all here for you. We wish only for your pleasure. In the corner with the sitar, we have Shahira, and the beautiful woman reading to Nixie is our resident bookworm, Farrah.' Georgette leant in so close Dianne could feel every warm word breathed in her ear. 'Nixie is blind, but watch out – she can see inside your soul.'

'Oh.' Dianne gulped as she observed the quaintly affectionate pair. Farrah wore glasses and nothing else. Nixie was clad in a pashmina like Dianne's, but tied just above her small breasts. She laid her cropped amber hair in Farrah's naked lap and listened to Maupassant's *Une Vie* read in impeccable French.

As if in response to Dianne's fond gaze, Nixie sat up and stared at her with blank blue eyes. Farrah stopped reading. Clutching her hand to her heart, Nixie said, 'I'm sorry about Jane. What a shame, after all those years.'

Dianne's throat closed up. If she'd attempted more than a nod, she would have wept, and she'd cried enough tears over that scheming harridan. She glanced at the other girls lounging on cushions around the room, one toying with the bauble swaying between her big breasts, one painting her toenails red, and one scribbling Venn diagrams into a notebook, but she did not receive any introduction to these three.

There was a velvet chaise in the middle of the room, and Francesca eased Dianne into it, stroking her hair and kissing her temple. 'You want to know somebody cares for you.' Francesca's smile filled Dianne's heavy heart. 'We all care.'

'It's true,' Nixie said, positioning herself like a sprite emerging from the shimmering depths of a blue pond.

Georgette sat at the edge of the chaise and nuzzled Dianne's shoulder. The warmth from Georgette's feminine form soothed Dianne's body and mind, and she felt an oncoming sense of peace. 'You want to tell us about her,' Georgette said, wrapping her soft hands around Dianne's belly.

It was true, absolutely. No matter how many times she told her story, compulsion drove her to tell it again. 'Jane wanted to go back to school. She wanted to earn her PhD.'

'I have one of those,' the ginger girl with the Venn diagrams chimed. Her smile faded when the rest of the harem stared her down. Bowing her head and snickering, she said, 'Sorry.'

'She returned to a life of academics,' Dianne went on. 'Academic subjects and academic people. Meanwhile, I worked. I worked overtime to support us, pay our rent, pay for her fees and books. In June, she finally completed her studies. And then she split.' Dianne felt at once weak and angry describing the wretched end to a six-year relationship. 'She left me a Dear John saying she'd fallen in love with another grad student and they were eloping and she knew I'd understand. Well, who does she think she is? No, I don't bloody well understand. How could she use me like that? How dare she?'

Georgette hugged Dianne so tight her large breasts pressed against Dianne's back. 'I'm sorry, babe. We all are. We're going to make you feel better.'

When the other girls crept forward, she knew she'd leave here feeling better. Georgette smoothed two hands around Dianne's waiting breasts and pressed them together while Francesca ran loving fingers through her hair. Little Farrah, with tawny hair to her knees, slipped like a sylph into Dianne's lap. That pixie body barely brushed her flesh. Her eyelids fluttered as Farrah planted kisses soft as butterfly wings over her lips. As Georgette's hands sculpted her breasts, Farrah's peaked nipples swept across her chest. She returned Farrah's kiss with perhaps greater ferocity than the girl anticipated, and Nixie snuck up to her side and stroked her thigh.

The combined sensations of fingers on flesh, lips on lips, hands on tits, and tongue on tongue, drove Dianne's arousal into the sunny realm of ineptitude. She could do nothing more than absorb pleasure. The girls – the beautiful, charming and sympathetic girls – toyed with her body and her desires. What could she do but enjoy?

Dianne felt as though she were falling into clouds when she set her back against Georgette's pillowy frame. Farrah tumbled forward on top of her, laughing as they kissed lips in birdlike pecks. Shahira sang softly, enticing an enchanting melody from the sitar while Francesca traced her fingertips across Dianne's cheeks and neck. It was true, what Madame had said – they recognised what she wanted and they gave it to her. And was there any seduction more entrancing than a serenade?

The girls to whom she hadn't been introduced sauntered over while Nixie pushed Farrah out of the way and opened Dianne's legs wide. As Nixie planted tender kisses across Dianne's thighs, the ginger genius took a finger in her mouth and sucked it. Dianne's body went from tingles to trembles. Pre-orgasmic shudders coursed through her and she writhed on top of, beneath, and beside the mass of beautiful women caressing her flesh.

Though Dianne couldn't see beyond Farrah's precious kisses, she could feel two sets of hands taking her two feet between them. When those resourceful women kissed her arches and took her toes in their mouths, her body bucked like a wild beast. Poor Farrah would have gone flying if Georgette hadn't released Dianne's breasts and held on to the pixie girl instead. For a moment, Dianne missed Georgette's sensual grasp – and then Farrah's nubile tits met her own and she was intoxicated all over again.

The girls at her feet were relentless. They took her toes in their mouths one, two, three at a time, running their tongues between, over and beneath. Dianne had never known a sensation so immediately fulfilling. Her body developed a mind of its own, jumping and rising as much as Georgette would allow. The tongues on her toes brought tears to her eyes. Her feet tried to escape, but the girls at the base of the chaise held her ankles tight and kept at them. Their saliva was wetter even than her convulsing pussy, and their mouths were hot as hell. When they sucked, Dianne felt like the disciple whose feet were washed in oil. She didn't deserve this much pleasure.

'Of course you do,' Nixie said, opening Dianne's sarong. 'You deserve everything and more.'

Before Nixie came anywhere near her pussy lips, Dianne writhed like mad. She lost control, and Georgette had to restrain her as she squealed and screamed, whipping her head side to side. She felt consumed by the women with their mouths around her toes. They'd brought her to the brink of orgasm and thrown her over the edge. The faster she fell, the higher she felt, until she couldn't bear any more pleasure. 'Stop,' she cried. 'It's too good. Enough, please.'

The girls let her toes fall from their mouths, and for a moment time stood still. All sensation ceased, except the constant sucking on her finger. When Farrah raised her head away from Dianne's and cast a worshipful gaze, Dianne's heart filled with warmth. It was emotion rather than passion that drove her forward.

'Thank you,' she said into the sparkling eyes at her feet.

Farrah slid away from Dianne's lap, but she didn't go far. Standing beside the chaise, she bent at the hips and licked a meandering path across Dianne's breasts. The sensation was so wildly arousing, she tossed her head back against Georgette. 'See, Dianne?' Georgette cooed. 'Didn't I say we'd take care of you? All we want is for you to be happy.'

'It's working,' she assured the mass of women. 'It's been a long time since I've felt this good.'

But Nixie made her feel even better. Scuttling between her legs, she pressed her lips to Dianne's wet slit and everything changed. The sensation of that lovely woman's mouth against her full and ready pussy lips made her feel at peace with life and connected to everyone in the room. Of course, she was in some way connected to them all – to the girls at her feet and the one sucking her fingers, to Farrah nibbling on her nipples and Georgette cushioning her from behind.

As Nixie moved her tongue slowly up and down Dianne's slit, Dianne looked up into Francesca's hazel eyes. This woman was gorgeous. She wore a sarong secured like a halter at the back of her neck, but she must have recognised the thoughts swimming through Dianne's mind, because she reached back and untied the knot. In one swift motion, the green fabric fell to the floor. Francesca grasped her olive breasts and pressed them together until their dark nipples almost met in the middle. They were perfect, round and perky, and her skin shone like it had been slathered in oil.

As Nixie's face moved faster between her legs, Dianne salivated for Francesca's breasts. She didn't have to wait long for Francesca to lower a tit to her mouth and drag its hard nipple back and forth across her lips. Dianne licked that dark bud, trying with each pass to trap it between her lips. When Nixie sucked her clit inside a warm, wet mouth, Dianne gasped at the intensity of sensation. Francesca took the opportunity to push her tit in Dianne's mouth, and as soon as it was there she seemed to feel the PhD's sucking intensify on her finger and Nixie's on her clit. She held her hand still, but writhed under Nixie's generous attack. She couldn't help herself – the harder Nixie sucked on her clit, the harder Dianne sucked Francesca's nipple. When she moved her hips in slow circles, Nixie launched a further assault, growling as she tore into Dianne's pussy like a beast. She gnawed and sucked and licked and raged. Dianne couldn't help assailing Francesca's tit with the same vigour. She must have bitten down just a tad too hard, because Francesca squealed and stole her tits away. Prancing to the other side of the chaise, she replicated Farrah's pose there.

Without warning, the PhD was at her mouth, kissing her with a desperate sort of passion. Dianne closed her eyes. She wasn't sure whose legs her wet fingers had fallen between, but they found a pussy and they rewarded it. When Farrah whimpered, she knew whose slit she'd found her way inside. She should have known by its tightness. As she fingerfucked the girl, Nixie moved away from her clit. Kissing Dianne's belly, she thrust long fingers deep inside. Georgette grabbed her hips and helped them buck back against Nixie's wildly thrusting fingers.

Dianne no longer had any control over her body – the women controlled it for her. They sucked it and reamed it and thrust it and fondled it. As Georgette forced her to buck harder against Nixie's fingers, the wave of orgasm knocked her mind off its feet. She screamed and shrieked and squealed and cried while the harem ravaged her body. They feasted on her. Even with her eyes closed, she could see them from above, pulsing, writhing, eating, sucking.

When she cried out one last time, the girls all seemed to know she couldn't handle any more. Georgette cleared them off, but they settled to the floor like loyal pets. As Dianne lay back against Georgette's consoling body, Nixie rested her head on Dianne's stomach, and the other girls cuddled in at her sides.

It must have been well over an hour later that Dianne awoke. Panic followed the peace that had followed the pleasure. How much would her slumber cost her?

'Nothing,' Nixie said without moving her head. 'We like you. We had no other appointments, so Madame let us keep you.'

'Oh.' Dianne smiled like a mother cat with her sleeping litter. 'Thank you,' she said to Nixie. 'You were all just wonderful. I never believed you'd know what I wanted before I did, but it's true. It's all true.'

Francesca petted her arm, but it was Georgette who said, 'We just love to give. We want to give you everything.'

'You did,' Dianne assured them. 'You asked about my life and you listened to my story, you comforted and consoled me, gave me confidence and reassurance, and topped it all with two full orgasms.' She greeted the generous harem with her warmest smile. 'You've given me all I've ever wanted.'

Hinged
by Angela Caperton

'Lost the key? What do you mean, you've lost the key?' A moment of real panic flashed through Veronica, though she had to fight back a fit of giggles at the sheer goofiness of her situation. Here she was, along with Gardner Peterson and Stewart Dirks, three-fifths of the Brenford College history department, in the back room of a sagging building a few blocks from the Laketown boardwalk, except Gardner and Stew weren't chained to the wall.

And neither one of the guys was wearing a chastity belt.

She rattled the chains and tested the limits of her movement. She might be able to scratch her hip if she struggled and stood on her tiptoes.

Stew probed his pockets and then turned them inside out. 'I don't have it.'

'Maybe Igor has a spare,' Gardner offered. He laughed openly, the bastard.

'He said he'd be back in ... what? An hour? Can you stand it that long, Ronnie?'

'I think so. The chains chafe a little, and the damned belt itches. Can you two see if you can get it off me?'

'Sure!' Stew answered with enthusiasm and caught hold of the metal band that circled Veronica's waist. The belt hugged her waist over her shorts, though both men had tried to convince her to lose them so she'd look like she was nude under the ancient device when they took the pictures. 'In your dreams, boys,' she'd answered with a grin.

No way, she thought, and she was glad now, the idea of the

137

old caretaker – the one Gardner dubbed Igor – returning to find her in a thong was seriously unappealing. Stew fiddled with the belt and Veronica fought the chains, trying to reach the band to help him. He pulled hard at the latch where the belt fastened.

'Ouch!' she cried. 'That hurts!'

'Wow, Ronnie,' Stew said, his voice broken with suppressed laughter. 'I'm so sorry. It's not budging. Your shorts are caught in the hinge. The goddamned belt is stuck.'

They'd taken the trip together, the first weekend of summer break, from Brenford to Laketown, an urban fieldtrip, Stew called it. Veronica admired his passion for mid-century culture, and because Gardner's uncle had owned an old concession just off the bad end of the Laketown boardwalk – shuttered since the 80s – the trip seemed a perfect launch to the summer. Laketown had a handful of historic buildings from the Civil War – Gardner's area of expertise – and a museum of Native American artefacts. And, of course the little resort town had Shelley's Lake and three good restaurants, all of which weighed into Veronica's consent to the trip, even though there was nothing professionally appealing there for a teacher of Medieval and Renaissance history.

That, and she liked both Stew and Gardner well enough to have hooked up with each of them her first year at Brenford. None of them had any illusions about relationships, and all things considered, that fit perfectly into Ronnie's life plan. Problem was, she could almost imagine herself falling in love with either one of them, and the risks of doing that before any of them had tenure were too high. At this point, it might end up with one of them employed and the other one moving on. She'd partied discreetly with each of them a few times since, but she would never let either of them go too far, even when she really wanted to.

Ronnie pegged the trip as a kind of test, but she readily dismissed serious thoughts in favour of celebration. At the end of the spring semester, they had all been granted tenure after five years of educating the minds of the future. The fact that all of them were tenured was more than enough reason to celebrate, and Ronnie was ready for anything. Anything, she told herself, wondering exactly what that meant.

They drove into Laketown early Saturday and rented adjoining rooms at the Wahoo Motel, a survivor from the 1930s that Stew said had once been a hideout for mobsters, and then they drove down to the boardwalk. The waterfront had fallen on to hard times in the 80s and 90s, but the strip of ancient weathered buildings had recently begun to show new signs of life, a couple of restaurants and a charter outfit with its bright nautical motif occupied the centre of it.

'Uncle Billy's place was down this way,' Gardner said, leading them down a narrow street that led inland from the shore road. 'I told you, he ran an attraction on Coney Island for almost 30 years before he retired here. This place was a junior version of his Curiosity Museum at Coney. Classic roadside stuff. The building's been padlocked since Uncle Billy died.'

They pulled up to an eroded curb and Gardner pointed to a white frame monolith, its windows shuttered with boards. Faded "No Trespassing" signs dotted the fence. A stooped, unshaven man of indeterminate age awaited them on the wide porch, jingling a ring of keys. Behind him the pink ghost of a garish sign promised "Fun and Thrills".

Stew leant over to Veronica and whispered, 'It's Igor!'

She choked back a laugh as Gardner climbed out of the back seat. 'You're from Parrish's, right?'

''S'right. Mr Parrish says you're OK.' The old man's eyes clearly indicated general disapproval as he handed a little ring of keys to Uncle Billy's prodigal nephew. 'That big one's for the front door. Not sure about the rest of them.'

Veronica and Stew joined the other two on the porch. Igor finally smiled when he saw Veronica in her shorts and tanktop. 'You got all afternoon. I'll come back in an hour or so to check on you. Don't take nothing, but if you see anything you want to buy, Mr Parrish says it's all for sale. Some of that junk you might be able to sell on eBay.'

With a parting leer at Ronnie's legs, the old man shuffled off to a battered Buick and drove away.

'OK,' Gardner chirped and tried the key in the big panelled

door. It turned easily and they stepped into the House of Curiosities.

Light filtered in through the boarded windows and their first steps raised dust. Gardner flipped a switch and dull luminescence emanated from ancient hanging ceiling lights to strain against the gloom. Veronica saw a counter, like a soda fountain, with a little kitchen behind it, shelves and bins, some of them still full of toys, a rack of grimy sunglasses, and a wide curtained doorway.

'I remember this,' Gardner said. 'I was like seven. The museum's back there.'

They spent a few minutes among the rubber sharks and suntan oil, but Stew's impatience pulled them back. Ronnie had no idea what to expect but she appreciated Stew's enthusiasm. This place was like a time-capsule to him and she shared his joy at the cheesy wonders of Uncle Billy's ten-cent museum – a Fiji mermaid, some bell jars that must have once contained ... what – two-headed calf embryos? Yellow newspaper clippings hung between the cases and racks, mementos of the Coney years.

'Back here,' Gardner called from another doorway. 'This was the best.'

Ronnie and Stew followed him back and, yes, Gardner was right. This was the best.

'Wow, my turn!' Ronnie said. 'All the way back to the middle ages!'

The big room looked like a silent-movie torture chamber: a wheel and a rack, an incongruous guillotine, chains and a brazier. 'There were wax dummies,' Gardner said, the disappointment plain in his voice. 'It was great.'

Stew moved around the room, wishing aloud for more light, but as their eyes adjusted, they could see well enough. 'What's this?' Stew asked. 'Is this what I think it is?'

Veronica laughed. 'It's a chastity belt,' she said. 'Let me see that.' Stew handed it to her and she examined it; a steel belt, hinged on one side and with an interlacing buckle on the other – a buckle that could be locked with a simple bar or a padlock. A curved triangle of metal descended from the centre of the band like a tarnished bikini.

'They're all fakes, right?' Gardner asked. 'There weren't really any chastity belts.'

'Well,' Veronica said. 'There were chastity belts but some scholars think they were just ... conversation pieces, that no one ever really used them for their alleged Crusader-era purpose.'

'I bet they were kinky toys,' Stew offered. 'Have you seen some of those antique dildos?'

Warmth slipped over Ronnie's skin. She'd done plenty of research into ancient sex toys. If they only knew ... Without hesitation, she put the belt around her waist and positioned the metal g-string over her crotch.

'Picture!' Stew called out and produced his camera. 'Get the shoes off, Ronnie.'

'And how about you take your shorts off?' Gardner asked, his grin wolfish.

Ronnie laughed as she kicked off her sandals and shook her head. 'I don't think so, but look.' She walked over to one wall. A pair of chain shackles hung from rusty rings. One of the cuffs still had a key in it. She tried the key and the cuff opened easily. Laying her left wrist in the metal bracelet, she closed it and heard it snap, and then unlocked it, slipping her wrist free. She tried the key in the right cuff, grinning at the opening click.

'Lock me up, boys,' she said. 'Truly a prisoner of history.'

Gardner and Stew looked at each other and smiled. Each of them took a wrist and closed the cold cuffs around her slender wrists. She felt the weight of the chains, the belt around her waist, and, yeah, she admitted it to herself. She was seriously turned on, in between the giggles.

She writhed in the chains as Stew took pictures but she couldn't quite manage the look of pain and desperation. When he showed her the shots, she looked like the Happy Heretic, but she also had to admit she looked pretty hot – her hair messy in her face, the tanktop stretched appealingly. She knew both men were getting off on this too.

'Let's wrap this up, boys,' Ronnie said, shaking the chains. They stood on either side of her, each with their hands on her wrists, and then they looked at each other.

'Where's the key?' Stew said first, as they discovered neither of them had it.

'It itches. The belt itches. And it's heavy,' Veronica said and her writhing took on new urgency. She hadn't expected the damn thing to be so weighty. The metal bands felt like they might be starting to cut into her hips. 'Can't you get the fabric out of the hinge?'

'I'll try,' Gardner promised and knelt beside her. He tugged hard at her shorts and she heard a seam rip. 'Sorry.' He didn't sound too sorry, Ronnie thought. 'No good. I can't get a good grip to pull.'

She hung there a moment, her breath a little more laboured. 'Do either of you have a knife?' she asked. 'Or maybe there are some scissors out there? Maybe you can cut part of it away.'

'Cut your shorts?' Stew asked, and then almost collapsed with laughter.

'I'm glad you think this is funny,' she chided, but she had trouble sounding serious herself. She smiled and stifled a giggle, the chirp doing little to help her imploring tone.

Neither of the men had a pocket-knife, but they rattled around the room to search for anything that might cut her shorts away. Before long, they left her field of vision to fan out into the other rooms of the museum and the shop. Stew returned with a pair of novelty scissors shaped like an egret. 'They seem pretty sharp,' he said, kneeling by the hinge.

He put his hand on her thigh right below the hem of the troublesome shorts. His hand burned like a brand and her breath quickened again. His fingers slipped under the leg as he manoeuvred for room and began to cut the fabric. The cool metal of the scissors slid up and a little release of tension spread over her abdomen as the material parted. The point pricked her once and she jumped.

'Sorry,' Stew offered, but she bit her lip and didn't spit out her chastisement. His hand worked inside the metal band, following the line of the cut.

'Jesus,' she mumbled. 'You just cut my thong too, Stew.'

Stew pulled at an end of the fabric and part of it came free.

He snipped again and drew out a length of lacy fabric. The metal of the belt stung her skin and she fought against her chains for a moment.

'It's no good,' Stew said. 'The hinge is still stuck.'

'Let me try,' Gardner offered eagerly, his hand almost trembling as Stew handed him the scissors. Snip, snip, and he pulled more of her lost shorts out of the chaste metal trap. She watched with amazing detachment as the remnants of her panties appeared in the palms of his hands. Before long, Ronnie realised she was, for all purposes, naked from the waist down under the ancient – probably fraudulent – device.

Both men knew it too. They looked at her with wide eyes, something almost feral glowing in the shady depths. 'It's still stuck,' Stew announced, as he pulled at the hinge. His fingers lingered everywhere they touched her and Ronnie stifled her approving grin. 'Let's try sliding it down.' Gardner proposed, nodding without confidence. Stew ran his fingers through his hair and nodded his agreement to the plan.

Ronnie only rolled her eyes.

One man on each side, they tried to work the band over the round swell of her bare hip.

'Almost,' Gardner said, when they paused, the sharp yelp from Ronnie stopping them as the band cut into her hip points. 'If we had some oil, I bet it would come.'

Or someone might, Veronica thought, working to control the hot twinges along her spine and slicking her pussy lips. Yes, someone might well indeed. She began to sweat and her tanktop stuck to the sides of her breasts, the nipples practically candles poking out of the frosting of her shirt. How long did they have before the old caretaker returned?

Stew went out of the room and returned with a dark plastic bottle. 'Coconut oil,' he said. 'It's pretty slippery. Um, I guess we better put it on for you, right?'

She looked at her hands, still bound by the chains, the cuffs cutting her wrists a little. 'Yeah, I seem to have a problem with my reach.'

They both filled their hands with oil and began to rub it into her hips and, reaching under the band, down her thighs. They both paused when their hands reached her bare ass, her nakedness unavoidable to their eager fingers. She pushed herself as far as she could away from the wall to give them access and they both oiled her backside, their hands incredibly hot, circling, kneading.

Ronnie groaned – her pussy as wet as Shelley's Lake, her breath ragged and she had a clear vision of these two magnificent men fucking her. Couldn't they feel it, couldn't they see the opportunity?

Stew, his daring spirit shining bright, touched her lower belly just above the belt. Ronnie groaned and drew in her stomach to let his hand slide down, oily, lubricating. Thank God she had a fresh shave, she thought as her pussy lips flooded with warmth.

Stew's hand brushed her mound and then lower, sliding just into the crevice, just above her clit hood. Yes, Gods, yes, Ronnie thought through dusty clouds of lust.

He looked up at her, his gaze ravenous and questioning.

'Get this damn belt off me,' she commanded. 'Fast.'

They gripped it together and pulled. It scraped and abraded her skin. Veronica pulled in her stomach and clenched her butt. It passed the hard points of her hips then she was free. Both men held on to it while she stepped out.

Naked from the waist down, she hung in chains before them. 'All right,' she whispered, resolute. 'I think you'd better fuck me now.'

Stew and Gardner blinked, and then looked at each other.

'Both of you,' Ronnie sighed. 'Right now.'

She let out a throaty chuckle. Both men looked like they were hiding flashlights in their shorts. She would love to have given both of them a little oral attention but the chains made that impossible. The best she could manage was a slow grind of her hips so they could see just how wet and ready she was for them.

Gardner and Stew looked at her. 'Maybe we should lock the front door,' Stew said.

'Hurry,' Ronnie groaned, then rattled her chains for emphasis. While Stew was out of the room, Gardner dropped

144

his shorts. His erection stood out at impressive attention. Ronnie bent her arms and caught her tanktop in her fingertips, pulling it up. Gardner took the invitation and attacked her breasts under the thin, satin brassiere. He went for the hook but her raised arms defied him. 'Another job for your bird friend,' she said, looking at the egret scissors. She didn't have to tell him twice. Snip, snip, and her breasts were bare, nipples aching for the attention she knew would come. Gardner had one tit in his mouth before she could catch her breath, and his fingers exploited her wet slit just as Stew came back into the room.

Power surged through Veronica. 'Come on, Stew. I'm pretty sure that's why I have two tits, but get your shorts off first.' On the surface it seemed silly for her to be calling the shots when she was the one in chains, but the two men seemed to need her direction and Veronica wasn't about to reject the opportunity to have them both.

Sweetly shy, Stew turned his back to show her his muscular butt while he dropped trousers. 'Now, Stew!' she growled.

Turning back, he showed he had a good inch on Gardner, the glorious uncut cock presenting an impressive standard. Ronnie grinned, remembering the interesting bend in the rigid length, her body shivering with the memory of his cock inside her.

She couldn't wait to have them both, a fantasy she had never remembered having before, though now the thought almost made her come – even though both of them had so far only worked on her breasts.

'Who's first?' Stew asked between nibbles.

'First?' Ronnie scoffed. She thrust out from the wall. 'There's room behind me, Gardner. See if you fit ... back there.'

He barely hesitated, her directions understood immediately. Gardner doffed his T-shirt, and squeezed between Veronica and the stone wall. The chains bit into her wrists, and her shoulders strained, but Ronnie wallowed in the sensation of Gardner behind her, his rock-hard, gloriously hot cock moulding into the cleft of her ass and her lower back. Stew stepped back, stroking his lovely huge rod, the tip weeping and shining, bouncing in anticipation. He growled, no scholarly annunciation, but a medieval lord's verbal brand upon his helpless slave. Professor Ronnie moaned in anticipation of reliving history.

From behind, Gardner nuzzled and bit her throat and the spongy head of his prick rubbed first against her well-oiled skin, then along her slit, bouncing off her clit. She needed no more encouragement and arched, precisely targeting his cock, capturing him in one thrust. Amazingly, she controlled the rhythm – she guessed he was in some kind of erotic shock, and that realisation spiked Ronnie's need. She ground against him four times, then thrust forward so he slipped out of her.

'Now you,' she told Stew. He didn't need to be told again. He caught her thighs in his strong hands and lifted her. Gardner's dick slid hot and slippery on her bottom, as Stew lowered her onto his monster cock, filling her, parting the flesh in delicious wholeness. She scissored him with her calves, the chains half-supporting her weight, the men holding her between them. Stew slid in all the way, that magical spot deep in her cunt shouting at the delicious contact. Gardner caught on and probed at her back button, fingering her ass, sliding his finger into the tight ring of her sphincter, teasing, coaxing until her ass lips released. Before she could think, Gardner slipped his cock in, coolly waiting as a passage opened through the tight gate. Wet with her juice and the coconut oil, he probed the tight depths of her ass.

Ronnie's senses flooded all input. She'd had anal a few times and never really liked it but this – this was cosmic. She set the rhythm at first but then her sensations relinquished control to the men who thrust into her. The wave built between them and she had no control over it at all. They fucked her hard, almost brutally, the chains singing in her ears, a chorus to their growls and grunts, her hands kneading the muscles of Stew's back, both men's hands all over her, worshipping her thighs and breasts and belly, Gardner's teeth in her shoulder, Stew licking her throat, kissing her rough and deep.

The tide rose, a surge deep as the sea. Gardner pulsed in her ass and Stew deep in her cunt. She counted one, two, three

146

beats, prolonging the moment, hanging over the depths.

The orgasm shattered time, brought castles to computers, obliterated the lines of language and art. She screamed, uncaring as to who might hear, who might see. Her body burst into colour, bright orange and vibrant blue, forbidden purple and sacred red. Pulsing hot shots of spew let her know they came deep inside her. The chains deafened her with the power of her thrashing. In moments, all that whispered through the museum was the harsh, mingled breath of the three of them, Ronnie skewered between the two men, their cocks pulsing in her ass and cunt.

'Goddamn,' Stew gasped when he slipped out of her.

Gardner kissed the slippery, sweaty back of her neck and he pulled her tanktop down over her tender breasts as he moved out from behind her. 'What are we going to do? Igor will be back any minute.'

Veronica knew he was right. As deliciously depraved as she felt, she didn't really want the old caretaker to find her, dripping from ass and cunt, chained to the wall.

'There were some cover-ups,' she said. 'Out by the cash register. They shouldn't be too musty to wear back to the hotel. I've got clothes there.'

'But the chains,' Stew protested. 'You can't get the cover-up on over those chains.'

Both men looked at her with sincere concern. Ronnie smiled. She saw in their eyes just how beautiful she was to them, just how much they still wanted her. The rest of the weekend would be heaven. After that, they had tenure; anything was possible.

'We have to get you out of those chains,' Gardner said.

'No problem,' she said her grin sly and knowing. She looked down at her bare foot on the dusty floor, curled painted toes pointing to a spot by the wall, where the key lay.

Exactly where she'd tossed it.

The Things Tour Guides Know
by Richard Hiscock

We were holidaying in New Zealand. Wanting to learn as much about the country as possible, my mate John and I decided to do a week tour and booked with a small company. Unfortunately most of the people were elderly so there were no wild parties like we'd hoped for.

One evening, having the night to ourselves, John and I decided to take a stroll along the water's edge, smoke a joint without having a lecture from some of the oldies.

We were just heading inland, back to the hotel when we came across a clearing surrounded by bushes. Voices whispered. Intrigued we snuck forward wanting to see what was going on. It was the tour guide Jeff with some chick. He had his cock out and she was sucking it like crazy. He was so big she could only fit half in her mouth.

Watching the two of them was really turning me on. I peered over at John and saw he was rubbing his cock absently. I focused back on the couple, observing the woman's mouth as it slipped over his enormous knob still trying to swallow his shaft. The more I stared the more I realised that I wanted to suck him off too, suck him into my mouth to feel his bulging veins against my lips, run my tongue along his shaft and see if I could devour him further than she could.

The idea of it shocked me. I wasn't gay so wondered where these thoughts were coming from. I gulped, tried to push the image away and focus on the chick instead, but my eyes kept going back to him. The way he pushed his pelvis forward had me thinking about his arse, how tight his cheeks would be in that stance. I visualised him naked with me on my knees sucking greedily – the image so erotic it had my cock throbbing.

She was sucking louder, gagging and slurping over his shaft. She tried to pull away but he held her head, demanding she continue. My hand stole down inside my board shorts to my own cock. It slipped over the knob which was oozing with precome. I peered over at John and saw him staring at me. I wondered if he was thinking what I was thinking but then hoped not; what would he think?

'Oh yeah,' we heard Jeff moan. 'That's great, baby. Now how about you get your gear off?'

She rose giggling. Sounded like she was a bit drunk. John and I eased back into the shadows watching her peel off her clothes. Man she had a great body. In the moonlight she looked like a goddess, her body sculpted, her hair cascading down over her back as she pranced about, keeping Jeff at bay as he lunged for her.

'Now you?' she purred.

He quickly stripped off while she stood back and watched.

'Here, lie on my shirt,' he said spreading it on the ground.

She did, legs splayed open while his eyes raked over her.

'You're a horny bitch, aren't you?'

'If you say so,' she giggled.

'You want me to fuck you?'

'What do you think?' Her legs were opening and closing, teasing him.

He fell to his knees between her thighs. Her legs wrapped around his back. We had a great view of his arse as his muscles clenched and contracted while he pumped her rhythmically.

John now had his own cock out of his shorts and in his hand stroking it lovingly. I had trouble tearing my eyes away from it and, when I stared back at Jeff's bare arse, the only thing I could think of was fucking it and – to make matters worse – he got the girl to get up on all fours and began fucking her doggy style.

'Oh fuck,' Jeff said. 'That's great. Ever had it up the arse?'

'No,' she whimpered. 'And there's no way that monster

would ever fit anyway.'

'Want to give it a try?' he coaxed.

'No,' she said, pushing back into him.

'I'd love to fuck her up the arse,' John mouthed to me.
I nodded.

'I won't hurt you if that's what you're worried about?'

'How can you be so sure?'

'I'm a tour guide. We know these things.'

'Yeah, right,' but I could hear the misgivings beginning to
fall away.

'Come on, I promise I won't hurt you,' he said.

She paused for a moment, clearly thinking. 'You sure? To
be honest I've always wanted to try but never been game.'

'Lean up against that tree,' he said.

He pulled her back by the hips towards him so her arse was
pointing upwards, then he fell to his knees and opened her
cheeks. We couldn't see her puckered hole but watched as he
licked at it, slurping, slathering her with his saliva.

'Fuck,' John mouthed, his cock rock hard in his hand.

'Easy now, baby,' Jeff said. 'Just relax.'

He was probing her with his knob, gently so as not to hurt
her. She was peering back at him over her shoulder.

'Promise you won't hurt me,' she said.

'Does that hurt?'

'No.'

'Good, I've just got the knob in. Now relax and I'll ease it
in further.'

Out of the corner of my eye I watched John. His mouth was
slack, his eyes wide. Jeff grabbed hold of the girl's hips with
both hands and pushed in further. She held on to the tree,
wiggled her hips back at him and widened her stance.

'Oh, yeah ...' she moaned.

'You like it?'

'Oh God, yes. I never thought it would fit. It feels fantastic.'

'It's not all the way in, baby. You want me to keep going?'

'Yes – please. I love it!'

I imagined my cock sinking into her arse. I'd never fucked
anyone up the arse – always wanted to but never had a willing

partner; maybe I could find out who she was and see if she'd allow me to as well, or maybe I could find myself a guy, slam it into him ... but there I was again, thinking about fucking a guy.

'Oh, yeah, harder,' she cried. 'Harder.'

My balls tightened. I needed to fuck someone too. A look passed between John and I as we watched each other while pumping our own cocks. Again I wondered if he was thinking what I was thinking.

And then, without a pause, I thought what the hell and fell to the ground at his feet. I pulled down his shorts and lunged for his cock. Grabbing at it with both hands I marvelled at the size of it. Tentatively I licked at it, once, then twice, my lips sliding easily over the tip and down the shaft. Nothing in my whole life ever felt as good.

'What the fuck do you think you're doing?' he hissed.

'Oh, God, sorry,' I mumbled. 'Don't know what came over me.'

'Who's there?' Jeff asked.

We scrambled out of there and hurried back to the hotel. In our room neither of us spoke for a while, then John broke the silence.

'You know I think we should forget what happened out there.'

'Sure,' I said.

'I believe you when you said you didn't know what you were doing.'

'Good.'

'So we won't mention it again, all right?'

'Fine by me.'

I was still embarrassed. How could I have got the wrong message? The way John had been handling himself and staring at me I was sure he was into some sort of experimentation. And to be honest he didn't push me away immediately – he did allow me to lick it before taking it into my mouth, but it wasn't until the next morning while I was in the bathroom that I knew he really was interested.

I'd shut the door while showering but noticed in the mirror

152

that John had opened it and was peering through the crack at me. I pretended not to know but I put on a good show, allowing the suds to slip and slide over me as I soaped myself.

I even dropped the soap and almost laughed to myself as I bent over and stayed that way a fraction longer than necessary, knowing he'd have a good eyeful of my arse. I know he's not gay either, but you know sometimes a little bit of experimentation can add some excitement to an otherwise boring holiday and I thought I'd go for it, push this to the next level. Turning off the taps, I wrapped a towel around myself and went back into the bedroom which we were sharing.

Removing the towel, I dried off my hair, making a show of shaking my cock as I did. I paraded around, acting as though I was searching for my underwear, the whole time I was so aware of his eyes on me and my cock began to grow under his scrutiny. I pretended not to notice.

The next thing I knew he was on his knees lunging for my cock. He sucked the knob into his mouth and I heard the intake of his breath. He slathered saliva over my shaft, licking it lovingly.

My eyes closed momentarily. I felt myself swoon and then, as he sucked me deep into the recesses of his mouth, my hands instinctively went to his head. I grabbed his hair and began to fuck his mouth rhythmically.

Oh God, I've never felt anything so fucking great in my life. It was like nothing I'd ever experienced before, which was true, but the feel of his mouth, his jaw sucking me hard, his tongue strong and knowing as only another man could.

My other hand now caressed his back, my fingers running lightly down towards the crack of his arse. He moved back, dropping my cock from his mouth; his eyes were glazed with lust.

'Get on all fours,' I whispered and he obliged.

It was a dreamlike experience – one I'll never forget – as I knelt in behind him, opening his cheeks to run a finger over the crack of his arse. I lowered my head, pooling saliva onto my fingers as I slathered up his hole.

Then with my cock gripped firmly in my hand I began to

inch it in. Nothing in this world has ever felt so good. John pushed back and I eased in further. A deep breath from him and another push from me and I was in to the hilt.

I began to push in and out and his soft moans of pleasure heightened my own excitement, but then a rustling at the window had us both freeze. I dared to look around and there was Jeff watching us openly.

'What the fuck?' I managed.

'Hey, don't let me stop you,' he said climbing the rest of the way in.

My cock was still up John's arse as Jeff made his way over. He opened his zip and, the next thing I knew, he had his cock in my mouth. I sucked on it eagerly, hungry for the feel of his hardness as I pushed my own cock in and out of John.

'Oh yeah, man,' he breathed excitedly. 'I was wondering how long it would take you guys to realise you were missing out.'

'What?' John said, peering back over his shoulder at us.

'You two? I saw you creep up on me last night and knew if you didn't try and join in or make some sort of contact with me that you might be into this. Plus it's been a long time since I've had a couple of guys to share an evening with.'

It was all too much for me to comprehend. I'd gone from one situation to another. I didn't care what he thought or knew. I was only interested in one thing and that was getting my rocks off.

It took me no time at all to come, the experience was so exhilarating, and when Jeff took over from where I left off, I lay back on the bed to watch. To say we had a night to remember would be an understatement.

John and I have an agreement that we'll never mention it to anyone and to be honest I've not been out with anyone else since. I'm waiting for him to realise that we're meant to be together and, in my mind, I'm reliving that experience until he comes to understand that that tour guide knew more about us than we ever had.

Casting Couch
by Charlotte Stein

The other guy she's got him to come in with is small, much smaller than he is. It's kind of dumb, really, because there's no way she's going to pick someone like that. Why would she want a short, skinny, little guy, when she could have someone big, and strapping, and awesome?

Like he is. He knows he's got the big leading man shoulders, the way most women like. And his hair is looking great today – really smooth and casually falling over his forehead. He smiles at her, to make sure she sees that he's got the wide, white, even teeth, and she smiles back in this great approving way.

His manager was right. Smiling is best. Smiling and good manly posture, you know, with your chest out and your shoulders straight – to show off all the pilates and weight work you've been doing.

And he has been doing it. He's been doing it so hard that he feels kind of light-headed, walking into her big, chilly office. But the tight black jeans with the fancy label and the tight black sweater with the even fancier label fit good, and that's what matters, really.

Or so his manager says.

'Benjamin,' he says. 'Make sure you always present a clean image to the general public. A clean, heteronormative image, at all times.'

And Ben is pretty sure he does. He has no idea what heteronormative means, but it sure sounds like him. Totally sounds like him. The little guy is looking at him funny, and it's making him sweat inside the clothes he kind of doesn't like.

'Hello, boys,' the lady says. Her name's something like Miss Miliver or Miss Mystifier or whatever, but he can't quite recall because she's staring right at him with these frosty blue eyes. They're so frosty he wants to stick his tongue to them.

Little guy is wiggling all over the place, next to him. Like he's too dumb to hide his excitement, when everyone knows that you're supposed to play it cool.

'So nice that you could come at such short notice. You both know that we're looking for a certain type of man, correct?'

His manager has said something like that to him. It's hard to recollect the details, however, what with all the nerves in his tummy and the need to throw up, again. He's not sure that Power Muscle stuff is really doing him any good.

'Uh, yeah,' the little guy says. He has this mean mouth and these mean tiny eyes, like a piglet – Ben isn't sure he cares for him, even before he's let out that funny sounding *uh, yeah*.

'Good. So could you both start by removing your tops?'

The little guy – who she calls Joe – starts doing it right away. But he's an idiot, because he takes his pants off too – right down to the underwear – and she never said to do that! Doesn't he know that you're only supposed to do what you're told?

And sure enough, she looks at him with narrowed eyes. Ben catches it, because he finds it best to really look out for what the other person is wanting, all the time. You've got to know, so that you can give your best to them and then they'll be happy.

When she says: 'Very good, Benjamin,' he feels a little zing of pleasure shoot straight to the base of his spine. See? He did good and now she's pleased. Piglet just doesn't understand.

'But you're a little ahead of the game, aren't you, Joe?'

At which, Joe just shrugs! Oh, he doesn't care at all. Anyone could see that.

She taps her clipboard, and after a moment of staring at both of them – him with his golden, shapely torso, and Joe with his little reedy thing – she notes something down. He really, really hopes that it's "Ben has excellent muscle tone", because, you know, that's totally true.

'Lovely abs you've got there, Benjamin,' she says, but this time it's not the compliment that gives him the little zing of pleasure. It's the way she says his name, like she's already got a relationship with him. She is the person who calls him Benjamin – not Benny or Ben or doofus.

It makes him feel funny, behind his knees.

'But you can take the pants off now too.'

He does so slowly, awkwardly. For some reason it makes him blush, even though he's taken his clothes off lots of times before, for photoshoots and stuff. Maybe it's because Piglet is watching him, and kind of smirking – like anything's going to be funny! He knows he's got strong thighs and long legs, and he never needs the sock his manager tells him to stuff down the front of his underpants.

From the look of Piglet, though, he sure needs a sock.

'Very nice,' Miss M says anyway, and then she makes a little gesture – a little twirl of her finger – that has him flummoxed, for a second. But fortunately Piglet gets it quick, and turns around for her only a second before he catches on and does it too.

Not that the time difference matters, because Piglet isn't half the showman he is. He doesn't even clench his butt cheeks, or flex those muscles around the shoulder blades like you're supposed to. And he's kind of scrawny everywhere too, as though he can't even be bothered to work out.

Though his skin does look really soft. Ben wants to give him that much. Sometimes, with all the tanning, his own skin doesn't keep quite as smooth as he'd like it. But Piglet is sort of silky looking, especially around his inner thighs and the curve of his shoulders – and he's got plump little cheeks too, which is nice.

'Well, you both have plus points, I must say,' Miss M tells them, and Ben is pleased because isn't that just what he was thinking? He's very fair, like that. 'But I think in order to decide if either of you are right for the parts we have available, I'm going to have to see full frontal.'

She raises an eyebrow, but all he can think is: parts! There's more than one part going, and she's really considering him! That's *awesome*.

'You are both OK with that, right?'

She's got a funny look to her – her left eyebrow is kind of cocked. And she's leaning forward so far he can see all the way down her top, to her big, big boobs. It makes sweat pop out on his forehead – though luckily the hair is there to hide it. He wouldn't want her to think he's looking at her boobs, and getting sweaty.

Especially not when he's going to have to show her his thingy, in a second.

'I'm OK with it,' he says, and shrugs one shoulder, because he is, as his manager often says, a very amenable sort of person. At which she looks very pleased, very pleased indeed, and she sort of sits back in her chair – but that's not really any better than before, because when she sits back her skirt rides up high where her leg is crossed over the other one.

He can almost see right up to her butt, underneath. And then she runs her tongue over the rails of her upper teeth, and that's even worse than the butt, somehow.

Plus the Piglet is naked. Joe is naked. He can tell, because when he tries not to look out of the corner of his eye, all he can see is pink, pink.

'Are you sure, Benjamin? Because it seems like maybe you don't want to.'

That shocks him out of whatever's messing him up. He can't possibly let her think that he doesn't want to do something! That would just be a disaster – especially when Piglet has done it.

So he strips out of his little underpants, and tries to think about things that keep his cock way, way down. All the way down, so there's not even a hint of weirdness like that time with the girl photographer, when she said *and could you bend over now please* and his body had gone all hot and cold and he'd thought about saying no, only that had just made it worse.

Her laughing had made it even worse than that. So had her telling him that he was adorable. Though the other stuff had been very nice – the stuff with her mouth on his cock and her getting him into bend into some really, *really* rude positions.

No matter what his manager said about not doing things like that, it had been totally awesome.

It's not so awesome thinking about it while here, however. It would be, if she were like that – but she's probably not and all those thoughts are making the blood rush south. And then, oh no then, Joe laughs and says: 'Oh my God, dummy popped a boner.'

He's pretty sure that by dummy, Joe means him. Which is absolutely mortifying, because he isn't dumb at all. He knows he isn't – his manager *says* he isn't. He's just *naïve*, that's all, just naïve and that's why he needs his manager's help.

Only then she says: 'Well. I guess you've got some catching up to do, don't you, Joe?'

Which is totally awesome. He can't stop himself grinning at her, and she grins right back.

'You're doing just fine, Benjamin. Rea–ea–eally fine.'

And she stretches the last word right out, because she's amazing. He wonders if it's possible to love someone, that quickly. His manager says no, but then Ben is pretty sure he only told him that to get him to focus on securing jobs, rather than all that messy relationship sort of stuff. His manager is always looking out for him like that.

'Thanks,' he says, kind of breathless – and doesn't even care that Joe rolls his eyes as he does something that makes Ben want to look straight forward at the wallpaper.

He wonders if Joe's really all that smarter than him, if he has to rub himself in order to get a boner. Because he can do it just by thinking about stuff, easily. Remembering the girl, with the rude positions. Remembering her saying that he had the stamina of an ox – yeah, that had been nice.

Thinking about the soft underside of Miss M's thigh, or, like – maybe she intended to show him her boobs! It could be. She's making soft eyes at him and she's got that look ... that look he finds hard to get hold of. Like she wants something, like she really wants something – but doesn't she know that he's only too happy to give it?

It makes him go funny behind the knees, to give it.

'What would you like me to do now?' he says, and his voice comes out real flat and soft, the way it sometimes does when someone's telling him what to do and that feeling starts coming over him.

She hesitates, however. She hesitates so much, he can feel himself starting to breathe hard. Joe is making frustrated noises, next to him, and they're making his skin prickle.

'I don't know, Benjamin. What do you think?'

Oh no – a quiz! He's terrible at quizzes. He usually fumbles the answers even when he knows them – though this time seems kind of different. Maybe because she's looking at him in that way and there's other stuff too. Other things that are going on that he can use to work it out.

She has two naked guys in front of her. And one of them's hard, the way she likes it. But the other one's not. What should the one who's succeeded do, to improve this situation?

'Do you want me to help him?' he says, and she smiles – a really big one.

'I think that would be very nice.'

Though for a second, he's sure he's got it wrong. Because she looks really, really surprised when he goes over to her and starts unbuttoning her blouse. Surprised – but not exactly mad, or anything. In fact – she laughs and kind of pats the side of his face, and tells him that he's one of a kind.

Which is awesome, but really – it just makes sense. If Joe's having trouble getting stiff, then he should know to look at her boobs. But now that Ben's over here, looking at him, he can see that it's going to take more than bare breasts.

Joe's all angry looking, and he's pulling on himself way too hard, and he's not even halfway there at all. His own cock is practically touching his belly, and he's pretty sure he's going to have to work on it in a second because his body's all hot and prickly and his balls feel achy and this is all just a little bit overwhelming.

But apparently, Joe needs something different. Joe says, 'I'd rather look at you, idiot.'

In this sneery, nasty sort of way. But that's OK. Because Miss M is running her hand over his back and right down over his ass and he's pretty sure that she'd like to see Joe, looking at him. She even says, 'Why don't you kneel down here, Benjamin?'

And she means, *you know*. Right in front of her but facing Joe, so that Joe can look at him while she moves him around with her hands. And the heel of her boot, in the small of his back.

Joe says, 'Oh my God, that's so hot.'

While he jacks his cock. And Ben is pretty sure that Joe means him. That nasty Piglet means that he, Benjamin, is hot, because he's kneeling on the floor and someone's got their hands all over him. And when she pushes him slowly forward until he's on all fours, and his ass is in the air, and he's groaning too because her hands are really firm, Joe gasps.

'Can I come on his face?' Joe says, and then he gets that weak feeling behind his knees again – especially because she's touching him in a really private place. Right between the cheeks of his ass, until he has to wonder if she's going to tell Joe to do something else, instead.

You know, like the thing that girl did with her tongue, only with a cock. Is it bad that the thought makes him want to jerk off? All the thoughts in his head make him want to jerk off, really, really badly. It doesn't seem fair somehow, that Joe is going to come on his face soon and he hasn't even gotten to touching himself at all.

Even if she's touching him, and it feels great. She's rubbing that strip of skin behind his balls now – after she's nudged his legs apart with her knee – and it's almost hurting, it feels so good.

But she still doesn't answer Joe, on the whole coming on his face thing. He can see Joe's legs real close to him, trembling around the thigh. The blur of his hand on his dick near enough that he can see it, without really looking.

Any second it's going to happen anyway, and all he can think is: *my manager is going to be really mad. I hope he doesn't do it in my hair. I wonder if it will taste like mine.*

Then Miss M says, 'Would you like him to come on your face, Benjamin?'

And sensation goes through him so hot and fierce, he's sure that he's done it on her carpet. Just like that, without anything touching his cock.

'You can say, you know. Joe here can wait, and not come, until you decide what you'd like. How does that sound?'

She's letting *him* choose? Not mean Piglet, or her, or his manager? *He* gets to choose?

'Uh ... uh ... I'm not good with decisions.'

Which is absolutely true. The ones that are popping into his head are probably not good for his career, at all.

'Oh, I think you are. I think you're much better than you think. So what's it to be?' she asks, and then *oh no* she reaches underneath him, and squeezes the tip of his cock. Heat grips him around the balls, the hips, the waist. Everywhere.

'I want to make love to you,' he blurts out, finally – because that's definitely true – but Joe laughs at him then and he thinks maybe Miss M is laughing at him too.

Only when she pulls at his body and gets him to turn around, her eyes are not frosty at all. They look warm with laughter, not mean. And she's only smiling a little bit, anyway – not giggling at him like the stupid Piglet.

'Why don't you kiss me first?' she says, and that's so nice! Yes, he'd like to kiss her while she reaches down and strokes his too-stiff cock – even though the sudden wet feel of her tongue thrusting into his mouth almost makes him go off.

As does the creepy nasty feeling of Joe's hand, shoving through his hair at the back. Almost pulling, but not quite. However, she then says, 'You be nice, Joe.'

As she mouths along his jaw line and fondles him in lots of places, eventually pushing him down until he's flat on his back, staring up at her and Joe – who's almost stopped tugging on his dick. It's a good job though, really, because the thing is now totally hard and really red, and there's already liquid leaking out of it.

For a second he closes his eyes, sure that said same stuff is going to drip onto his upturned face. But then he can feel her messing around with his cock, and he has to look at her, instead, as she rolls a condom down the length of him.

162

She does it like she really, really knows what she's doing. Not like him, when that little model girl from Russia had said – *just jerk off while you eat my pussy, OK? No sex.* Because he'd taken too long with all those slippery bits of rubber.

But it was all right in the end though. She had made a lot of noise, when he licked back and forth over her clit, and she'd said lots of nice things like *you're much better at this than you should be.*

He'd wanted to tell her that it's because he always knows what to give people, but then she'd turned mad because of the come he'd gotten all over her sheets.

At least there's no danger of making a mess here. Miss M has her thighs either side of his body, and she's got hold of his covered prick, and suddenly she's sliding down, down until he has to dig his nails into the pile of the carpet, and think of other things.

'You're doing *really* well,' she says to him, but he can tell he is because he's big and hard, and both of those things are making her look flushed and happy.

He can see through her sheer bra that her nipples have gone all stiff, and though she still seems restrained and calm, she's moving up and down on him already.

Oh, it feels nice. And her moaning – her moaning feels nice too. Even Joe's gasping feels nice, as he crouches over him and starts really jerking himself off. So close to his face too, which should be gross and yet somehow isn't at all.

It's all fine, when a wet pussy is sliding up and down his cock, and Miss M is telling him that it's all right, it's all right, just before she starts fucking him really hard.

Joe looks down at him with eyes that don't seem quite as mean, and asks, 'That feel good?'

Which seems friendly. He nods, and Joe grins, which seems even more friendly. So friendly that when Joe kind of tilts his hips and the head of his cock gets very close to Ben's mouth, it doesn't seem like much of a hardship to turn a bit, and stick his tongue out.

More than stick his tongue out, really. He licks the shiny tip, just a little bit, just to see what it tastes like, and then Miss M gasps his name and Joe's thighs tremble helplessly, so he just has to do it again.

This time, when Joe asks, the question isn't directed at Miss M.

'Can I come on your face?' he says, and it seems OK that his hips buck upwards, when Joe does so. That's OK, right? It'd be nice, if they could all come together – surely?

But although he says yeah, it's still kind of unexpected when Joe grunts and jerks forward and does it, right over his mouth. Some even gets inside, and it tastes salty and weird and almost exactly the way his own does, only this is much more exciting because it's someone else's. Someone else has come all over his face in this really rude way, while another person rides his cock in a lovely office where he's supposed to be having a professional audition.

He's not sure such thoughts are supposed to make him have an orgasm. But they do, anyway. His back arches right up off the floor and he has to kind of hold himself really stiff, because it's so strong it almost hurts. And he knows he makes these really embarrassing noises too, all these grunts and hard sounds that make Joe giggle.

But Miss M doesn't giggle. He's pretty sure she's coming too, because he can feel her pussy tightening around his cock in this great way, and she's shaking all over and saying *oh oh oh*.

When he finally works up the courage to open his eyes, she looks very, very pleased with him. She's all red and her lips are parted and she's breathing hard, and when she runs her hands over his sweaty body, she does it like she appreciates him a whole lot.

It makes him fill up all over with warmth.

'You can go now, Joe,' she says, which makes him feel even warmer. 'We'll call you.'

Joe seems kind of mad about that, but he stands up and shoves his clothes on, and soon it's just the pair of them, in her professional office with the nice blinds.

And then she leans over, and *licks* all the come up off his face. Actually licks it, all slow and deliberate and with her hand cupping his jaw.

'Did you like that?' she says, when he's all clean again. He can't remember the last time someone seemed so concerned with him liking things. But she must be sincere, because she helps him to stand up and takes off the condom and then – oh, even better. Then, she cleans his cock too.

Also with her mouth.

Of course he gets hard again – which she seems really pleased about – but she doesn't seem to want to do anything more. Not yet, at least. Instead, she gives him this awesome fluffy robe and makes him sit down in the nice chair and brings him honey and lemon. Which is much nicer than the other girl and the Russian girl or even his manager, really.

'Are you comfortable, Benjamin?' she says, and he nods. Because that seems best. 'Good.'

Which is nice, but he's still squirming. He's squirming now because of all that stuff, and what if ...?

'Did I get the job?' he says – probably in a rude way too. Now she's going to be mad, because he's not polite. 'It's just that – if I didn't, I think my manager's going to be angry. I mean, I almost sucked someone's–'

He's kind of glad that she cuts him off.

'Your manager would be angry, that you did things you wanted to do?'

What does she mean? Of course he would be!

'Well ... yeah.'

'You did want to do them, didn't you?'

He flushes red, but it still comes out in a funny breathy rush. 'Yes.'

'And you'd like to do more of it, with me?'

'Uh ... maybe ... can I do it without telling him?'

But she just laughs, and looks away at some pictures she has on her big desk.

'Don't be silly, darling,' she says. 'Why would you have to not tell him anything? He's not your manager any more.'

Which seems really odd, it does. Even though he knows exactly what she means, and goes weak behind his knees and thrillingly warm through his chest, before she explains it.

'I'm your manager now. And I know you're going to enjoy

165

your career a whole lot more, with me at the helm. Don't you think?'

The Favour
by Leslie Lee Sanders

Jenna Madison rang the doorbell and nervously waited for Brandon Stone to answer. She had no idea what he looked like but by her husband's description of him he used to be six feet tall, dirty-blond and have an ass like a football player. She attended many football games with her husband and considered herself a suitable judge for judging Brandon's ass.

The doorknob jiggled and twisted and Jenna gulped in anticipation. When the door opened there stood a very tall, handsome blond man. Her eyes immediately focused on his full lips and steel blue eyes. She smiled.

'Hello, I'm Jenna.' She offered her hand. 'Donavan's wife.' When the attractive, god-like figure before her dipped his eyes and tilted his head in confusion she did the same. 'You are Brandon, right? We chatted online a few days ago.'

He relaxed and a smile replaced his confused frown. 'Of course.' He shook her hand. 'Come in.' Jenna entered his lovely dwelling. 'I haven't heard from Donavan in years. How is he? Where is he?' he asked.

Jenna dropped her head to hide her bashful smile. 'He doesn't know I've found you. I wanted to surprise him.'

'Ah.' Brandon nodded. 'From what I remember, Donavan didn't like surprises.'

'He still doesn't.' Jenna snorted. 'But he would love a good one and I'm determined to make this a great one.'

'Yes, go far and beyond.' Brandon chuckled. 'I like that.'

'Anything to save my marriage,' Jenna mumbled. She stared at the beautifully polished hardwood floor.

167

Brandon sighed. 'Is everything OK?'

'Donavan says it is but I get the feeling things are changing.' Jenna looked up into the beautiful stranger's eyes and immediately regretted sharing her fears so soon. Just because Donavan and Brandon used to be best friends doesn't make Donavan instantly her friend – let alone her therapist. 'Sorry, I didn't mean to–'

'No, that's OK.' Brandon smiled. 'Would you like to have a seat or something to drink?'

'No, thanks.' Jenna ran her fingers through her long hair nervously. 'My husband used to talk about you a lot. He has some cherished memories of you two that he sometimes reminisces about and I thought it would be a great idea to get you two back together.'

Brandon smiled. His eyes softened and a glint of happiness swept across his face. 'Cherished memories, huh?' He smiled as if he was reminiscing himself.

'Most importantly,' Jenna said, interrupting his thoughts, 'I came over to ask a favour. A huge favour.'

'A favour? OK?'

'This is a favour that definitely deserves to be asked in a face-to-face conversation.'

Jenna looked into her husband's soft hazel eyes as they lay in bed and gave him a quick peck on the lips. 'You know there isn't anything I wouldn't do for you.' She ran her fingertips softly up and down his sculpted abs and played with the coarse curls of his dark chest hairs.

He continued to gently fondle her bare breast with one hand and closed his eyes, bathing in the afterglow of their sex. 'There's isn't anything I wouldn't do for you too.'

'Then why don't you want to try something new to spice things up?' she asked, still staring into his relaxed face.

'Do you really think we need to spice things up?' he asked, and finally looked her in the eye. 'I think things are fine the way they are.'

'We do the same things in bed,' Jenna complained. 'You're getting bored.'

'I'm not.'

'You are. You're just in denial.'

Donavan laughed, his chest rose and fell rapidly with each chuckle. 'You're worried over nothing.'

'You don't talk dirty to me like you used to,' Jenna frowned. 'You stopped pulling my hair when you're fucking me from behind, and you don't even sneeze after you've come like you used to. That tells me you didn't come as hard as you should have. Things are changing.'

'Would you like me to talk dirty to you and pull your hair *now*?' Donavan smirked.

'Are you going to get behind me and fuck me like I'm a dirty little whore?' Jenna grinned devilishly. Instantly her juices began to flow between her legs.

'Come here.' Donavan ordered and pulled Jenna against his chest. Immediately his tongue swept past her lips and licked against hers. One hand cupped her ass and the other tangled tightly in her brunette locks. 'You're going to feel what it's like to have a huge hard cock in your tight little pussy.'

'Yes, give it to me, big boy,' Jenna breathed. 'Fucking give me more.'

'I bet you want to taste my big cock on your tongue, don't you?'

'Yes.'

'You want my tongue on your wet pussy too, huh?'

'Yes,' Jenna whispered. 'Now get me really wet and tell me what your friend is doing to me.'

'Ah, yes,' Donavan whispered. He gasped when Jenna nibbled his bottom lip and held her tighter. 'He's standing behind you licking your neck.'

'Where are his hands?' Jenna instantly imagined blue-eyed, dirty blond Brandon standing behind her sensually licking her neck, causing heat to swirl around her sensitive areas. She liked that image but she liked the heat even more.

'He's wrapping his arms around you,' Donavan said. 'One hand is cupping your breast and the other is between your legs.'

'Ooh,' Jenna moaned. 'And where is his dick?'

'It's pressed against your ass wanting so bad to enter.' As Donavan said the words he pressed his full erection against Jenna's thigh.

Jenna imagined Donavan standing before her, pressing his body against hers as he was pressed against her now, kissing her mouth while Brandon stood behind her playing with her shaven pussy. She imagined Brandon's hand leaving her wetness to find Donavan's hard cock to stroke it, using her juices as lubricant. She wondered if her husband had the same image in his head.

'What is your friend doing to *you* while he's pressed against me?'

'This is all about you, babe,' Donavan pulled her hair causing her head to fall back and expose her neck. He kissed her neck and whispered, 'We're only pleasing you.'

'No, you need pleasure too,' Jenna said. 'Maybe he's jacking your hard cock waiting to stuff it into his watering mouth, yes?'

'We're just focusing on your body right now,' Donavan said.

'Come on, baby,' Jenna whined. She tried to hide her disappointment but probably failed. 'He wants to touch you too, the way he did in high school.'

'But I'm not in high school any more,' Donavan said.

Jenna sensed the defensiveness in his tone and separated their bodies enough to look into her husband's beautiful hazel jewels. 'You used to talk about the things you and the amazing Brandon Stone used to do in high school all the time and you liked talking about your high-school trysts. It used to get you off. Why not now?'

'By the tone of your voice I'm guessing we're not going to fuck any more, am I right?' Donavan sighed.

That must have been his attempt at changing the subject but it wasn't going to work. Jenna knew better. 'You're worrying me,' Jenna said. 'You're not the same.'

'Brandon and I ended in high school,' he said. 'We graduated and went our separate ways. I haven't seen him since and, if you must know the truth, it only confirms that that life I once lived is completely over. There's no reason to go back.'

'You were happy then and it made you hot and horny to tell me the experiences you had with him. It's dirty and gets me off too. No need to stop now.'

'It's over. It's about time I let it go and stop living in the past,' Donavan said. 'Brandon's moved on and so should I.' Donavan exhaled slowly and stared at the ceiling, a look of dissatisfaction on his face.

Jenna suddenly wondered if the look on his face was from the change in mood or because he suddenly realised he and Brandon had moved on and started separate lives. She worried if secretly meeting with Brandon would help her and Donavan's marriage like she had envisioned or instead hurt it. She rested her head on his chest and they both lay in bed in silence.

The day went on as any other. By the time nightfall arrived, Jenna and Donavan were snuggling on the living room sofa watching a movie. Their movie watching was interrupted by a knock on the door. Jenna immediately began to get giddy as she'd been expecting her special company all day.

Jenna answered the door. Brandon wore a nice black silk shirt that clung to his chest muscles perfectly and dark fitted blue jeans. He looked amazing. Jenna couldn't wait for Donavan to set his eyes on his high-school buddy.

'Come in,' Jenna said and stepped aside.

'Thank you.' Brandon smiled genuinely and walked into their comfy home.

Donavan came around the corner and, as soon as he set eyes on Brandon, he stopped in his tracks. At first the look of utter shock swept his face and finally a bashful smile appeared.

'Brandon? Brandon Stone?'

'That's me,' Brandon said and laughed.

'Jesus, it's been a long time,' Donavan said and met Brandon with a huge hug. 'A long time.'

'Nearly ten years,' Brandon said. They separated and Brandon stared into Donavan's eyes with such giddiness. 'You look good.'

'Thanks, I try,' Donavan said.

Jenna stared back and forth between the two as they looked each other over with a smile on her face to match theirs. She never had seen her husband so excited, so thrilled.

'So, what are you doing here?' Donavan asked.

'Jenna found me online and I couldn't pass up a chance to see you again,' Brandon said. He smiled wider and hugged Donavan again. 'I missed you.'

'Me too,' Brandon glanced at Jenna. 'I missed you too.'

'You look more handsome than Donavan described,' Jenna said. Donavan's cheeks were redder than a ripe apple. 'Why don't you have a picture of yourself online? It'll make it easier for high-school friends to get reacquainted with you.'

'I like to separate my personal life from my cyber life,' Brandon said. 'I'm single right now and I do a lot of online dating.'

'You date a lot. How frequently?' Donavan asked with a more serious look on his face.

'Maybe once a week,' Donavan said. 'But nothing serious for years now. We don't ever make it to the next level. They just don't have what I'm looking for.'

'And what are you looking for?' Donavan asked.

'More than just sex.'

'Wow, you've changed.' Donavan laughed.

Brandon joined him. 'Yeah, ten years will do that to you. But I'm not the only one who's changed.'

'Yeah, I've been married for five years now,' Donavan said. 'Could you believe that?'

'You used to say you would never get married,' Brandon said. 'You said that living the life we used to live was too much fun to let it go and settle down. You wanted to live it for ever.'

'You remember that?' Donavan said in disbelief.

'That's not all that I remember,' Brandon said, with a flirtatious smile on his lips.

Donavan chuckled nervously, a behaviour Jenna had never witnessed from him before. 'Well, I found the perfect girl who's too much fun to pass up. I had to pin her down for life before someone else did.' Donavan winked at Jenna and she smiled.

'She's quite a catch,' Brandon said. 'You're a lucky man.'

Jenna took that compliment as her cue to get things moving toward the most amazing night her husband would ever experience. 'How about some drinks?'

Hours had passed and the atmosphere in the living room became calm and romantic. The television was off and the only light source were a few candles Jenna had lit to set the mood for high-school reminiscing. Brandon and Donavan had reverted back to their years as rebellious high-school kids by making a game out of who could drink the most beers. They were tied at six each while Jenna lagged behind with just three. Either way her plan had worked because they were all much more relaxed and the laughs just kept on coming.

'We had a great time in high school, didn't we?' Donavan said.

'We did,' Brandon said. 'But what 18-year-old boy wouldn't have as much fun as we did when every girl wanted them.'

'They wanted *you*,' Donavan corrected. 'They just went along with me to get at you.'

'No,' Brandon disagreed.

'Yes, you were the popular Brandon Stone,' Donavan said. 'You knew what all the girls were saying about you. You know why they called you Stone.'

'Because it's my last name,' Brandon said to Jenna but couldn't hold back his laughter.

'I thought it was because of how hard your dick got when you were horny,' Jenna said.

Brandon stopped laughing and looked to Donavan, a half-full bottle of beer in his hand. 'She knows, huh?'

Donavan nodded. 'She knows everything.'

Brandon flirted with his eyes. 'What else do you know, Jenna?'

Jenna looked back and forth between her husband and his best friend. 'I know that at first you two used to take turns fucking girls while the other watched and then you moved on

173

to fucking them at the same time.' She licked her blushed lips slowly, enough to announce what was on her mind. 'I also know that after you two got bored of fucking girls you turned to each other.' She said in a low seductive voice as she twirled her finger around the hard bud of her left nipple that poked through her top. 'But because Donavan was a little shy about it, he wouldn't let you fuck him so you just sucked his dick until he came in your mouth. But you, eager for pleasure, allowed Donavan to do whatever he wanted to you including fucking you, the amazing Brandon Stone.'

When Jenna looked back at Donavan he had his sexually enticing eyes pinned on Brandon while he rubbed his palm over his jeans where his growing hard-on began to tent. Jenna grinned, loving the direction their little chat was going.

Brandon must have taken Donavan's bold behaviour as a prompt because he stood up and pulled Jenna up to stand before him. She and Donavan both watched as he pulled his shirt over his head, revealing his incredible sculpted abs. He stared into Jenna's eyes as he unbuttoned and unzipped his jeans. He stepped out of them slowly and sensually.

Jenna eyed Donavan. He seemed to be enjoying the view as much as she was. She grinned at Brandon, hinting at her dirty thoughts.

'I'm going to fuck you.' Brandon pulled Jenna's shirt over her head and dropped it to the floor. 'I'm going to fuck you and your husband all night.'

Jenna exhaled, feeling the heat of desire in her throat. She stood in the middle of the living room wearing nothing but a pair of panties and a skirt. Her voluptuous breasts were exposed to the cool night air and her nipples immediately stiffened.

Donavan came to her side and smiled at her briefly before closing his mouth over her hard nipple. Jenna closed her eyes and savoured the sensation. Chills raced down her spine. Donavan sucked her nipple for a full minute before he let it pop from his lips.

Brandon took over and clamped his full lips over the same nipple to give it a good suck. Jenna moaned in delight. 'I can't

174

wait to be fucked by two huge cocks,' she whispered. 'But, baby, I want to see you fuck this pretty boy first.'

Brandon looked up into Donavan's eyes. For a second they stared at each other's facial features and Jenna watched them in silence. She could see how Brandon admired her husband's hazel eyes and chiselled jaw. Donavan let his hand glide along the side of Brandon's face as he stared at his pouty lips. Before a second passed, Donavan pulled Brandon closer and pressed his lips to his. Jenna had a close-up look at their tongues licking and gliding against one another's. It aroused her immensely to be sandwiched between two hot men who obviously had the hots for each other.

'You want to fuck me?' Brandon breathed into the kiss.

'I want to fuck you so bad,' Donavan said and bit Brandon's bottom lip.

Jenna saw Brandon melt instantly. His eyes fluttered although they were half closed and his body relaxed as he panted and moaned. The fantastic thing was that Jenna knew exactly how he felt. Donavan had kissed her like that before and she had done the same.

She took advantage of her position and ran her palm up and down the length of Brandon's hard cock. Although he still wore his black boxer-briefs she still admired his girth. Donavan ripped his own clothes off hastily. Completely naked, he moved to position himself behind Brandon. Quickly, Donavan turned and pushed Brandon against the nearest wall and pressed his dick against Brandon's ass. Jenna was amazed at how quick yet uniform Donavan and Brandon moved. She was left in the middle of the room alone but her attention was on how Donavan manhandled Brandon. She felt she was right there next to them.

Donavan thrust his groin against Brandon's ass as he placed Brandon's hands over his head and pinned them against the wall. Jenna squeezed her thighs together as her juices started to flow.

'You want me to fuck your ass?' Donavan whispered against Brandon's shoulder. 'You want to feel how deep my dick can go?'

'Put it in me,' Brandon moaned. 'God, I need it.'

With that order Donavan obeyed. He quickly hooked his fingers into the rim of Brandon's boxer-briefs and pulled them down over his ass and to his thighs. Jenna blushed with heat as she witnessed her husband lick his finger and slide it between Brandon's ass cheeks, and what a great ass he had. For her being the judge, Brandon definitely had a tight, lean, football-player ass.

Donavan twisted and glided his finger in and out as Brandon squirmed in pleasure. 'You want more?' Donavan asked. 'You want me to spread you more?'

'Yes,' Brandon growled. 'Give it to me.'

Donavan pulled out, spit on three fingers and eased them all back in between Brandon's tight ass cheeks. 'You like that? You want more?'

'Fuck me, Donnie.' Brandon placed his forehead to the wall and begged, 'Fuck me now.' Donnie was the nickname Brandon had given Donavan in high school. Maybe he begged for it then the same way he was begging for it now. The thought of it definitely was a turn-on for Jenna.

Donavan removed his fingers and left Brandon briefly to fetch a condom from his pant pocket. When he returned to him, he placed the condom on, lubed his cock up with saliva and slowly pressed it inside his high-school buddy.

'Fuck yeah,' Brandon cried. 'God, I fucking missed this. All this time ... I needed you.'

Donavan moved his body in waves as he slowly fucked Brandon's tightness. 'I missed this too. I wanted this for so long.'

Jenna made her way over to her husband. She kissed his muscular back and ran her palms over his flexed arms. She had never been so aroused in her life. Watching her husband fuck his male best friend lit a fire in her hotter than any fantasy ever had. Her desire burned so deep she felt the heat on her skin. She pressed her pouty lips against Donavan's ear. 'I want you. I want you both to treat me like I'm your dirty whore.'

Donavan paused. Jenna watched him pull out of Brandon and pull the latex from his swollen cock, dropping it to the floor. In no time Donavan's lips were pressed on hers. She moaned as his tongue licked hers. She gasped when his hands found her ass and squeezed. She nearly collapsed when the amazing Brandon pressed his body against the back of hers. His stiff cock pressed against her lower back and smeared it with sticky precome. But nothing was more thrilling than suddenly feeling Brandon's cock prod her wet pussy entrance. She would have collapsed in sheer bliss if she wasn't securely anchored between two gorgeous bodies.

'Fuck her,' Donavan demanded. 'Fill her pussy up with your cock and fuck her good.'

Such dirty talk made her weak in the knees. The deep-throat groans and grunts coming from Brandon as he fucked her hard and fast were enough to stimulate her sexual senses. Moreover, her husband demanding another man to fuck her while he assisted in the fucking was overload on her sanity. She wanted to come but she didn't want to give in to the pleasure without having a thick cock down her throat first.

She bent over, allowing Donavan to support her as she took his hard-on in her mouth, past her lips, along her tongue and down her throat. Before long, she was being fucked simultaneously by the amazing high-school buddies. And, boy, was it bliss. Finally, she gave in to her pleasure and let an orgasm rip through her body. Brandon was next to do the same. She felt the warmth of his juices inside her as they collected at the tip of his condom. As Brandon panted for air, the taste of Donavan's hot, bitter semen hit the back of her throat. It was bliss, indeed.

During the afterglow of incredible sex, Brandon excused himself to the bathroom. Jenna lay naked on the sofa, glistening with a light layer of sweat as Donavan held her in his arms. The cool air brushed her skin and made her shiver slightly. 'This was the most amazing night. I hope you won't get angry with me.'

'I had a great time.' Donavan kissed her lips. 'Why would I get angry?'

Jenna exhaled as she confessed, 'I searched for Brandon

online in order to ask him a favour.'

Donavan lifted an eyebrow. 'A favour?'

Jenna flashed a guilty look. 'I knew you weren't over him. I knew you had unspoken feelings for him that were jeopardising our sex life and possibly, sooner or later, our marriage. I couldn't let that happen so I–'

'So you sought him out to ask him to fuck me?' Donavan said, with an all-knowing grin. 'At first he forgot that he was supposed to meet you, but when you mentioned me all sorts of memories came back to him, right?'

Jenna was astonished. 'How did you know?'

He smiled. 'I admit. I was surprised when the phone rang and it was him on the other end. But what didn't surprise me was when he told me he had met with you and about the favour.'

'He told you? Why?'

'He thought I would be upset with a surprise. He knows I don't like surprises.'

So you were pretending this whole time?'

'No, my feelings are real,' he said. 'Everything I ever felt about Brandon is real. But instead of surprising me with *my* fantasy fulfilled, we fulfilled yours. I hope you're not angry with me.'

'I had a great time.' Jenna kissed his lips. 'Why would I be angry? Besides, I think Brandon knows he's getting more than just sex with you. There will be other nights like this one.'

'I would like that,' he said and sneezed so loud Jenna nearly jumped out of her skin.

A sneeze that put everything back into perspective for Jenna. Her marriage hadn't changed one bit. It had always been ... perfect.

As You Wish
by Heidi Champa

'So, Todd is going to be there?'

I rolled my eyes. I had casually mentioned that my ex, Todd would be at the party and he had been talking about it non-stop.

'Yes, Jake. Todd is going to be there. Is that a problem?'

'No. No problem. Just curious.'

I sniffed at that notion. 'Just curious.' I couldn't figure out why, but Jake had become obsessed with Todd. I had told him there was nothing to worry about, nothing to fear from an ex. But, he seemed to be oddly keyed up for this party. I chalked it up to his fragile male ego, but there seemed to be something else lurking under the surface. I tried to ignore him and just have fun. But Jake had other plans.

He was staring again. I kept catching him from across the room. It was obvious that his eyes were glued to Todd and me, despite his attempts to look casual. He was transfixed, registering our every move. I tried to ignore it, tried to hold a normal conversation with my ex-boyfriend. A guy that he had assured me he was *not* jealous of. I was beginning to think Jake had lied to me. My friendships were important to me, and he claimed he understood. The way his eyes moved over the two of us, it was clear to everyone that he was anything but understanding.

My anger simmered all evening, but I held my tongue. I decided instead to torture Jake. If he was jealous, if he was upset, then I would give him something to be upset about. When Todd ran his hand down my back for no reason, I didn't shy away. I stood a step too close, reached out to touch his arm when I laughed. I flirted, gauging Jake's reactions to my brazenness. But his expression didn't seem to change. He just watched us, no visible signs of anger in his eyes. By the end of the night, I was livid, and when I kissed Todd goodbye I opted for his lips rather than his cheek. Jake was standing right next to us when I pressed my lips to Todd's. I turned to him, accepting my coat from his waiting arms. Nothing. Not even a hint of panic.

We rode home in silence, as I was unable to find the words to pick a fight with him. I went about my routine when we got home, as he was clearly not willing to start the conversation either. As I stood by the sink, brushing my teeth, he appeared in the doorway. Still watching me.

'You're mad at me, aren't you?'

I spit out the toothpaste in my mouth and stared at his face in the mirror. Again, there was no readable expression.

'I'm not. I'm just confused. Are you going to tell me why you were staring at me all night? Why you watched Todd and me like a hawk? You said you were OK with us being friends.'

I grabbed my lotion and started rubbing the cool cream over my dry legs. His eyes watched me, and he started to move closer until he stood behind me. He pushed my hair away from my neck and kissed the exposed flesh. I stopped moving my hands across my legs, not knowing what else to do. His hands moved down my sides, lifting the hem of my nightgown, exposing my panties. His finger traced circles over my stomach as his mouth continued to evade my questions with kisses.

'Answer me, Jake.' He reluctantly stopped nuzzling my neck, and looked at me in the mirror.

'I liked watching you. Besides, what did you expect me to do – you were flirting with him. Face it, Trish. You *wanted* me to watch.'

I opened my mouth to object to his observations, but he turned my head and covered my protest with a kiss. He spun me around to face him, reaching under my flimsy cotton gown to rub my breasts. He caught my hard nipples between his fingers, pinching slightly. He stopped, looking back into my eyes.

180

'Come on, Trish. You knew I was watching, and you did all that smiling and touching on purpose. What were you doing – trying to teach me a lesson?' His smug smile made me angry. I tried to pull away, but he held me close to him.

'You don't trust me, do you? Yeah, I wanted to teach you a lesson. I wanted to make you even more jealous.'

'You think I was watching you because I'm jealous?'

I nodded but he just smiled. My attempts to upset him had clearly backfired. In fact, they seemed to be having the opposite effect. I could feel his erection pressing into my thigh. Again, I tried to get away from him, but he just pulled me closer.

'You and Todd are cute together. I bet you made a nice couple.'

I was confused by his remarks; even more confused when he crushed my mouth with his. He pulled back; the sparkle in his eyes was unmistakable. He turned me around, our eyes meeting again in the mirror. My nightie was bunched up at my hips, and he was grinding his cock into my ass. Even with clothing between us, I could feel him twitch. His eyes stayed glued on mine.

'I've always wondered about the two of you. What you were like together.'

His hand rubbed my nipples back into stiff points. Teasing me, I could feel my pussy getting wet. Despite my lingering confusion, I gave in to his touch.

'Why would you say something like that?' I could barely get my words out.

'Watching the two of you doesn't make me jealous, Trish. I like it. That is why I was watching in the first place. I was fantasising about the two of you. Fucking.'

On the last word, his hand slipped into my panties, finding me wet and open. His finger eased inside me without effort, without resistance. My mind was still swimming with this new information, but he wasn't done yet.

'I could picture you, wrapping your legs around his back, right there on the couch. I can tell by the way he looks at you that he still wants you. Not that I blame him. Come on, admit it. You still want him. Just a little bit.'

Another finger slid inside me and my panties were long gone. I was aware of his eyes still watching me, still holding mine in the mirror, but I had lost focus. Everything was blurred and hazy. His fingers were replaced by the head of his cock nudging against my cunt. Again, his words ran over me and left me reeling.

'I bet he was the first guy to really make you come, am I right? That is why you are so attached to him. He's the one, isn't he?'

He may not have wanted or even needed a reply, but I gave him one. I nodded, acknowledging the truth that Jake had spoken. Todd wasn't my first love, but he had given me my first orgasm. Passion had never been our problem.

As Jake fucked me slow, my mind travelled back to Todd and me; flashes from random fucks from many years ago. Maybe I did still want him. Forgetting him completely never seemed possible. I would have been lying if I had said I hadn't thought about him over the years.

'You're thinking about him right now, aren't you?'

I wondered if he could really tell, or if he just knew me better than I thought. I managed a nod as he slid deeper inside me.

'Good, I'm glad. I'm glad you're thinking about him. Because, I can't stop thinking about the two of you. Every time you say his name, or wear that old T-shirt of his. God, Trish. It's driving me crazy. I want you to fuck him again. I want to watch you fuck him. I need to see it. I know it's not what I'm supposed to want. But I can't help it.'

I could barely breathe, the air felt so heavy. I couldn't believe what Jake was saying, what he was doing. His request surprised me, made my pussy tighten around his cock even more. Jake's cock pulled out of me almost completely, before driving back in deep. He brought me back to him, back to the moment, and to his statement.

'Say you will, Trish. At least say you want to. I need to hear you say it.' As he fucked me harder, I tried to find the courage to form the words.

'I want to, Jake.'

'Want to what? Say it.'

'I want you to watch Todd fuck me.'

Before my words were even out of my mouth, I was coming. So was Jake, his hands digging hard into my hips. He had barely pulled out, when he picked me up and carried me to the bed. He wasn't finished with me. He dove between my legs, devouring me greedily. As his tongue flicked my clit and brought me to yet another screaming climax, my mind again went to Todd. One more time with Todd. Could I – for Jake?

It seemed so simple, too easy. I guess I shouldn't have been shocked that Todd agreed to fuck me. Just like Jake said he would. I didn't want to believe that he had been right, that Todd still wanted me. But it seemed to be true. The fact that he had no objection to Jake watching did surprise me. When I presented him with the idea, he didn't seem fazed at all. In fact, he too seemed turned on by the idea of showing Jake how he used to fuck me. And, now that it was actually going to happen, I couldn't stop thinking about it either.

Todd would be arriving any minute. Jake had never seemed so calm. He sipped his scotch and sat in the chair in the corner of our bedroom. I paced. The doorbell rang, and I jumped. Jake stepped up to get the door, like he was expecting any normal delivery. He was acting like this was something we did every day.

I looked up and there they were, both standing in the doorway. It felt like a movie all of a sudden. Like it wasn't going to be me at all, but some character who would know just how to handle this. Jake dimmed the lights and retreated to his seat. Todd stepped closer to me, standing just a few inches away. There was no easy or smooth way to do this. Nothing could ease the tension. No cute or clever thing to say that could get us all laughing. There was no way to do it, but just to do it. Todd seemed to agree, wrapping his hand around my neck and pulling my face to his. His mouth covered mine. As my lips parted, I realised just how long it had been since someone else had kissed my lips. It felt foreign, yet so familiar.

I could feel Jake's eyes. I wondered what he was thinking – if he was having second thoughts. As Todd kissed my neck, I stole a last glance at Jake. He sat back in his chair, his eyes barely visible in the dim light. I saw the corners of his mouth go up, and I felt myself start to relax. This was what he wanted, and I was going to give it to him. Todd's sucking mouth and teeth scraped the soft flesh of my neck and I couldn't help but cry out. Pulling my hair slightly, he exposed my neck further, opening me up to him. He manoeuvred me closer to the bed.

Todd was pulling his shirt over his head and mine soon followed. He laid me back on the bed, his mouth closing around my nipple before my head hit the pillow. I grabbed his shoulders and arched my back, feeling his tongue pass over my tight flesh again and again. I looked over at Jake, his face as intense as his stare following Todd's mouth. I could feel sweat starting to form on my back, and Todd's hand slipping into my pants. Knowing he would find me wet, knowing how sure and steady his fingers always were, made me moan out loud. As soon as he touched me, he breathed into my ear.

'God, you are so hot. Still as wet as I remember. You missed me, didn't you?'

I couldn't speak. Todd pulled his hand out, just long enough to strip us both naked. I felt his hard cock against my leg and his hand went right back between my legs, straight to my clit. I spread my thighs. Jake had moved forward in his chair, his erection visible through his pants. I couldn't look for long, as Todd kissed me hard, bringing me back to him. I pushed my hips into his hand, feeling his fingers slide deeper inside me. He looked at me, and I could remember the last time I had stared up at him from this place.

'Do you want me to lick it?'

This time he spoke so Jake could hear him. He hadn't asked me that in so long, but the question still sounded so right.

'Yes.'

Todd disappeared, his hands pushing my thighs apart. His tongue ran all over my slit. I looked right at Jake, his eyes finally on mine. His cock was in his hand, his breath laboured. Todd sucked my clit into his mouth, pushing his fingers deeper.

184

He still knew just what I wanted. I couldn't stop the moans coming from my mouth and I could hear Jake sigh in response. But, just as I was ready to let go, Todd stopped licking my pussy, letting his fingers lazily trace over my wet folds. Only one wet finger moved slowly in and out of me. He looked at Jake, forcing him to break his stare into my eyes.

'What do you think, Jake, do you think she's ready to get fucked?'

I gasped, my hand clutching at my chest. I heard Jake get up from the chair and walk towards the bed. He was staring down at me; at Todd's finger pushing in and out of my wet pussy. He sat on the edge of the bed, his eyes never leaving mine.

'It looks like it, but maybe we should ask her. Come on, Trish, we want to hear you say it. Tell us. Are you ready to get fucked?'

I could barely stand the heat coming from my pussy. Hearing them talk about me like that made me clamp down on Todd's finger. I knew they were both waiting for me to answer, I just wasn't sure I could. I looked back and forth between them. Todd and Jake; my past and my present. Even though it was Todd's cock I was waiting for, it was Jake's eyes I met first.

'Fuck me. God, fuck me.'

Todd eased his cock into me, and I watched Jake's eyes follow his every thrust. My legs wrapped around his back, just like Jake wanted. Every move Todd made was so familiar, but everything was different now. His cock was moving slowly, his mouth swallowing all my moans. It was just all too much to take, too much to handle. I didn't want to look, but I knew I had to. I had to see Jake's eyes.

But, instead of finding him on the edge of the bed, he was right next to me. I watched as he stroked his cock with his fist, his tempo slow and deliberate. His eyes met Todd's, and they both stopped moving. I should have known Jake couldn't just watch.

'Get on your knees, baby.'

Jake's voice was wobbly, but he smiled down at me, waiting for me to move. I rolled on to my stomach, my muscles weak and shaky. Todd pulled my hips back towards him, his cock sliding easily back into my waiting pussy. My head hung down, my eyes closed, my body taken over by Todd's slow pace. Jake pulled my chin up, our eyes meeting briefly before I focused my gaze on his stiff dick.

'Open your mouth, baby. Suck me.'

I had sucked Jake off a million times before. Todd had fucked me a million times before. But nothing could have prepared me for how different it felt to have them both at the same time. My mouth closed over Jake's swollen cockhead; his hand immediately grabbed my hair. I let my jaw relax, let Jake fuck my mouth. It was such an overwhelming feeling, being taken by two men at once. They worked together, Todd holding back while Jake moved faster than usual. I felt the familiar bite of Todd's fingers, digging into my hips. He must have been close, but he kept the same pace. I could hear Jake straining in front of me, his whimpers coinciding with the long sweeps of my tongue on his cock.

I was so close, so ready to turn my body and my pleasure over to the two of them. Todd reached around and ran the thick pad of his thumb over my clit. My moans caught in my throat, unable to move past Jake's stiff prick. I looked up at him to find his eyes shining down at me. When I did, it was over. I was coming. Coming with Todd, but coming for Jake. It didn't take long for Todd to join me, his body covering me, groaning into my back with his release. Jake waited another second before following suit, filling my mouth with his hot come. The three of us came to a halt, Todd the first to disengage. Disposing of the condom, he left Jake and me on the bed, holding on to each other, a sweaty heap, breathing hard. We both looked up at him in the bathroom doorway, but none of us said a word.

Just as in the beginning, there was no easy way for the night to end. Todd dressed and laid a gentle kiss on my lips. I stayed motionless, naked and heavy on the bed. Then it was just Jake and I. He wrapped his body around mine. He didn't say anything. I felt my eyes grow heavy and right before I fell asleep he breathed one last word into my ear: 'Beautiful.'

Belonging
by Justine Elyot

He understands my needs, and so does she.

We have been together so long now that they can anticipate me, give the order before I have to act out my frustrations, arrange a new scene before I even know I want one.

We had had a few weeks of equilibrium now: me sleeping in the spare room, making them breakfast, then spending the day at college or in the library before rushing home to give the house a swift once-over and putting dinner in the oven.

They both work hard, so our evenings had been spent quietly, me on a cushion at their feet while they shared ice-cream and watched TV and played with my hair. Perhaps I was a little restless the night before, perhaps I had yawned a bit too ostentatiously or rolled my eyes at yet another re-run of *NCIS*.

Whatever it was, Paul had noticed.

'Delicious,' he said, stretching contentedly and pushing the plate of eaten eggs and toast away from him. 'That will set me up for a long day. Oh, by the way, Tamara.'

I stiffened and my hands rose out of the dishwater precipitately, dripping soap bubbles. *By the way, Tamara.* That always led somewhere ... interesting.

'When I get home, I want you in full uniform, ready to serve.'

Deep breaths; somehow, although I am always expecting this, it always takes me by surprise.

'Yes, sir,' I said, my voice low.

'You are not looking at me, Tamara. You need to look at me when you speak to me.'

'I know; I forgot. I'm sorry, sir.' I spun around, agitated at the idea of displeasing him.

'Tut tut, Tamara.' Danni was grinning as she spritzed on perfume and dropped it into her Prada clutch. 'It isn't like you to be disrespectful.'

'I didn't mean ...'

'I know, sweetie. Never mind. We'll sort all that out tonight. Have a nice day now.'

She kissed me on both cheeks and fled to her breakfast meeting.

Paul, always slower and more deliberate in his movements, pushed back his chair and picked up the jacket that was slung over the back of it.

'You know you need this, don't you?'

'Yes, I need this, sir.'

'Good girl.' He held out one arm, inviting me into the sanctuary of his chest. I stood, trembling slightly, against the solidness of him, my cheek enjoying the cool silk tie it rested upon. 'Now behave yourself today, hmm?' He slapped my bottom in its satin bathrobe and kissed the top of my head. 'Goodbye.'

On days like these, concentration on my academic work is, well, academic. I gave up early, went to the pool, then wandered around town window-shopping and planning the evening meal. It would have to be special. It always had to be special on such nights.

Thus it is that at ten minutes to seven, I am shoving casserole dishes into the oven, turning down the dial on the steaming vegetables, whisking up egg whites and uncorking a bottle of one of the nicer merlots from the rack, all while endeavouring to keep my hair, make-up and uniform pristine. Not an easy task, but thankfully I have years of practice behind me.

There. Everything that can be done in advance is done. The table is laid, the lights are low and the house is spick and span. I check my face in the mirror, tug down the brief, clingy skirt, though I know it is designed to ride up and expose my stocking tops, pick up the silver tray with its two perfectly mixed gin

188

and tonics, and stand by the front door.

I have been staring at the coat rack for only a few minutes when I hear the low purr of Paul's car engine. I wonder if he and Danni are returning from work together – they usually do on nights like these, but sometimes she has unavoidable commitments which mean she has to taxi home.

No, she is with him. I can hear voices, high and amiable, getting louder along with the scrunch of gravel that documents their footsteps. The key turns in the lock and I hold out the tray, keeping it balanced on the flat of my palm.

'Ah, thank you, Slutworth,' says Paul lightly, using my "special" name. He takes both the glasses from the tray and hands one to Danni. 'Now hurry along to the parlour for your inspection.'

I return the salver to the kitchen, make sure nothing is burning or overboiling, then I present myself in the "parlour" – the living room on less formal nights. Danni is reclining cross-legged in her favourite armchair, listening to the ice cubes clink in her gin, but Paul's dominating presence radiates from the centre of the room. He has his Master of the House face on. I stand as expected, spine straight, head slightly bowed, hands clasped behind back.

'Face,' he says, and I look up. His fingers cup my chin while he scrutinises my *maquillage* – sweeping eyelashes, scarlet lips. He runs a smooth hand along my smoother hairline, following it to where it disappears into a bun whose severity is dissipated by the frippery of white lace ribbons that trail down from it.

'Good.' He turns attention to my sheer white blouse, undoing the top pearl button, all the better to plunge his hand into my cleavage and check that I am wearing regulation underwear. The cupless rubber basque is breathtakingly tight, and obviously he would have seen my rouged nipples through the whisper-thin fabric of my blouse, so you could argue that this is an unnecessary formality. If you dared argue with Paul, that is. I wouldn't.

I gasp when he pinches each nipple then exhale at the withdrawal of his hand.

189

'Good. Now lift your skirt, please.'

I hitch it to the waist and stand silently while he casts his eye over my nude shaved pussy and white thighs, contrasting with the black suspender straps that dig into them. At a wave of his hand, I turn to display my bared bottom. No knickers is a rule that does not only apply to nights like this. I am forbidden to wear them in any other than emergency circumstances.

'Yes, that seems to be perfectly in order, Slutworth. Now take yourself over to your mistress, for closer examination.'

The heels I totter over on are high and slim, but I manage to maintain the correct posture until I arrive at Danni's negligently crossed legs. She puts down her gin, leans forward and casts a sharp eye over my pubic triangle.

'Spread those legs, Slutworth,' she commands icily. I position my feet wide apart, still holding up my skirt, awaiting the crowning moment of my inspection.

Her hand snatches at me and I feel the perfect polished ovals of her fingernails glide along my labia before she tests the size and protrusion of my clitoris with the pads of two fingers.

'She's very wet, Paul. Dripping wet, in fact.' Danni swishes around in my private places – though I am not supposed to think of them as private any more – until her fingers are thoroughly coated with my juices, which I am then made to lick off.

'Disgusting little slut,' she croons, smiling at me, her brilliant blue eyes narrow as a cat's. 'Turn around and face Paul.'

I do so, then I feel her press her knuckles into my slit, hard against my clit.

'Ride them, Slutworth, while I prepare your back passage.'

Face flaming, and knowing I have to look Paul in the eye throughout the performance, I begin to sway and lurch on her knuckles, which she twists a little underneath me, creating an exquisitely tense friction. Once I am bucking in earnest, hearing the little sucking sounds of my sex fitting around her hand, she begins the second part of her task. One cool, lubricated finger begins to circle my anal pucker, slow and steady in contrast to my frantic frigging motion.

My brow damp, chest heaving, I strive to reach the moment that will end this dance of degradation, even as I fall deeper and deeper into pleasure. Danni slides two fingers up inside my bottom and wiggles them there so that I feel held fast between her front and rear invasions.

Paul crunches on an ice cube, smiling encouragingly at me throughout.

'Ride a little harder, Slutworth. Show us how much you want it. Show us how much you need it. So much that you gave yourself to us, to be our very own free fucktoy. You must need this very, very badly.'

Danni rotates her fingers in my bum and I come with a mighty rush, my legs weakening so that it is only my posterior prong keeping me upright, along with the supportive set of knuckles I am spending myself on. The moment I dream of and crave is so fleeting, but for just those few seconds, I experience the keenness of my surrender, my submission to them at full force; an abandoned rapture that lifts me beyond my body.

'Well done,' they chorus, their voices warm and thick. I have pleased them.

'Now present yourself for the plug, please,' adds Paul, and straight away I am clicked back into my reality of service and obedience. I lower myself slowly on to my knees, feeling Danni's fingers retreat back down my passage until they are out again, then I place my head on my folded arms, so that my bottom is raised and exposed to my mistress' liking.

Over the years, the plugs have increased in size and width. Their current favourite is a challenge to accommodate; it stretches me to the point that I can only waddle, legs bowed, rather than walk with the gracious poise I studied for so long. They don't seem to miss my elegant gait though, and I think they prefer me this way.

Danni likes to take her time over this operation, pushing in a little way, then pulling out again as my unwilling ring contracts and tries to expel its visitor. She proceeds with a great deal of soothing and clucking noises, telling me I am doing well, that I needn't think she is going to stop, that I need to feel this level of fullness because it is good for my submission.

'I know it feels uncomfortable, sweetie,' she says, while I puff and grimace and yelp. 'It's meant to feel that way. Little sluts like you need to know that their bottoms don't belong to them, isn't that right? Their bottoms and their pussies and their tits belong to their owners. And sometimes their owners' friends. So hold tight, Slutworth, and take it all the way in.'

It finds its space and seats itself, the wide base peeking rudely from my rear hole.

'Good. Now you're ready,' says Danni with satisfaction, slapping one cheek before pulling my skirt back down to my stocking tops.

'And so is the dinner, I think,' remarks Paul, sniffing the air. 'Something smells delicious – something apart from Slutworth, who smells like a bitch in heat, as usual. Shall we take our places at the table?'

I concentrate all my attention on preparing and serving the dinner, carrying each porcelain dish to the table, then ladling a little of each offering on to my owners' plates, pouring the wine, adding the condiments. All of this is testing work with spike heels and a bumful of plug, but I manage to get through without any spillages or mistakes.

While they eat, chatting lightly about their respective days at the office, I stand at the side of the table, between them, at attention. Every now and again, one of their hands wanders, perhaps to the seat of my skirt or the stiff nipple that is visible through my shirt. After I serve Paul some extra steamed vegetables, he has me crouch under the table between his knees, unzip his trousers and take his cock in my mouth.

'Slutworth is behaving very well tonight,' he comments as I suck away.

'Yes, she is, isn't she? If she carries on like this, it'll be hard to find anything to spank her for.'

'And that would never do,' chuckles Paul.

'Can you believe it's been five years?' I pause briefly in my fellatio. Really? Is this an anniversary of sorts?

'Who told you to stop?' Paul's tone is severe, then it relaxes again when I resume my mouthwork. 'Yes, five years ago today we met her in the museum restaurant. What a pretty little waitress she was. You noticed her before she even took our order, didn't you?'

'I told you she was special. Told you she was corruptible.'

'And you were right. The way she reacted when you told her off for knocking over the salt cellar ... it told us all we needed to know.'

'That little bitten lip, that tremulous look, the gabbled apology.'

'And then we got chatting ... between courses ...'

'Met her at the end of her shift ...'

'Took her out for cocktails ...'

'Took her home ...'

'And she's been here ever since. Excuse me.' Paul pauses to ejaculate in my mouth. 'And we're very happy to have her.'

'Very lucky to have her,' says Danni and I melt, halfway through swallowing my own repast.

After I have served them chocolate and amaretto soufflé, they send me into the kitchen to make coffee and feast on leftovers before we all repair to the ... parlour, for the post-prandial entertainment.

I reflect, as I eat, on five years of loving service. Five years of feeling wanted, of safety and security, of having people I can tend to and who tend to me. What most would regard as a form of bizarre imprisonment has set me free, released me from mundane anxieties so I can complete my academic work, further my career ambitions, concentrate on my dreams.

The irony is worth savouring, as is the coffee, but when it has been poured and the petits-fours offered around, my contemplation time is at an end and I must await my next order.

'Well, Slutworth.' Paul smiles expansively at me, looking relaxed and sated, making me feel proud that I have conferred this air of satisfaction on him. 'Like I said earlier, you have been an exemplary maid tonight. I can't find any fault with you at all.'

'Perhaps we should let you off your spanking.' The look in Danni's eye is mischievous. I'm not a masochist, don't enjoy pain in the least, but without a spanking the evening will feel incomplete and I will sleep badly. Which she knows.

'Oh, is that a quivering lip?' teases Paul. 'Don't worry, Slutworth. You'll sleep on your stomach tonight. After all, we could say that we owe you a birthday spanking. Five years. That calls for a ... celebration, doesn't it?'

'Yes, sir,' I say gratefully.

'Take yourself over to your mistress and use your tongue to pleasure her, Slutworth. I'll attend to your spanking while you work.'

My eyes widen – this is a new tack. I have never been asked to do this before. But I do not query his wish, and I scuttle forward, arrange myself between Danni's cobalt-coloured pumps and say the words that are second nature to me.

'Please, ma'am, may I serve you with my tongue?'

'Of course, Slutworth. One moment.' She stands, long legs shearing away above me, and removes her knickers, laying them down next to her espresso cup. Then she arranges herself in the armchair so that her delicate quim is at my eye level and I shuffle forward, snuffling like a pig seeking truffles, and give her pale pink clit a kiss.

'You will need to stand for this,' says Paul from behind me. He hoiks me up with an arm beneath my ribcage, makes me hold on to the arms of the chair and bend down to lick Danni's lips. I feel the strain on my calves and the backs of my thighs, but I know why Paul is doing this – my bottom cheeks are stretched perfectly taut and my skirt has risen to the very crest of my buttocks, revealing my pale suspendered thighs to his view. The wide bulb of the butt plug is especially inescapable now, and I squirm a little, trying in vain to find a more comfortable stance. I do not leave off my licking though, for once I have started I must not stop. When Paul lifts my skirt to bare my backside, I push my face further into the strong-scented juices, half-hoping he will remove the plug, and half dreading it. In the event, he leaves it in.

I ply my tongue hard as he runs his hands over my vulnerable half-moons.

'Five unforgettable years,' he croons. 'Let's have two

strokes of the paddle for each year, shall we?'

I am not expected to answer, of course. Although I simultaneously worship and abhor his hard wooden paddle, I cannot clench my buttocks in anticipation of the first stroke, for the plug has them stretched beyond that capacity. Instead I thrust my tongue inside Danni's cunt, smashing my face into her flesh, so that the first stinging smack of the paddle forces the breath out of me and on to her swollen clit, giving her the pleasure and the benefit of my pain.

She writhes beneath my groans, enjoying them for the sensation they afford her as well as the knowledge that I am submitting to her husband's discipline, a twin stimulant to which she is addicted.

The paddle falls inexorably, heating me up, sending tremors beyond my flesh and inside me, where the plug transmits the impact to my widespread walls. After only three, I know that I am dripping wet, my cunt as hot as my bum cheeks, pushing out for more, more pain, more gain, more steps on the road to what I need.

I am gorging on Danni, sucking and devouring her, almost frantic with the strength of my appetite. I can hear her harsh breaths, her swearing, feel her scratchy nails against my shoulders, digging in. And I can hear the heavenly crack of the paddle against my hot skin, hear Paul's count in that slow, steady way he does it, hear my hoarse cries, muffled by their cunt gag.

On the ninth stroke, I cannot stop myself, I put my hand between my legs and begin to rub myself furiously. On the tenth, I come, and so does Danni, wrapping her thighs against my ears, holding me tightly between her legs so my mouth is imprisoned in her spread, spent centre. Paul drops to his knees behind me and begins to paw and kiss my burning bottom, twisting the plug to draw out my orgasm even longer. His arms clasp around my waist and he sinks his lips into my neck, marking it as his possession.

We lie like that, exhausted but happy, for some time, gathering ourselves without hurry. I know that later on I will be taken to their bed and comprehensively fucked until we are raw and sore and unable to continue. I know that we will spend the rest of the night in each other's arms, thanking whichever unnamed deity is to thank for the way we all came together. With Paul and Danni I have found the thing I never thought I'd have – a place where I belong.

Three to Tango
by Josie Jordan

The pounding techno shakes the ground beneath my feet. I'm buzzing with excitement and at the same time shivering with nerves.

Tia points down on to the dance floor below. 'Guy in the blue top?'

I shake my head. 'Not my type.'

All of a sudden, her hand grips my arse. 'Yeah?' she spits, over her shoulder. 'What do you think you're looking at?'

Used to this by now, I turn to see who her victim is this time. It's the group of guys behind, who are backing nervously away.

Tia glares at them. 'They were eyeing up your legs, Lauren.'

'Were they now?' It's hardly the best way to go about achieving my mission, but I know she means well. Her hand remains there for a moment even after the men have disappeared. When she turns to face me, my eyes are drawn to her lips, part open and showing her cute little teeth. I'm very tempted to kiss her. Yet I'm pretty sure that if I did so, she would recoil. The whole "bi" thing is just a game she plays to wind men up.

All the same, when I told her what I wanted for my 30th, after far too many vodkas last weekend, she surprised me. 'I'm up for it!' Her response was instant and all nonchalant, like it was no big deal. She even blew me a jokey kiss.

When her hand returns to the railings, I can't decide if I'm disappointed or relieved.

Which is strange, because I'm not bi. In fact I wasn't attracted to women at all until I met Tia. Somehow she intrigues me.

As for the other thing I'm hoping for tonight? I barely dare admit it, even to myself. To meet The One: my elusive soulmate. Near impossible perhaps, given that I haven't the faintest idea what I'm looking for.

'How about that one then, the Beckham lookalike?' asks Tia.

I laugh. 'The one in the white shirt? I can't see the resemblance.'

A new track begins and the crowd roars.

'Yay! I love this tune,' I say.

'Come on then, let's dance.'

We hurry downstairs and push our way on to the dance floor just as the melody comes in. The strobe lights flash, everyone goes crazy and I'm happy again – for now at least.

As we dance, a dark-haired guy catches my eye. They say if you see someone dance, you can tell what they'll be like in bed, and he's dancing with pure passion.

Noticing me watching him, he shoots me a smile.

'Don't look now,' I shout to Tia. 'But check out the guy in the black T-shirt.'

A moment later, she gives me the thumbs up. We dance our way over to him and he turns his body to face mine. His dark eyes sparkle at me every time I look at him. We dance closer and closer until his fingers brush mine. Above the stage smoke, I can smell his shampoo. When Tia gets behind him, pressing herself up to his back, he seems startled but not displeased.

One of his mates hones in on Tia. 'Fuck off!' she mouths.

I bite my lip as the poor guy fucks off, looking offended.

Tia returns her attention to the guy in front of her, helping herself to a feel of his arse.

It's now or never. Leaning in close, I shout, 'Want a drink?'

He raises his eyebrows as though he can't believe his luck. 'Sure.'

His palm wraps around mine to lead me to the bar. Not to be outdone, Tia grabs hold of his other hand.

'What's your name?' I ask as we wait to be served. The music is quieter over here, but we still have to lean towards each other to make ourselves heard.

'Matt.'

'I'm Lauren.' Our eyes meet and I feel a spark of desire. 'And this is Tia.'

Men generally don't know quite what to make of Tia. Tonight, for instance, she's wearing a short dress in a white semi-transparent sort of fabric. Cute. Yet she's teamed it with silver-studded biker boots and over-the-top smoky eye make-up. Kind of a bride-of-Dracula look. It sums up her personality completely.

We take our drinks to a booth. Matt slides in between Tia and me. I shuffle up until I'm right next to him, letting my bare arm rest against his as we chat.

He's softly spoken, with an air of quiet confidence. His hair is closely cropped, making him look sweetly vulnerable and a few years younger than he probably is.

I knock back half my drink and say softly, 'You're gorgeous, Matt. Isn't he, Tia?'

Tia voices her agreement.

'Are your legs as sexy as your arms?' I ask next. My heart thumps as I reach down to his denim-clad thigh.

He blinks.

Tia's hand goes to his other thigh and remains there. She grins. 'I reckon so.'

His eyes widen in surprise.

I pluck up all my courage. 'Want to come home with us tonight, Matt?'

His jaw drops. He sets down his drink and looks from me to Tia. 'You serious?'

I nod, not taking my eyes from his face.

'What is this? Some kind of fantasy?'

'You could say that.'

He draws in a slow breath. 'OK. I'd better tell my mates I'm leaving.'

Tia and I stand up to let him get out. We exchange looks.

'Think he'll come back?' I ask.

Tia cackles. 'I hope so. Nice choice, Lauren.'

He returns wearing a leather jacket and a dazed grin.

We're silent in the taxi. Nerves on my part – and Matt's, I guess. As for Tia, it's hard to say. She's not really the nervous type. When I turn her way, she's gazing out of the window with the faintest of smiles.

Matt gives me a shy sideways glance. I feel that spark again as our eyes meet. He starts painting little circles on my palm with his thumb. Wow. I'd never realised quite how sensitive my palm could be. It's as though he's touching me *there* instead. The inside of my knickers is getting wetter and wetter.

He jumps. I look down and see that Tia has her hand on his cock.

I think the taxi driver has clocked what's going on. He gives us a strange look as we climb out.

As soon as we're inside, Tia and I set about preparing gin and tonic. Matt watches us from the sofa. I hand him his drink and he downs it immediately.

'Are you hot, Matt?' Tia teases.

'Let's cool him down.' I kick off my heels and climb astride his lap.

He sets his glass on the side table and clasps my waist, watching to see what I'm going to do next. Fishing an ice-cube from my glass, I slide it down his cheek. When it reaches his lips, he parts them. I like that he's prepared to let me be in charge. It takes some confidence for a man to sit back like this.

I ice his bottom lip and kiss him hard, like I've wanted to since I first set eyes on him. After the initial chill, his lips warm up rapidly. He's delicious. There's a hint of stubble on his upper lip. I trail my tongue over the bristles.

Tia is next to us on the sofa. 'Want a taste, Tia?' I ask.

I lean back to give her access. She dives in and plants her mouth onto his. While they're kissing, I take his hand and place it on her ample chest. Watching my face, he slides his fingers down the front of her dress. Tia kisses him harder in response.

Both of them are breathless when she pulls away. His hands settle on my thighs, where my dress has hitched up. I peel off

200

his T-shirt to reveal a smooth chest with taut abs. 'Nice,' I whisper and kiss him again.

Tia's hands roam over his nipples. I feel him flinch and I smile to myself. She must have an ice-cube.

'Take off Lauren's dress,' she says in his ear. 'And her bra.'

While he unzips me, she sticks her hand inside his fly and pulls out his cock. She giggles. 'You've gone all hard, Matt.'

He pulls my dress over my head. I reach behind to unclip my bra and shrug it off my shoulders. He lowers his lips to my tits, sucking as much flesh as he can into his mouth. His hot tongue laps my nipples.

His eyes flick upwards to mine. I sense him wondering how far this will go. In response, I wrap my fingers around his cock and tug the warm flesh gently up and down. Things are getting pretty heated. As much as I want him right now, I want to make this last. I prise his hands from my waist and climb off.

In a flash, Tia has stripped him of his jeans and boxers. His generously proportioned cock, fully erect now, juts up towards the ceiling. 'Mm,' she says, approvingly. She glances at me. 'Want to watch us, Matt?'

My heart speeds up another notch. I've always wanted to do this. With shaky hands I lift off her dress and bra. We press our bodies together. Tit to tit, lip to lip. Her small fingers weave through my hair. She smells of vanilla and coconut.

Back on the sofa, Matt has his hand around his cock.

Tia's warm tongue slips into my mouth. And just as I'm getting used to kissing her, her hand skims my thigh. Before I know it, her fingers are inside my knickers, her slim forefinger probing into me. I gasp. It's so much softer than a man's fingers.

She has me so turned on that my inhibitions are just melting away. I reach into her gusset and explore her hot sticky centre.

At the sight of Matt stroking himself up and down, I say, 'Let's go to bed.'

Taking Matt by the hand, we lead him down the corridor to my king-size bed.

'What are we going to do to you then, Matty boy?' asks Tia, kicking off her boots.

She and I fall to the bed on top of him. We take it in turns to kiss him, holding his broad shoulders to the mattress.

He has Tia's right breast in one hand and my left breast in the other. 'Fucking hell,' he mutters, 'I can't believe this is happening.'

Neither can I. 'Hold him down, Tia.'

She grabs his arms.

Taking an ice-cube from Tia's glass, I put it in my mouth. 'Spread your legs, Matt.'

His cock is fully exposed and oozing a clear bead of liquid. As I wrap my lips around the tip, he inhales sharply.

Tia clamps her hand over his mouth. 'Shh.'

Slowly I suck up and down his swollen length, relishing his salty taste. His flesh is burning hot and he's still squirming at the ice. I pin his ankles to the bed with my feet. I can't get all of him into my mouth, but I give it my best shot. He gives a low groan as the end of his cock touches the back of my throat. Reluctantly I pull away. 'Want a go, Tia?'

She and I swap places. All she has on is a lacy black g-string. She kneels over him. As her scarlet lips descend, I slip her g-string over her hips. She has the sexiest bottom, full and round.

I take his tongue into my mouth and suck it hard as she sucks his cock.

'I want you, Matt,' I tell him, wriggling out of my knickers.

Panting from Tia's efforts, he traces up the insides of my leg and pushes his chunky forefinger into my folds. I raise my hips to his hand, wanting more. A second finger joins the first. As his fingertips caress my insides, he rubs my clitoris with his thumb, searching my face all the while. His desire is plain to see and hear.

I let him take me to the brink, then I pull away, gasping. 'We're going to fuck you, Matt.'

Tia lifts her mouth from his cock to add: 'All night long.' She gives him one last fierce suck that makes him arch his back. 'Pass me a condom, Lauren.'

As she rolls the rubber on to him, she looks at me with a grin. 'It's *your* birthday, Lauren. You can go first.'

I'm aching to have him inside me. Still, I hover over him, trying to prolong the moment.

'Come on,' he begs.

Tia and I exchange amused looks.

She slaps the side of his face. 'Patience!'

Inch by throbbing inch, I slide down the length of his cock until my bottom rests on his strong thighs.

'Oh God!' he groans.

I hold there a moment, taking in the solid warmth of his flesh.

Alongside, Tia watches on. I take Matt's hand. 'Fingerfuck her, like I'm fucking you.'

Tia's mouth opens wide in surprise as he pushes his middle finger inside her. I start moving on him again. Up and down, feeling that rounded helmet burrowing inside me.

I move harder and Matt gives Tia another finger. Her breaths are coming closer together. The sight of her flushed face as his fingers thrust in and out of her turns me on even more. 'Give her your tongue, Matt,' I urge.

Tia climbs in front of me. She presses herself to his mouth, holding herself open to him with one hand, clasping her other hand to the back of his head. I grip Matt's hips and start fucking him as hard as I can. His hands tighten on Tia's plump buttocks.

He's breathing really hard now.

'He's about to come,' Tia warns.

He's not the only one, but I slow right down. I want Tia to come first. 'Make her come, Matt.'

He grunts in response and I see his head moving faster from side to side.

'Mmm,' Tia breathes.

I reward him with a quick thrust of my hips, before returning to slow slides. He bucks his hips for more.

'Hold him to the bed, Tia,' I say.

She pins his arms down with her knees. He tries to pull them free, but she won't let him.

'I'm so close,' she says and I reach around to cup her breasts. 'Shit, Lauren,' she breathes and I start moving harder on Matt again.

I don't know how much longer I can hold back, but then Tia shouts out. With her still sitting over Matt's face, I start to fuck him really hard. I dig my nails into the sides of his buttocks as the pleasure soars back up to a crescendo. And then the whole of my insides are clenching in violent, almost painful spasms. Wow.

A second later, Matt's cock seems to swell inside me. His whole body jerks from the bed and he gives a muffled cry.

When Tia climbs off, he lies there, looking stunned.

Tia chuckles as she gets up. 'I think we've blown his mind! Shit and I think that blew mine too.'

His cock softens inside me. Reluctantly I climb off. I'm so turned on that I'm already plotting what I want to do next.

Tia and I stretch out on the bed.

Matt props himself up on his elbow. 'Have you two done this before?' he asks when he's got his breath back.

'Mind your own business,' says Tia before I can answer. 'Why, have you?'

He looks horrified. 'What, you mean with two guys? No way! Nor two girls. Although I have to say I've dreamt about it – what guy hasn't?'

Tia snorts.

'Whose idea was this anyway?' he asks next.

I smile shyly. 'Mine.'

He studies me. 'And why me?'

I flush. 'I guess I liked the look of you.'

He traces his finger across my lips. 'And?'

It's not just that he's totally gorgeous. I like his quiet manner; the way he sat back, letting us take control like that. He's a big guy and he could probably overpower us any time he wanted, but he was happy to play along. Could this be more than just a one-night stand? Still, he must see me as some sort of crazed nymphomaniac. 'And you didn't disappoint,' I reply finally.

He breaks into a smile.

Tia yawns. 'Why is it that guys are so into the whole two girls thing? Is it because you think you might learn something from watching us, or because you're too lazy to do all the hard work yourself?'

Now he looks embarrassed. 'I don't know.'

Tia smiles wickedly. 'So let's see what we can teach you.' She reaches down my bare belly and I gulp as her expert fingers go to work on me again.

She knows exactly what she's doing. Instantly my body floods with new rushes of pleasure. Two minutes and I'm on the brink again.

She stops.

'No!' I moan.

'Well don't just bloody lie there,' Tia says to Matt. 'I've done nearly all the work for you.'

He sits up and sticks his face between my thighs. His dark eyes rest on mine as his tongue makes tiny rapid circles on my clit.

Tia remains kneeling behind him. With a naughty smile, she lowers her mouth to his buttocks. He makes a yelp of surprise. She nipped him.

Pleasure builds in my stomach.

I can tell from Tia's laughter that she's up to no good back there. Matt's body jerks to the side but his tongue keeps moving. She must have her fingers in his arse. The thought of this is what sends me over the edge. I pull his face to my crotch and explode around it.

'You can get your revenge on her now,' I tell him weakly.

Matt turns round to face his tormentor.

Tia grabs hold of his newly swollen cock. 'Well, hello ...'

While she wriggles another condom on to him, I say, 'She likes it from behind.'

I'm torn between jealously and fascination as he presses her shoulders to the bed and eases his cock into her. I can see the lust in his eyes.

Mm,' she breathes.

'Screw her nice and hard,' I say.

'Don't worry,' he mutters. 'I'm going to.'

I've heard my neighbours at it through the wall, but actually seeing it right in front of you is something else entirely. I stroke my fingers over my throbbing clit as his cock ploughs into her. Tia's boobs swing back and forth. She's shoving herself onto him, taking all he can give.

The mattress rocks beneath me as their hips shunt backwards and forwards. I can't believe I'm lying here watching this. I can see them, feel them, hear them and smell them as they fuck. I'm concerned he won't last, yet he appears in control – for now at least.

Tia starts making little noises. This seems to spur Matt on, for he grips her hips and speeds up a notch. Her moans reach a crescendo. She buries her face in the pillow and cries out into it.

With his cock still buried deep inside her, Matt's eyes return to mine. I feel a thrill of excitement as I realise what he's thinking. I nod my head a fraction. He pulls out of Tia and she collapses to the bed.

Shaking with desire, I reach for another condom. Matt's cock twitches as I put it on him.

'How do you want it?' he asks gruffly.

Tia rolls over to watch. I kneel up against the headboard and arch my bottom towards him, looking at him over my shoulder.

With a faint smile on his lips, he grabs me by the waist and shoves himself inside me. 'Like this?'

I can't believe how good he feels. My insides are still hypersensitive and he's even harder than he was the first time. 'Yeah, just like that.'

He pushes in and out, but I need more, so I start touching myself again. He finds a steady rhythm. Yet just when I'm getting somewhere he stops.

'You OK?' I ask breathlessly.

'Yeah. Just give me a minute.'

I feel him shuddering with the effort of holding back.

'Let me,' says Tia. Kneeling in front of me, she slaps away my fingers and replaces them with her own. As she rubs my clit back and forth, I tilt my head back onto Matt's broad shoulder. I can feel his cock ticking away inside me. There's something deeply erotic about knowing he's about to go off in there.

Tia lowers her lips to mine and presses her tongue deep into my mouth. Matt starts moving inside me again. I close my eyes, almost there. Tia's soft fingertips are about to bring me off. I suck hard on her tongue. As I feel the stirrings of my third climax of the evening, I say to myself: *Happy birthday.*

One week later. I'm lying in bed with my new lover. It's three in the morning and we're spooning, about to make love for the third time. Neither of us will be getting much sleep tonight.

Matt's a sweet boy. Tia and I might give him a call some time. For tonight though, the lips pressing into the back of my neck are softer than any lips I've ever known. I've finally found what I was looking for. And do you know what? She was right there in front of me, all along.

Wrong Number
by Jean-Philippe Aubourg

Sarah swore as she climbed out of bed and staggered next door to the phone. It was 11.30 p.m.! She had forgotten to unplug it before settling down.

Sarah ran a business from home, a home she had only recently moved into. The phone company had installed a business line with a lovely number, a collection of successive digits, easy to remember. So easy to remember, she was dealing with customers of its former owner – an escort agency.

It had evidently been an agency which specialised in providing women at short notice, usually between two and four in the morning. After the third call in the small hours she had taken to unplugging the phone at night, but still had to deal with the punters who called during the day – men who frequently just grunted, 'What girls have you got available?' Most became flustered and could not get off the phone fast enough when she told them it was a wrong number. Had she not already circulated the phone number to all her clients and prospective clients, she would have asked for a new one, and was hoping the calls would dry up.

Now she cursed herself for forgetting to pull the plug. At least once she had disillusioned this latest gentleman he would not call again. She picked up the receiver and said in a resigned voice, 'Hello?'

What she did not expect to hear was the voice of another woman, and a young woman at that. 'Hello? I hope you can help me. I ... I'm looking for ...' She seemed nervous, but determined. Sarah was about to explain, but the woman managed to get the rest of her sentence out before she could say anything. 'My boyfriend and I are looking for a woman to join us. He wants to see me with another woman, and none of the other agencies have a girl available tonight.'

Sarah was nonplussed. There was a moment's silence while she took in the request and gathered her thoughts. 'I'm sorry, but this isn't an escort agency any more. It's a private house'.

'Oh no!' The woman sounded very disappointed. 'But you were my last hope! I've tried all the other agencies, and they can't find us a girl at short notice. It has to be tonight, my boyfriend's going away on Monday, and I wanted to give him a treat before he left.' Then he's a very lucky man, thought Sarah, and he should count his blessings that you would even consider doing this. 'Are you sure you can't help us?'

'I'm sorry,' said Sarah, 'I really can't. As I said, this is a private house!'

'OK, sorry to have bothered you. Bye.'

'Bye.' Sarah replaced the receiver, pulled the cable from the wall and returned to bed. Instead of what she normally felt – annoyance and revulsion – she felt something different. Admiration for the woman prepared to go to such lengths for her boyfriend, regret that she probably would not be able to give him what she wanted ... and, to her surprise, excitement.

All the previous calls had given her a window on a world she did not like the look of: unattractive, aging men, cheating on their wives, or so socially inept they were not able to find a sexual partner without paying for it. But not this. A couple – presumably happy and attractive – who wanted to introduce, temporarily, a third person, to heighten their enjoyment. Sarah picked up her book and tried to read again, but her mind wandered.

What did they look like? She sounded late 20s or early 30s. Maybe he was going away because he was in the army, all muscular, with short hair and tattoos? Was she dark or, like Sarah, blonde? Thin or curvy? Was her pussy natural, trimmed or shaved ...?

STOP IT! Sarah could not believe she was thinking like this! She was a hard-headed businesswoman, not some sex-crazed nymphomaniac, or a call girl! But still, what would it be like to be sandwiched between two lovers?

Sarah liked to think she had enjoyed an adventurous sex life. There had been several boyfriends, and during a six-week experiment, a girlfriend. It had not ended because she was desperate for sex with a man, but because the girl had been the wrong person for her to be with. She had not ruled out trying it again, if she met a woman with whom she clicked.

Right now she was between partners of any sex, devoting her energy to her business. She was also between the sheets and it was getting on for midnight. Time to sleep. She turned out the light and rolled over, closing her eyes, and trying to drive out any erotic thoughts. She found her right hand snaking down her front, to the hem of her nightdress, then underneath, and into the soft little burrow of her sex. What would it be like? Just once? I might not get such a golden opportunity to try it again?

Sitting up and throwing back the covers, she switched on the light. She stood in front of the wardrobe mirror and slowly lifted her nightdress up and over her head. She looked critically at her body. A pretty face with a small nose and slightly pointed chin. Blonde hair which fell to her shoulders, curving slightly at its ends. Breasts that were a nice handful, neither too big nor too small. A slight bulge to her tummy, barely noticeable, but there nonetheless since she had started working from home and stopped going to the gym. Legs that were not the longest, but still shapely. A neatly trimmed pubic thatch. She turned to look at her bottom, an apple-shaped bum which flared out from her hips, then back in at the thighs. Yes, if you were paying for a woman, and this one turned up on your doorstep, you would be happy enough.

For several days after the event, Sarah tried to work out why she did what she did. She had not had sex for ten months, but she had gone for longer spells and not been this daring. Was it wanting to get a closer look at the world which had been slightly revealed to her, to pull back the curtain and look at the full picture? Was it a latent desire to be with a woman again? Or that a threesome was one of the fantasies which delivered the most powerful orgasm, when she relaxed with her vibrator at the end of a long day?

Whatever caused her to do it, what she did was to plug the phone back in and press 1471. The caller had not withheld her number. Sarah pressed the number to be put through, swallowing hard and trying to fight the rising tide of excitement she was getting from doing something that was just so *wrong*!

The phone rang several times, and Sarah was about to conclude that the woman had given up her search and switched off her phone, but suddenly it was answered. 'Hello?' said the now-familiar voice.

'Er ... hello.' Now it was Sarah's turn to be tongue-tied. 'It's me ... the person you called about half-an-hour ago? You thought this was an escort agency?'

'Yes, but look, I'm sorry I disturbed you. It was a genuine mistake. The agency's site is still up and they have the number on. If you've called to have a go at me, it's not really my fault ...'

'No! No, not at all!' Sarah could hear her voice cracking, and knew it was now or never. 'What I called to say was ... well, to ask ... if you were still looking for a woman to join you?'

The words seemed to hang somewhere along the line between them for several seconds, before the woman answered. 'But I thought you weren't an escort agency?'

'I'm not.'

'So why would you ...?'

'Put it down to a dare I've made with myself. Look, describe yourselves to me, and you could have your wish tonight.' Sarah may have been horny, but she still had standards.

'Oh, OK. I'm 29, my name's Carla. I'm 36-26-36, and I've got long brown hair. My boyfriend is called Steve and he's 35. He's in the army, and he's being posted to ...'

'That's OK, give me your address and I'll be right there.'

Just 45 minutes later Sarah was standing on the doorstep of an unremarkable terrace house. While the rest of the street was in darkness, dim lights burned behind the curtains of a downstairs room and another upstairs. Her tummy lurched as she realised she was expected. She had prepared herself in record time, and wore her sexiest little black dress, a new pair of hold-up stockings and her highest black heels. Her hair was wildly brushed out, and she had applied the simplest make-up.

She raised her hand to ring the doorbell, but hesitated. Just what was she letting herself in for? She was no escort girl! She was a hard-working self-made woman, not a sex toy for a lustful couple! It was not too late; she should get back in her car, drive home and forget this moment of madness.

She saw her finger, with its deep red-painted nail, ringing the doorbell. It was as if a part of her she had no idea existed had taken over the rest of her body. The bell rang, an electronic reproduction of the Westminster chimes of Big Ben. Sarah felt herself churning and knew her whole body was trembling, even as she saw the shadow appear behind the frosted window of the front door. The shadow grew larger until it filled the window, then the door was opened and a young woman was facing her.

'Sarah? Hi, I'm Carla.' She was as she described, attractive with long dark hair that swept down over her shoulders. Her curves were barely hidden under the navy blue silk robe, which seemed to be all she was wearing. 'Come in!' Carla stood aside to let Sarah pass along the hallway. 'First on the right. Steve's waiting for you.'

The room was lit by a single lamp, and was filled with soft music. Steve stood to greet her. He was tall – about six-two – and his fair hair was short and military. He too was wearing a robe, the masculine version of Carla's. 'Hi,' he said, holding out a large hand to shake Sarah's. 'Look, thanks for coming. Although we're still not sure why you did.' You and me both, thought Sarah. 'But we're very pleased you felt you could join us.'

'It'll be my pleasure – I hope!' Sarah replied. God, she thought, now I'm even talking like a tart!

'Wine?' Carla had followed her and walked to a small table with an open bottle of red and three glasses on it. Sarah nodded and Carla poured the drinks, then handed them round. She and

Steve sat on the sofa, while Sarah took her place in a single armchair.

'This is the first time we've tried to do anything like this,' Carla explained. 'And to be honest, this is not the outcome we expected. But I hope whatever happens we'll all be satisfied at the end of the day. Or should I say night!' All three laughed, feeling the slight tension in the room start to dissipate.

'So what do you want to do?' asked Sarah. There was no point beating about the bush.

'Nothing you aren't comfortable with,' said Steve, his nerves making the words come out a little too fast. 'And if you want to stop, just say so.'

'Thanks,' said Sarah, 'that's very reassuring. But I hope it won't be necessary. So what exactly did you have in mind?'

'Well, since we're all a little on edge, how about an icebreaker?' Carla took a long swig of her wine, set the glass down and stood up. She undid the cord around her gown and let the garment fall to the floor. As Sarah had suspected, she was naked underneath.

The girl was hot. Her breasts were large, with dark red nipples, standing up in her growing excitement. Her ribcage tapered to a flat tummy, then her figure flared out to wider hips, back in to smooth lean thighs and calves, all the way down to feet which had nails painted in the same dark green as her fingernails. She put her hands on her hips, contrasting those green nails even further against creamy skin. She parted her thighs, showing a sex which bore no hair at all, and lips which were smooth and closed, inviting exploration.

Carla smiled at Sarah, obviously happy for the other girl to appreciate her beauty. Turning on her heels, she sank to her knees next to Steve. Sarah had a perfect view of her bottom, a smooth peach which curved out and back in just the right proportions. Carla deftly untied the cord of Steve's robe and flicked each end aside. Her hands went back to the robe and lifted first one seam, then the other, folding them back to reveal her boyfriend's body.

He was as fit as her, maybe more so, with the six-pack stomach and chest of a man for whom physical strength was a

214

vital part of his job. His penis was large, almost fully erect and already at least seven inches long. His balls were no disappointment either, already tightening in excitement. Carla took his shaft in her delicate fingers and ran them lightly up and down, making Steve sigh and his weapon twitch. She turned her head and looked at Sarah. 'So we don't disappoint?'

All Sarah could do in reply was to whisper a hoarse 'No!', which seemed to amuse both of them, judging by their smiles. Carla turned back to Steve and lowered her head. Flicking out her tongue, and making sure Sarah still had a perfect view, she ran it up and down Steve's length, very gently at first, then a little harder, until she was sliding the whole flat surface across his skin, in between flicking his glans with the tip. Steve closed his eyes and groaned, as he became even harder, then threw back his head as Carla knelt up, bent forward and sank her mouth down on him.

His whole cock disappeared between her lips and a loud sucking sound as she pulled in her cheeks forced another louder groan from him. His breathing quickened as she moved her head up and down, her fingers circling the base of his tool and squeezing in time with her head movements.

Sarah watched in awe. She had given her share of blowjobs, but this woman was an expert. She wondered if her oral talents would be as good when it came time for her to join them.

Oh! The reality of what she was doing hit her again. She was expected to undress and join this couple, and probably have sex with both of them! In the cold light of day this would be an outrageous suggestion but the growing stickiness she could feel in her expensive silk panties told her there was no way she was backing out now.

Carla pulled her head away with a long, final suck, followed by a few short rubs with her fingers. Giving his glistening head a final kiss, she turned to look at Sarah again. 'He's as hard as he's ever going to be,' she said, her voice low and sultry. 'Are you ready to join us?'

Sarah nodded. Standing on legs which were a little shaky, she reached behind her, looking for the catch of her dress. 'Let me help,' said Carla, standing and walking behind her, her large breasts jiggling as she moved. Sarah felt her fingers on the catch, then the zipper, glad of the help as her own hands were now quivering. She heard the burr of the zip, and felt the material part across her back. She shook her shoulders and the dress fell forward and down, exposing her in her underwear.

Steve, who was now massaging his own erection, let out another groan of appreciation. Sarah had chosen her emerald green Agent Provocateur set, bra and panties edged with cream lace. She felt the material between her legs slipping over her sex as she raised one foot, then the other, to step out of her dress. Carla picked it up and carefully folded it over the arm of the chair, before Sarah felt her hands on her shoulders. Then there was hot breath and lips on her neck, then Carla's tongue running from below her ear, to her bra strap, then back again, just as it had on Steve's penis.

'I believe we were looking for a girl willing to have sex with me,' she whispered in Sarah's ear. 'Shall we take this to the bedroom and see if we've found one?'

Sarah slipped around to face Carla, feeling her arms slide around her shoulders as she moved. She kissed Carla full on the lips, feeling her mouth open and opening hers in response. They French kissed for what felt like an eternity, before Carla broke away and stepped back, taking Sarah's hand and leading her out of the living room and up the stairs. Sarah was aware of Steve following them, throwing off his robe as he did so.

Sarah was drawn up the narrow stairs and into a room off the landing, evidently the couple's bedroom. It had been laid out for the night's sport, a red bulb glowing in each bedside lamp, a dark blue duvet cover, and condoms and lubricant next to one of the lamps. Sarah was being seduced and she loved it.

Carla let go of her hand and sat on the edge of the bed, leaning back on her hands and parting her thighs to show off her shaven sex. 'So?' she asked, 'ever sucked a pussy before?'

'Yes,' Sarah answered, then coughed as she realised how dry her throat had become, 'but not for some time.'

'Cool!' Carla smiled mischievously. 'This is my first time, but I've always wanted to try it. And Steve's always wanted to see me try it! How would you like me?'

'Lying back on the bed.' Sarah realised she had been given control over this beautiful woman, the power to use her body as she wished. It was quite a responsibility, but one she knew she was up to.

Carla climbed on to the bed and rested her head on the pillow. She lifted her knees and planted her feet flat on the duvet, her creamy thighs parted, her labia opening as she did so. Sarah swallowed hard and climbed on to the bed alongside her, then reached up and took one of the other pillows. She pulled it down and slipped it under Carla's bottom, the brunette obligingly lifting herself up then sinking back onto it, her pelvis now raised above the rest of her body.

Sarah slipped down the bed and knelt between Carla's knees. She placed a hand on each one, as she looked at her target. Carla's vagina was beginning to pout, and looked delicious, and she was almost tempted to dive straight in, but she knew it would taste so much sweeter with a little teasing. Leaning forward, she kissed Carla full on the mouth again and ran her lips down her chin, her throat and between her breasts. She lifted her head to first her right nipple, then the left, sucking hard on the swollen buds and hearing her gasp as she did so. Her mouth continued its journey, from Carla's breasts, across her tummy, and finally into the Promised Land.

She planted dozens of little kisses on the soft flesh just above the labia, which Carla had shaved smooth, evidently not very long ago. At the same time, Sarah's hands had wandered down Carla's thighs, and her fingers were now touching the swollen lips. She pushed the index and second finger of her right hand gently between them, then parted them. Sarah placed her mouth on the soft flesh she had exposed and sucked gently. Another groan told her she was hitting the spot. Pointing her tongue, Sarah ran the tip up and down Carla's inner labia. Now she heard Steve, who was watching from the end of the bed, groaning more loudly than Carla.

She set to her task with relish, pushing her tongue further and further inside Carla, now using the fingers of both hands to open her, exposing as much soft dark red flesh as possible, savouring Carla's musky taste.

Suddenly Sarah felt the bed dip behind her, and realised Steve had joined them. She felt her knickers being pulled aside at the crotch, and heard a condom packet being ripped open. Then his large hands were all over her bottom, squeezing it, slapping it, kneading the buttocks and eventually pulling them apart. She felt his thick tool nudging her own sex, as if asking permission. She gave it with a wiggle of her hips. Steve plunged home, even as she pushed her index finger fully inside Carla, flicking her tongue repeatedly over her clitoris.

Steve took her hips and fucked her hard, forcing Sarah to bury her face in Carla's sex, licking, slurping and eating her greedily. She could feel the woman building to orgasm, and with the amount of stimulation he had enjoyed, Steve would not last long.

Carla came first, a wild bucking climax which mashed her pussy against Sarah's mouth, filling it with moist flesh. The sight must have sent Steve over the edge, as he grabbed Sarah's hips even tighter and pulled her back onto his prick, almost using her like a sex toy to bring himself off. She felt him explode and pulse as he filled the condom, still pushing her back and forth to drain the last few drops. Then he collapsed alongside a semi-conscious Carla. Sarah crawled up the bed and lay on her other side, an arm thrown across both her lovers.

Half-an-hour later it was her turn to scream and thrash, as she lay naked on her back, Carla making too good a job of cunnilingus to have been telling the truth about it being her first time. Steve lay next to Sarah, fondling and sucking each of her breasts in turn, as his girlfriend sucked and licked her to climax.

Sarah awoke late. Steve and Carla were next to her, their bodies entwined. Silently Sarah slipped up and out of the bedroom, to find the bathroom.

As she stood in front of the mirror, still naked, teasing her hair back into some kind of style with her fingers, the bathroom door opened. She turned to see Carla, also naked. 'Morning. Or should I say, afternoon!' said the brunette.

'Oh! Have we slept late? Good job it's Saturday!' Carla

stood behind Sarah and the women looked at themselves together in the half-length mirror. One of Carla's hands cupped Sarah's right buttock, while the other snaked around her waist and its palm gently pressed Sarah's left nipple. Sarah giggled and turned to kiss Carla gently on the lips.

'Steve gets deployed on Monday.' There was a note of sadness in her voice. 'He'll be away for six months. It's a long time, but it'll pass, and I've sent him off with a wonderful memory. But in the meantime, I'm going to need some comfort myself. I was wondering ...' and she paused a little, and angled her head to look at Sarah's face, rather than her reflection, 'How would it be if I were to dial the wrong number again?'

Sarah turned to face Carla, took her face in her hands and kissed her tenderly and deeply. 'Consider me your personal call girl! Now let's go and send your soldier boy off in real style.' Taking her by the hand, Sarah led Carla back to the bedroom. From now on Sarah knew she would be leaving her phone plugged in.